D1007937

Praise for the Vampire Memories Series

Memories of Envy

"Hendee has a gift for intricate psychological plots, and her characters are some of the best in current fantasy. Their motives and interactions are thoroughly convincing. The series can be enjoyed as single novels or an ongoing story."   —*Booklist*

"Dramatic . . . part soap opera, part supernatural thriller, Hendee's series will satisfy readers looking for bloodsoaked pathos."   —*Publishers Weekly*

"A real page-turner. The characters really came to life for me. . . . I hope they're around for many books to come."
—Fresh Fiction

Hunting Memories

"A gripping tale. The action moves the story along while the characters, with their skills and secrets, keep the reader's full attention. *Hunting Memories* is a must read in the series, and it provides many answers in the overall story line. I'll be looking forward to the next book in the Vampire Memories."   —Darque Reviews

"One of the year's better vampire novels, what with realistic characters, including ghosts and vampires, who have plausible problems; an intriguing, if standard, plot; historical literacy; and a style of writing that encourages turning pages. Both fantasy and romance fans should enjoy Hendee's commendable effort."   —*Booklist*

"Filled with action, a bit of politics, and plenty of character-building interactions, this is a strong addition to the series. . . . Those looking for an alternative to Patricia Briggs or Ilona Andrews won't be disappointed with Hendee's newest series."   —Monsters and Critics

continued . . .

"An enjoyable and creative (not just of new vampires) cocktail cleverly blending urban fantasy . . . with strong horror elements . . . a thriller of a vampire tale."
—*Midwest Book Review*

"Barb Hendee . . . knows her vampires."   —BSCreview

Blood Memories

"A satisfying story line coupled with engaging characters, fast action, and a hint of things to come make this a winner."   —Monsters and Critics

"A good vampire story for the Halloween holiday, the story is fast-paced and intriguing."
—*News and Sentinel* (Parkersburg, WV)

"Well written . . . a fascinating tale with wonderful characters and delicious villains who solicit the readers into loathing them. The story line is character driven although there is plenty of action throughout. . . . Vampire subgenre [fans] will enjoy this work as an exhilarating tale of death visiting the undead."   —SFRevu

"A terrific vampire stand-alone thriller that fans will enjoy . . . the story is filled with action, but also contains a strong cast who ensure vampirism in the Northwest seems real. . . . The heroine especially is an intriguing person. . . . This [is] a fine tale that the vampire crowd will appreciate."   —*Midwest Book Review*

IN MEMORIES WE FEAR

A VAMPIRE MEMORIES NOVEL

BARB HENDEE

A ROC BOOK

ROC
Published by New American Library, a division of
Penguin Group (USA) Inc., 375 Hudson Street,
New York, New York 10014, USA
Penguin Group (Canada), 90 Eglinton Avenue East, Suite 700, Toronto,
Ontario M4P 2Y3, Canada (a division of Pearson Penguin Canada Inc.)
Penguin Books Ltd., 80 Strand, London WC2R 0RL, England
Penguin Ireland, 25 St. Stephen's Green, Dublin 2,
Ireland (a division of Penguin Books Ltd.)
Penguin Group (Australia), 250 Camberwell Road, Camberwell, Victoria 3124,
Australia (a division of Pearson Australia Group Pty. Ltd.)
Penguin Books India Pvt. Ltd., 11 Community Centre, Panchsheel Park,
New Delhi - 110 017, India
Penguin Group (NZ), 67 Apollo Drive, Rosedale, Auckland 0632,
New Zealand (a division of Pearson New Zealand Ltd.)
Penguin Books (South Africa) (Pty.) Ltd., 24 Sturdee Avenue,
Rosebank, Johannesburg 2196, South Africa

Penguin Books Ltd., Registered Offices:
80 Strand, London WC2R 0RL, England

First published by Roc, an imprint of New American Library,
a division of Penguin Group (USA) Inc.

First Printing, October 2011
10 9 8 7 6 5 4 3 2 1

Copyright © Barb Hendee, 2011
All rights reserved

ROC REGISTERED TRADEMARK—MARCA REGISTRADA

Printed in the United States of America

PUBLISHER'S NOTE
This is a work of fiction. Names, characters, places, and incidents either are the
product of the author's imagination or are used fictitiously, and any resem-
blance to actual persons, living or dead, business establishments, events, or
locales is entirely coincidental.
   The publisher does not have any control over and does not assume any responsibility for author or third-party Web sites or their content.

chapter one

PORTLAND, OREGON

Midautumn was approaching, and even at night, the trees lining Naito Parkway were glorious in their shades of red and yellow. Sunset came much earlier in the Northwest once summer gave way to fall.

Eleisha Clevon ran along the river, laughing once as she turned to see her companion coming behind.

"Eleisha," he called out in a heavy French accent, "what are you doing?"

"Catch me!"

Tonight she almost felt like the teenage girl she appeared to be, wearing jeans, canvas sneakers, and a loose sweater. Her dark blond hair whipped across her face in the cool air as she glanced back once more, just in time to see her companion bolt forward, his body moving so fast it became a blur.

Before she'd run two more steps, he cut her off. His hand shot out and pressed against a tree trunk a few inches from her shoulder.

"What are you doing?" he said again.

Eleisha looked up into Philip Branté's face, seeing his eyes glow in surprise. He was so tall, she had to tilt her head back.

She didn't answer and ducked under his arm, dashing away, laughing again. In all her 187 years on this earth, she couldn't remember ever being able to *play* with anyone the way she could with Philip. Tonight, she wanted to show him how much he had changed her. The sight of her running and laughing might confuse him at first, but he was catching on.

"Eleisha!" he called.

Then he stopped talking and ran after her, darting around her easily, leaning down, and throwing her over his shoulder. A stocky man in a baseball cap passed by and glanced over, but Eleisha was still laughing, so the man just shook his head and smiled. She and Philip must have looked like two lovers playing by the river.

Maybe they were.

"Okay, I've caught you," Philip said, turning in a slow circle. "Now what?"

She didn't bother struggling—it would have been pointless—and ran her hands down the back of his Armani coat. He leaned over again and put her down, studying her face intently as if unsure of her identity.

But he didn't look displeased. He just looked intense, with little idea of what to say or do.

"What is this all about?" he finally asked, his accent thicker than normal. "*Pourquoi?* Why are you so different?"

His skin was ivory, and his eyes were a shade of light amber. He wore his red-brown hair in layers down to the top of his collar, and he wore the long Armani coat to cover the machete fastened to his belt.

"I'm happy," she answered.

And she was. Until last spring, she'd lived an almost completely solitary life as a caretaker for an aged, damaged vampire. But then everything changed, and now she was living in an old church with Philip, along with another vampire, Rose de Spenser, and a telepathic mortal, Wade Sheffield. She wasn't alone anymore.

And they were looking for others like themselves, vampires in hiding, who didn't want to be alone anymore either.

At first, this transition had been like a shock of cold water for Eleisha—almost painful—as it had been for Philip, and they'd not always been good company for each other, but that, too, had changed, and throughout the past month he'd become more and more aware of her loneliness, of her need to talk about the past . . . and he'd listened.

She loved him for it.

They'd come out here to feed tonight, and she knew this area was his favorite hunting ground. She hadn't fed in more than a week, and she was hungry, but she also wanted to please him, to make their existence interesting for him. Philip was easily bored—one of his faults—so she tried to keep him entertained.

"Do you remember the game we played a few nights after moving here?" she asked. "Where we tried to outdo each other in the hunt . . . competed for whose prey was a bigger risk?"

"You hated that game. You argued with me."

Yes, she had, but she hadn't completely trusted him then. Back in their separate worlds, for nearly two hundred years, they had both killed mortals to feed. The rapidly turning wheel of recent events had taught Eleisha that she didn't need to kill to feed, that she could replace a victim's memories and leave the person alive—unconscious but alive. She'd taught Philip how to do this.

He was a predator by nature, and *this* had been the hardest adjustment for him. But he'd done it. He'd become so skilled with both his telepathy and his self-control that she never worried anymore. She trusted him now.

"Chicken?" she asked, teasing him like a mortal.

He raised his eyebrows.

"New rules," he said, switching gears as quickly as always. "I choose your prey for you. You have to win with whomever I pick." Philip lived in the moment. That was another thing she liked about him. She tended to dwell too much on the past.

"Done," she said. "But then I get to choose yours."

He flashed a smile—somewhat disturbing, as he did this so rarely. "Done," he repeated.

Without another word, he turned and headed for Front Avenue, slipping around the far side of the Marriott. She followed, moving behind him, wondering what he was up to, but she took pleasure in his expression as he scanned the sidewalk. He was enjoying this.

Although it rained a good deal in Portland, especially in fall and winter, tonight was cool and clear.

Together they watched a wide variety of mortals walk past: groups of teenagers, old couples, young couples, and any number of people alone as they hurried by. Philip kept stock-still, just watching, until he suddenly pointed toward the exit from a parking garage.

"That one," he said quietly.

A tall man with an expensive haircut and a tailored suit was heading across the street at an even but determined pace. He carried a computer case in one hand and a stack of enlarged cardboard charts in the other. Even from this distance, Eleisha could see his eyes were hard and focused, as if he were reviewing a speech in his head.

She wanted to groan.

She'd never been good with corporate sharks, and Philip knew it.

He turned his head and flashed another smile, trying to parody her voice. "Chicken?" When she hesitated, he said, "Better hurry or you'll lose him before you start."

"Pick someone else," she urged.

"No."

The man was halfway across the street, heading for the hotel's glass doors. Eleisha's sensible caution kicked in, and she wondered about the wisdom of suggesting this game for Philip's amusement. In spite of her newfound sense of happiness, she took the cautions of hunting seriously, and there were several essential components that could never be forgotten. For one, the victim had to be left someplace safe, someplace where he could not be hurt or robbed while unconscious. Eleisha almost always lured the person into a car so she could lock the doors and let him wake up on his own in a secured place. That wasn't an option here.

And for another, victims were always chosen with deference to the particular vampire's "gift." Within a few nights of becoming undead, a specific element of the vampire's previous personality developed into an overwhelming aura, which could be turned on and off at will. Eleisha's gift was an aura of helplessness. So now she always chose people who were either sympathetic or protective.

Corporate sharks were neither; they tended to care about only themselves and their bank accounts.

"Better go," Philip said almost gleefully.

Eleisha wanted to kick herself. Creative thought and improvisation were integral components to winning this game. But where could she possibly take this man so they could be alone, and that she could still leave him in safety? She couldn't just lure him into an alley and leave him there. If he was coming from the parking lot across the street, he didn't have a room at the Marriott. He was probably here to give some kind of presentation.

Giving Philip an exasperated look, she headed out and, cutting the man off before he reached the doors, reached out with her mind to pick up any stray surface thoughts. She almost stumbled at the desperation hidden behind his impassive face.

Can't lose this one.

Too much on the Visa now.

Lose the house if this fails.

At least the card cleared at the desk.

She tried to unjumble his thoughts, realizing as she searched that he did have a room at the hotel, but he couldn't afford valet parking—which was the only option at this hotel. He'd gone to his car to get a few last-minute items for a sales pitch.

Eleisha hurried toward him, knowing this was going to be impossible without leaning heavily on her gift, but she threw pride to the wind.

"Sir, please," she said, holding up her hands and letting her gift flow. "Please help me."

For just a second, she worried he wasn't even going to stop—not even going to look down—but he did.

"I don't have time for—," he started, and his eyes locked on her face.

She was dressed all wrong, looking neither like a damsel in distress nor a pretty street urchin. For God's sake . . . she was trying this in a pair of canvas sneakers and one of Philip's old sweaters that hung halfway to her knees.

"Please," she said again, turning up her gift and watching his expression alter slightly. He would see her as helpless, fragile, alone, and in desperate need of help. She clouded his mind, his judgment, and played upon any sense of humanity he still possessed.

"I need a place to hide, just for a few hours," she said, moving closer, pitching her voice to a tone of fear, hoping Philip could see how difficult this was from where he stood.

"Hide?" the man repeated, his eyes glassy now. Up close, his suit looked cleaned and pressed, but not new. She normally didn't require anywhere near this much influence over a victim—and it was hardly sporting—but she didn't have a choice here.

"Just for a few hours," she said again. "Someplace no one will find me. Can I stay in your room?"

This was lamest thing she'd ever suggested to a victim, and any sane person would have told her to call the police and walked right past her. But at the moment, he wasn't sane. He wanted only to protect her. He'd do anything she asked.

"All right," he said, sounding dazed. "But I have a pitch to make. I can't miss it."

"When?" she asked, surprising herself that she cared.

"Half an hour . . . in the Klamath room."

Half an hour? He wasn't going to make that.

He led her inside the hotel and to the elevator, as if taking a strange girl from the street to his room— just because she wanted a place to hide—was the most normal thing in the world, and Eleisha began feeling uncomfortable about the whole situation, again wishing maybe she hadn't suggested this.

He led her to the sixth floor and used his key card to open the door to his room. They entered, and she closed the door. At this point, she would put him to sleep, feed, and then alter his memory so he'd have no recollection of ever having seen her.

But she looked at the printed charts and the computer case, and she remembered his stray thoughts about losing his house and how his nearly maxed Visa card could barely cover the price of this room.

"Okay, you're safe here," he said, readjusting the charts. "I have to go."

She reached out and touched his face. "You're tired. You need to sleep."

Like a clock stopping, his eyes closed, and he fell back onto the bed, with the computer and charts beside him. Eleisha looked at his wrist. She was hungry, but she couldn't do this. If she fed, he probably wouldn't wake up soon enough, and he'd still be weak.

Instead, she reached inside his mind and took him back to the moment he'd crossed the street. She put in a different memory. He'd found the charts in his car, but he'd forgotten the computer in his room, and he'd hurried back up to get it. He never met anyone. He never saw anyone on the way up. Then stress and exhaustion had overtaken him briefly.

"You'll wake up in forty seconds," she whispered. "Do you understand? Forty seconds."

She slipped out the door. He would make his presentation.

All the way back down in the elevator, through the lobby, and into the street, she wondered what on earth had possessed her to instigate some game that played with people's lives—just to entertain Philip.

But when she came around the building and saw his face, she knew why. He looked animated, interested . . . amused.

"That was tragic," he said. "No style. No improvising. You just used your gift. I can do better wearing a gunnysack without any pants. I can do better without even turning on my gift."

But his voice held no cruelty. He was having fun.

"Really?" she said. "Have you forgotten that *I* get to choose the target?" She started walking, glancing back. "You just wait."

Wade Sheffield was on the bottom floor of the church, doing curls with a set of free weights he'd bought last month.

He'd been living here, since the previous spring, with three vampires and a ghost. He was probably the only mortal in the world more comfortable with the undead than he was with normal people, but he'd been able to read minds all his life, and "normal people" did not enjoy his company.

So now the five of them were trying to make this old brick church into a home. They nicknamed the building "the underground."

The main floor comprised a large sanctuary, complete with stained glass windows, and two offices. Wade had refurnished one office, and Rose had turned the other into her bedroom.

The upstairs was not currently in use, but it sported six rooms that had once been engaged for Sunday school classes, and later, these would be used to house any lost vampires they found.

The basement consisted of a three-bedroom apartment where Wade, Eleisha, and Philip lived, and an industrial-sized kitchen that the old congregation had once used for potluck dinners. But over the summer, Wade had been turning this area into a home gym. He'd started with a simple weight machine and then moved to free weights.

In the early days of their mission, he'd believed that being educated, telepathic, and competent would be enough to make him indispensable to the group.

He'd been wrong.

Now he was working out twice a day, and Philip was teaching him how to use a sword.

After finishing a second set of curls, he was sweating, and he dropped the weights into their rack, half turning to look at the doorway; tonight he was feeling anxious, even frustrated.

Their last attempt to locate a lost vampire in Denver and bring her home had ended in complete disaster, but after a few weeks of mental recovery, Eleisha had seemed ready to "get back on the horse" and try again—or so Wade thought.

Again, he'd been wrong.

Their strategy was for Wade to search out any on-line news stories of homicide victims drained of blood or of living people checked into hospitals with cuts or gashes that did not warrant an unexplained amount of blood loss. He'd once worked as a police psychologist, and he knew a good deal about *where* to search for such stories. Then, they would attempt to make contact, travel to meet the vampire, and try to bring him or her safely home to the church.

Since the end of the summer, Eleisha had always expressed polite interest in any possible stories he mentioned, but she didn't press him, and she didn't seem eager for him to find a new lead. He wasn't sure why. She should be pushing him, even working with him, doing everything she could to launch a new mission. This entire underground had been her idea, her vision, in the first place.

Had her last failure shattered her confidence? Was she afraid to try again?

To make matters worse, lately, she seemed interested only in spending time with Philip.

Well . . . Wade didn't know why that made matters worse. He just knew it bothered him.

Grabbing a towel, he wiped off his face and arms and headed back toward their basement apartment. He didn't stop there and went straight to the stairs, half jogging up to his office on the main floor.

He liked this room with its old, used desk he'd

picked up in downtown Portland. He liked the book-shelves and all the maps and his computer. The walls were cream, and the window overlooked Eleisha's rose garden.

Dropping into the desk chair, he moved his mouse, and the computer screen lit up. Tonight he was de-termined to find something—anything—to get them all out of this current state of limbo and back into some kind of action.

Opening his Internet home page, he started, as usual, with the online *New York Times*, skimming quickly as his mind had instinctively learned to stop on specific words or phrases. When he found noth-ing, a memory tickled the back of his mind, and he switched over to London's *Evening Standard*.

"Anything at all?" A masculine voice with a Scot-tish accent sounded from behind him.

Wade didn't even bother turning, but he glanced up.

"Not yet."

Seamus de Spenser stood looking over his shoul-der. Seamus' body was transparent as always. Though long dead, he looked like a young man, his brown hair hanging to his shoulders. He wore a blue and yellow Scottish plaid draped across his shoul-der and held by a belt over the black breeches he had died in. The knife sheath at his hip was empty.

He was Rose's nephew, and he'd died the same night she was turned—but he'd come back as a spirit, forever tied to her.

Seamus was a key component of their strategy. Once Wade located a possible location, he sent Seamus to investigate. As a ghost, Seamus could zero in on a vampire—or anything undead—once he was in the general vicinity. Unfortunately, he couldn't stay too long, as his spirit was tied to Rose, and the longer he stayed away from her, the weaker he became.

He and Wade worked well together, but Wade always wondered what they might look like to an outsider . . . the two of them studying the computer screen. Wade, in his early thirties with a slender build, viewed his own appearance as common. His only outstanding feature was a shock of white-blond hair. He hadn't cut it in more than six months, and it hung down the back of his neck. But how did he look with a six-foot-tall, transparent Scottish Highlander leaning over his shoulder?

"I've just switched to London," Wade said.

In midsummer, they'd come across a strong lead there: a news story about a "wild man" who'd attacked a woman in an alley and tried to bite her. When the police ran to intervene, their own dogs had turned on them, allowing the attacker to get away. Wade had been certain he was onto something. But Seamus hadn't been able to find anything in London, and he'd come back home on the brink of exhaustion.

"I keep telling you," Seamus said. "You're always looking in the major papers. Find a way to access smaller papers . . . from smaller towns."

"I know what I'm doing."

Vampires didn't live in small towns. They needed a large population to hide their feeding practices.

Seamus started to say something else, but he stopped as their eyes hit the same headline at the same moment.

WILD MAN STRIKES
OUTSIDE BRITISH MUSEUM

As if unaware of what he was doing, Seamus began reading the story aloud. "'Late Tuesday night, a second bizarre attack took place in Bloomsbury. According to the police report, although the museum was closed, the sound of screaming brought two security guards running toward the street where they found a "dark-haired man with tattered clothes" pinning a woman against a streetlamp and biting her throat.'"

Seamus stopped.

Wade looked up at him again. "'Biting her throat,'" he repeated softly. Then he took over reading. "'Two security guards, whose names have not yet been released, moved to intervene. The man broke off his attack and ran. As they pursued, three cats seemed to come "from nowhere" and attack the guards, leaving bites and scratches severe enough to send both men to the hospital. One is expected to require cosmetic surgery. . . .'"

Wade stopped reading as the story moved on to recount the woman's injuries, complete with blood loss.

"There's something in this, Seamus," Wade said, shaking his head. "There must be."

"I tried before and couldn't pinpoint anything," Seamus answered, almost defensively, as if Wade were accusing him of failure. "What if it's just a madman who *thinks* he's a vampire?"

Wade tried to keep his tone even. "Then how do you explain the dogs turning on their own handlers in the first story? How do you explain these . . . these cats jumping in to fight off pursuit? No, there's something here."

"What do you want me to do?"

"Can you search again? Try again?"

Seamus floated a few feet back. "If you think it will do any good, I can go tonight. But I searched the entire city last time and found nothing."

He didn't sound hopeful that a new search would bring different results.

"Do you want to tell Rose good-bye?" Wade asked.

"No, you do it for me."

Wade nodded and looked at Seamus. "We're onto something." He paused and, not sure why, he added, "Find him."

Seamus tilted his transparent head to one side. Then he vanished, teleporting to London.

Philip followed Eleisha up Eleventh Avenue to the Gerding Theater at the Armory. Refurbished rock-work on the sides of the building loomed several stories high.

The emotions bubbling beneath his skin were so

varied, he wasn't sure what to think or feel. A part of him was thrilled at the change in Eleisha tonight. She'd always worked hard to keep him entertained— he knew that even if he didn't acknowledge it. But her methods normally involved finding movies he might like or reading detective novels aloud (so she could do the voices) or playing cards with him.

She had never run along a river, laughing and calling for him to catch her, and she'd certainly never suggested playing a "game" while hunting. He liked that she was trying so hard to please him. He liked being the center of her world.

But this game, along with her spirit of semiwild abandon, was dangerous for him.

Eleisha was cautious and careful and sensible, and for the past few months, he'd clung to her steady nature. He'd been trying so hard to *be* the man she already thought he was. Since returning from Denver, he hadn't slipped out alone and killed anyone while feeding. He'd denied himself this need for her sake, and for the sake of the underground. He was slowly beginning to see the value of a structured community built on mutual trust.

To his surprise, the longer he'd hunted "her way," the easier it became . . . and the less often he was hit by a hunger to inflict fear and death. He was gaining control.

Tonight, he feared that by trying to please him, she was unwittingly washing that control away. The first time they'd played this game, he'd been the one to suggest it—practically forcing it on her. But what had started out as mere fun ended with him nearly killing a woman in a dressing room at Macy's.

For him, the joy of hunting had always culminated in his victim's death, and he'd been working hard to train himself to view hunting as nothing more than a necessity. Tonight, Eleisha was making it a sport again, and good sport ended only one way.

And yet he couldn't call this off; he wouldn't. She was trying so hard to please him, and he loved for her to please him more than anything else. He fought his instincts and vowed to keep himself in control.

"In here," she said, walking through the main doors.

"You're hardly dressed for the theater," he murmured.

"We're not going to the theater."

Philip glanced at a clock on the wall of the large main lobby. It was after nine o'clock, and the main shows normally started at eight. He wondered what Eleisha was up to. He'd half expected her to head straight for the nearest gym and point out a lesbian carrying her own hockey stick.

"Down there," Eleisha said, pointing. "The posters for new shows are downstairs."

Several people milling about inside the ticket office glanced over, but no one said anything. Eleisha headed for the large curving staircase and led him down to a lower level. They emerged into what appeared to be a smaller lobby with large closed double doors at the far end. Posters for current and upcoming shows lined the walls.

She began looking at the posters. "Intermission won't be long," she said quietly, although they were the only two people down here.

He looked at the closed doors and realized what she was doing. There was a show in progress. Even the ushers had gone inside, and she was pretending to be checking out plays to attend in the future. People probably did this all the time. Eleisha's shabby handling of her own victim may have been embarrassing, but she was certainly proving more creative in picking out his.

The doors opened, and people began pouring out, heading off to get drinks at intermission, use the restrooms, or take advantage of the water fountains. Within seconds, the empty lobby was packed with people, and the silence was replaced with a low roar of voices all discussing the disappointing performance of the lead actor.

At the moment, Eleisha was not paying attention to anything being said about the show; instead, she watched the rush of people carefully. The line at the ladies' room was already long, but she just kept scanning, and Philip felt his excitement begin to grow. Whom would she choose?

The level of dress here varied widely from women in evening gowns and heels and men in suits, all the way down to a few people in torn blue jeans. The latter annoyed Philip. He believed in dressing up for the theater.

Ten minutes passed, and Eleisha had not said a word. He began to fidget, wondering again what she was up to. The lights flickered, signaling that the show was about to begin.

"Eleisha," he whispered.

"Shhhhh."

A couple carrying nearly empty glasses of white wine came down the stairs, heading casually toward the doors as if wishing to finish their drinks first. Late-middle-aged and balding, the man wore a dark gray suit with silver cuff links. The woman, younger than he, was lovely, dressed in a black silk blouse over a long silver skirt. Diamonds glittered in her ears.

"Her," Eleisha said, "but you have to draw her away from the man before they go back inside, and you have to leave her somewhere safe."

He already knew that last rule, but he was surprised by Eleisha's choice. Philip had no trouble seducing attractive women—that was his usual mode of operation. Did she think it would be difficult for him to lure the woman away from the man before they reached the doors? Or . . . was she simply still trying to please him?

He *was* pleased.

Who wouldn't be?

He didn't hesitate and stepped to one side of the lobby as people continued pouring back into the theater. He waited until the man and woman were almost to the doors, and then he reached out telepathically.

Your wallet is missing. It's in the ladies' room.

He had no idea if she'd even gone to the restroom before going for her drink, but it didn't matter. She stopped and frowned, glancing down at her black beaded handbag.

It's not in there. It's in the ladies' room.

"Go ahead to the seats," she told the man. "I think I left my wallet in the restroom."

"Your wallet?"

"Yes, you go on. I'll be quick."

Philip knew the impulse he'd placed felt natural, as if she would never consider doing anything else, and she hurried over to the ladies' room, disappearing inside. The lobby was now empty, and the ushers were about to close the doors.

Philip glanced down at Eleisha, and then he walked right into the restroom. The woman was looking inside the stalls in confusion, as if unsure why she'd come. She was the only person here—except for Philip.

She gasped when she looked over and saw him standing there.

"Forgive me," he said. "I'm in the wrong room."

He turned on his gift.

Philip's gift had always made hunting easy, especially in situations like this. He exuded an overwhelming sense of attraction—and his face did the rest. He kept his gift turned down to a minimum, not leaning upon it nearly as hard as Eleisha had.

The woman stared at him, her voice wavering. "I should . . . I need to . . ."

He increased his gift slightly, clouding her mind. "No, stay here."

She focused on his face, listened to his accent, and

he backed her inside the large handicapped stall. She let him.

Up close, he could see she was a little older than he first thought, but still lovely, with shining brown hair and delicate features. This felt like real hunting . . . the way he used to hunt, and he could feel the tension building in his chest. Hunger hit him like a wall.

He was driven by an urge to pin her against the bathroom stall and turn off his gift so he could absorb her fear before he drained her. He wanted it so badly, he started shaking.

Eleisha should not have suggested this—or he should have refused.

He fought for control. "You're tired," he said, "so tired. Go to sleep."

She dropped into his arms. He crouched, still holding her—still shaking—and forced himself to carefully puncture her wrist with his teeth. Warm blood flowed down his throat, and shadows of her memories passed through him.

He saw a luxurious kitchen with granite countertops. He saw her preparing for dinner parties, smiling at numerous people even though she was tired . . . and drinking more than she should to compensate. Then he saw her sitting alone in a dining room, looking down at the roasted game hens on the table getting cold as she waited for her husband . . . and she drank too much while waiting.

He swallowed just enough blood to strengthen himself, and he jerked his mouth away, closing his eyes and reminding himself that Eleisha was standing just outside the restroom. He had to stop now.

Opening his eyes again, he dug through the woman's bag and found a bottle of Chanel N°5, which struck him as somewhat dated but pleasant. The glass of the bottle was thick, so he smashed it against the floor, breaking it into pieces. He used one shard to connect the holes between his teeth marks and then dropped it on the floor. Reaching inside the woman's mind, he altered her memory. She'd come in, found her wallet, noticed the perfume in her bag as she put the wallet away, and decided she needed a small spray. Taking the bottle out, she'd slipped on a wet patch of the floor, shattered the bottle, and landed on some of the glass, cutting herself. Then she'd passed out.

Philip backed out of the stall, forcing himself away. He walked away from the bathroom, leaving the unconscious woman behind.

But as he came into the lobby, Eleisha saw his face, and her expression turned to alarm.

"What's wrong?" she asked.

"Nothing."

"Is she all right?"

He nodded, and her alarm shifted to concern.

"You did well," she said. "Much better than me. That was smart to wait until everyone was gone and then send her to the ladies' room." Her hazel eyes were so worried for him, for his happiness. He wanted to grip her face in both hands.

"Yes, but . . . ," he started.

How could he tell her that games like this were torture for him, that they only reminded him of what he'd left behind? She was trying so hard.

"It's nothing," he said. "Let's go home."

By the time they reached the church, Philip was feeling a little better. After all, he *had* managed to control himself, and the cravings inside him were beginning to fade. Eleisha moved ahead of him to the front doors, her hair swinging across her back.

"Oh, Philip, I bought us some Alfred Hitchcock movies," she said.

He frowned. "Who is that?"

"A wonderful director, very unique."

Philip didn't like how that sounded. If the word "artistic" came out of her mouth even once, he would revolt.

"Don't worry," she said. "We'll start with *Psycho* tonight and then watch *Vertigo* tomorrow. You'll like them both. I promise."

"Oh . . . all right."

Usually, when she said he'd like something, she tended to be right, and she'd introduced him to a number of films, books, and musical CDs that had surprised him. Suddenly, he began to feel much better. All things considered, in spite of his internal struggle, tonight had been not been dull, and now Eleisha had planned to watch a movie called *Psycho* with him. He was happy.

As they headed through the sanctuary and

through the door behind the altar, she'd just begun chatting about something involving the use of light and shadow when Wade stepped from his office.

"I sent Seamus back to London," he said without even a greeting.

Something in his voice caught Philip's attention—a hard determination.

"Why?" Eleisha asked.

"Come look at this."

A feeling of trepidation began to grow in Philip's stomach as they followed Wade into the office and Eleisha pulled up a chair so that she and Wade could look at the computer screen together.

From where he was standing, Philip could see the headline.

WILD MAN STRIKES
OUTSIDE BRITISH MUSEUM

The trepidation turned into a knot as Eleisha began silently reading. She stopped and looked at Wade. "Again . . . ," she said. "Almost the same story."

"Except this time the woman suffered blood loss. Even if Seamus can't pinpoint a signature, I think we should check this out ourselves."

"Where's Rose? Does she know yet?"

"No. She's in her room, and I didn't want to disturb her," he answered.

Philip just hung back by the door.

Eleisha finished scanning the story, but her face was unreadable when she looked over at Wade and nodded. "Yes, we have to go. But how long do you want to give Seamus first? We shouldn't leave until we've let him finish his search. He might learn more this time."

"Agreed. We should give him at least a few days," Wade said, reaching for a map. "But I think we should get a hotel in this area. It's central, and it's close to several Tube stations." He pointed down, but Philip didn't bother looking.

Wade and Eleisha continued their discussion, and all plans for watching the Hitchcock film evaporated. Philip understood. This was their purpose; this was why they'd bought the church in the first place. Wade's job was to locate a lost vampire. Eleisha would make contact and establish trust. Philip would provide protection.

He understood.

But he also couldn't help dwelling on the memory of the past few months, when Eleisha hadn't seemed interested in anything but him. Now they were about to launch a new search, a new mission, and a part of him couldn't help feeling that he'd just lost something.

chapter two

VALE OF GLAMORGAN, WALES

Julian Ashton walked through the long dining hall at Cliffbracken Manor, noticing cobwebs in several corners and reminding himself to contact the Cardiff agency to arrange for a more competent maid. The last two had been hopeless, and he vowed that if he could engage someone capable, he would not feed on her.

Good help was hard to find, and he couldn't deny that Cliffbracken was gaining a rather dim reputation for disappearing servants.

He walked down the darkened hallway to his study, his favorite room. The fire he'd built earlier burned in the hearth, making the aged chairs and couches look almost new in the soft yellow light. A pile of maps and newspapers completely covered a

round table in the center of the room. He leaned
down to examine several of them.

Julian was a large man with a bone structure that
almost made him look heavy. His dark hair hung at
uneven angles around a solid chin, and he pushed it
back, away from his face, wondering where to start
first.

His nights had taken on a kind of routine while
he waited for Eleisha to find a new lead. He usually
woke, built a fire, went to the stables, took his horse
out for a long ride, and then he would come back
here to do research. Wade and Eleisha were taking
so long to find someone new to track that he'd decided to try to take matters into his own hands, just
to see what he would find. So he'd begun subscrib-
ing to international newspapers. He decided to start
with Germany tonight and picked up a copy of *Der
Spiegel*.

He'd just begun reading when the air beside him
shimmered, and a transparent teenage girl appeared.

She was his spy, Mary Jordane.

In addition to her being transparent, the most striking things about her were her spiky magenta hair and
shiny silver nose stud. Thin, with a hint of budding
breasts, she was wearing a purple T-shirt, a black mesh
overshirt, torn jeans, and Dr. Martens boots.

"They've sent Seamus back to London," she
blurted out immediately, and seemed about to rush
onward.

Mary had never lost her penchant for babbling
the instant she appeared.

"Slower!" he ordered.

She pursed her mouth and glared at him. By performing a ritual séance, he'd called her from the other side, manipulating her cooperation with a mix of promises for the future and threats of sending her back to the gray, in-between plane where he had found her. However, recently, the nature of their relationship had begun to change, and he sometimes wondered if she now *enjoyed* working for him. The very thought made him uncomfortable, as he wanted only servants who feared him, but he needed her too much to send her back.

"To London?" he asked, knowing the question would jar her from pouting.

"Yeah, I listened while Wade talked to Eleisha in the office. They had the computer up. That wild man from last summer attacked someone else."

This got his attention. He'd been hoping Eleisha would continue to investigate that lead. He believed one of the elders may have escaped him and gone feral. It was possible.

Two centuries past, Julian's kind had been far more numerous, and they'd existed by four laws. The most sacred of these laws was "No vampire shall kill to feed." They'd retained their secrecy through telepathy, feeding on mortals, altering a memory, and then leaving the victim alive. New vampires required training from their makers to awaken and hone psychic abilities, but Julian's telepathy never surfaced. He lived by his own laws, and so the elders began quietly turning against him.

His own maker, Angelo, tried to hide this news from him, but he *knew*. He heard the rumblings, and he acted first, beheading every vampire who lived by the laws, including Angelo—who would have turned against him sooner or later.

Julian had left a small crop of younger vampires, untrained vampires like Eleisha and Philip, alone. They were not telepathic, did not know the laws, and were no threat to him.

Then with no warning, Eleisha suddenly developed fierce psychic abilities, and she began actively looking for any vampires who might have escaped Julian's net and remained in hiding.

She'd found several vampires who didn't count, such as Rose de Spenser, an uneducated creature who knew nothing of her own kind.

But Eleisha had also found Robert Brighton, a five-hundred-year-old elder who practiced the four laws like a religion. Robert had come out of hiding for Eleisha, who was so very easy to trust. Julian could not allow him to contaminate the others, to start the whole nightmare over again, and so he'd tracked Eleisha down and taken Robert's head.

That Robert had survived and hidden for so long told Julian he couldn't possibly be the only one. Now Julian was simply waiting for Eleisha to find more elders, to lure more of them out . . . and to lead him right to them.

Had she finally found another elder?

"Is she preparing to leave?" he asked.

"No. Wade wants to wait and see what Seamus

can track down first. But he says they're definitely going this time, whether Seamus pinpoints something or not."

"Wade?"

This was an oddity Julian had been noticing in Mary's reports. More and more in the past few months, Wade seemed to be making the decisions and giving the orders. Why would Eleisha—or Philip for that matter—ever take orders from a mortal? Julian wasn't certain what this meant, but it bore watching.

"You want me to alert Jasper, tell him to be ready to move?" Mary asked.

Julian's brows knitted. He rarely gave much thought to Jasper Nesland—a young vampire he'd created to serve him.

"No, not yet. Just go back to Portland and keep listening. Come to me as soon as they purchase tickets."

"Okay."

She sounded disappointed about something. He wasn't sure what, but he didn't give it any thought.

"Go," he ordered.

The air shimmered again, and she vanished. Julian began digging through the newspapers, looking for the most recent issue of the *Evening Standard*. He wanted to see the article Wade had found.

Eleisha sat in her nightgown before the mirror at her dressing table. She picked up a silver brush and absently ran it through her hair—with several things on her mind.

First, she was hungry and now wondered about her wisdom in not feeding when she'd had the chance. Since Julian had proven himself a danger to any of the lost vampires they found, Philip had strictly forbidden Wade, Eleisha, or Rose from going out alone at night, and they had all agreed to this.

Eleisha had reason to believe that for now Julian was no threat to her, but Philip hadn't changed his mind.

If she told him she needed to go hunting again, he'd want to know why, and then she'd have to tell him what happened tonight, and it would spoil any enjoyment he'd taken from the game they'd played. If she tried slipping out alone, his reaction would be worse.

She didn't know what to do.

But also, for months now she'd been dwelling on a specific memory she'd seen in the mind of another vampire, Robert Brighton. He had existed for hundreds of years in the company of a woman named Jessenia whom he loved—no, more than loved. He'd been *in* love with her. Due to Eleisha's youth spent as a servant, followed by nearly two centuries as a caretaker, she'd never experienced any of the things Robert had, and seeing his memories with Jessenia had been a revelation. Eleisha sometimes closed her eyes and relived what he felt as he touched Jessenia, kissed her . . . while joining his mind to hers.

Apparently, the love of vampires was different from the love of mortals, but just as physically intense.

Such acts were foreign to Eleisha.

They were foreign to Philip.

She knew he'd had lovers when he was a mortal, but something happened to him when he was turned, and as a result he couldn't remember anything—anything at all—of his mortal life. It was as if he'd been born the night he was turned. After two hundred years, any remnants of humanity that might once have remained with him were long gone.

She ran the brush through her hair again.

The bedroom door opened, and Philip walked in. He glanced at her nightgown in surprise. "Dawn's still an hour away."

He wore jeans and a black T-shirt. Philip was quite possibly the most handsome man she'd ever seen—or anyone had ever seen for that matter. But she didn't care what he looked like. His appearance was just part of his gift, something to fool mortals. He could have been disfigured, and she'd have loved him the same. When she was with him, she didn't feel alone.

"I know," she answered. "I just felt like getting ready for bed early."

Looking at his reflection in the mirror, she could see he was unhappy about something—probably the impending trip to London and everything that went along with such a search.

"I'm sorry about the Hitchcock film," she said, not sure what else to say. "We'll watch it tomorrow if Seamus hasn't come back yet."

He shrugged. Philip had never been skilled at

speaking. No matter what he was feeling, he often didn't know how to put his thoughts into words, and he'd shared enough of his memories with her that she understood how much this disability frustrated him. He wished he could master verbal communication.

Eleisha turned in her chair, looking around. This room pleased her in a way no other bedroom had before. She liked that it was halfway underground. She liked the antique sloped ceiling and the cream-colored walls and the white trim. The bed was covered in a white eyelet comforter and a ridiculous number of Philip's pillows. He technically had his own room, but he never slept there.

"Philip," she began, uncertain how to even broach the image in her mind. But they could be leaving for London as early as tomorrow night, and then they would all be embroiled in a difficult search. "I wanted to try something new tonight . . . to try showing you a memory."

He dropped down into the chair beside her bed and pulled his boots off. "You've shown me memories."

"Not like this. I want to try showing you a memory I saw in someone else."

He stopped moving, and the muscles in his arms tensed. "Who?"

"Robert."

As soon as she said it, she'd let out a secret she couldn't take back. Philip looked up, and she wasn't sure what she saw in his eyes. Anger or anxiety? Maybe both.

"Robert showed you his memories?" He bit the words off. "How many?"

She stood up and hurried over, crouching down beside him. Sharing memories was a deeply personal act. "More than he wanted. We got locked inside his past, and they just kept coming. Don't be angry." She put her fingers on the arm of the chair. "Philip, do you remember the gypsy girl you once saw with him, way back when you were first turned? Jessenia?"

He wasn't ready to stop being angry yet and didn't answer. He just looked at her.

"They spent hundreds of years together," she went on. "They were close like us . . . but different." She had no idea how to explain the next part. "They shared more than we do."

His tight expression relaxed slightly. "What?"

"I can't . . . tell you. I don't know how. Will you let me try to show you the memory? It happened about a week after Jessenia turned him."

Philip glanced away, and his jaw twitched. "Eleisha, I don't want to see anything from Robert's life. I don't know why you are—"

"Please. This isn't about Robert. It's about us."

She didn't know why this was so important to her, but she couldn't stop dwelling on that one memory, and she needed to show it to Philip. She needed him to know.

He let out a frustrated sound, like a growl, and stood up, moving to the window to make sure the oversized shade was drawn and the heavy curtains were closed. If they got lost inside a shared memory, the sun could rise before they came out.

He pulled his T-shirt over his head and dropped it on the chair. Then he sat on the bed, putting his back against all the pillows.

Eleisha went to him quickly. He didn't want to do this; he didn't want to try this. But if he was even half-willing, she wouldn't let the chance go. Once he saw what she'd seen, felt what she'd felt, he'd understand.

"Remember how Robert's gift was protection, how he made people feel safe," Eleisha said quickly. "Jessenia's was a sense of adventure. She infected people with a seduction of adventure."

Eleisha crawled up beside Philip and grasped two of his fingers, reaching her thoughts into his while simultaneously letting her mind flow back.

Philip was accustomed to Eleisha's communicating feelings to him through memories, and he'd never minded before, never worried about it before. But she'd never looked this intense before either—and she'd certainly never begged.

He wanted to stop this before it began, but how could he refuse? She asked so little of him.

So he let her grasp his fingers, and he opened his mind, feeling her inside him immediately. Normally, during a shared memory, he would be sucked away into her past, seeing through her eyes and reliving the experience through her.

But this time, when he closed his eyes, he felt her

struggling for a few moments, and then the scene changed.

To his shock, he was looking out through Robert's eyes.

He became Robert.

Robert had decided upon a journey to France, so he and Jessenia made their way to the coast and found passage on a ship to cross the Channel. Once settled in their cramped quarters below decks, he looked forward to the crossing. Jessenia made every moment enticing, and he was still reveling in his newfound existence with her.

So much was new to him now.

The air was nearly black outside the small porthole, and he felt sharply aware and awake. Somehow, she seemed different to him tonight. She kept studying his face almost as if she were hungry. He never tired of looking at her. He loved the sight of her thick black hair.

She looked to be about nineteen years old, with the pale, glowing skin of someone who seldom went outdoors. Her nose was small, and her mouth was heart-shaped. She wore a forest green skirt and white blouse with a thin vestment over the top, laced up tightly. She was slender and her hips were narrow, yet the tops of her breasts swelled above the laced vest. Gold rings dangled from her ears, and bracelets clinked on her wrists.

She came to him, sitting beside him on his bunk. "I can feel your gift," she said. "It's getting stronger."

So much she said was still a mystery.

"I love your gift," she whispered, "as you love mine."

She reached up and kissed him. He pushed her back to lie on the bunk, and he pressed his mouth down hard over hers, running his hands down her slender waist as she moved her hands up to grip the nape of his neck.

In spite of his desire, his body did not respond in its usual way, and he ran his hand over the tops of her breasts. His need for her, his urgency grew, but his body betrayed him.

Then . . . he felt Jessenia inside his mind, her thoughts reaching for and entwining with his. Her sense of adventure and her joy in journeys suddenly became part of him, drawing upon him; as he thought of them together in strange places, a feeling of fierce protection began to build inside. No matter where they went, no matter what they saw or what they did, he would protect her, from people, from the sun, from poverty, from everything.

Her passion for adventure began to combine with his desire to protect . . . inside him . . . inside her . . . until he could no longer tell the difference. The joining and meshing of half-mad drives went on and on in waves through his body until he felt it build to an almost-intolerable bubble. Then it burst, and his body shuddered in a shock of intense pleasure. Jessenia was still gripping the nape of his neck, and she gasped aloud—as if she still needed to breathe.

"Robert," she was saying over and over in his ear. "I knew, I knew."

He pressed his nose against hers. He was still shaking.

He had never imagined emotions like this, drives and needs like this. She had been inside him, and he inside her.

What had she done to him?

Her body began to relax beneath his, and she turned her head to one side.

"I knew as soon as I saw you," she said.

"No!"

Philip jerked away, gasping, as if he, too, needed to breathe. He pulled away from Eleisha and jumped up off the bed, running both hands through his hair. He couldn't go on with that memory, feeling that intimate connection of others.

"No," he said again, pacing toward the dressing table.

"Philip."

The sad quality of her voice made him whirl back around. She was curled up with her arms around her knees. She looked small and forlorn.

"What does it mean?" she whispered.

And then he wasn't angry or even anxious anymore. She wasn't trying to force him to see or experience something he didn't want to. She genuinely hadn't known how to explain her questions. If there was one thing Philip understood, it was the inability to speak thoughts. She'd seen—and felt—something she couldn't comprehend, and she'd wanted to share it, wanted his help.

He took four strides back to the bed. Dropping down, he pulled her up against his chest and held her there. In his mind, he could still feel Robert pressing his mouth on Jessenia's—as a mortal would—and how much Robert had liked it. He could still feel their gifts meshing into each other and the intense pleasure that followed. Philip had often kissed his victims before feeding, but he'd never felt anything like Robert had. Kissing was just a prelude to feeding, something he did to relax a victim right before he shut off his gift and reveled in the onslaught of fear.

"Philip, what does it mean?" Eleisha whispered again, pushing her face against his shoulder.

He gripped her tightly. "I don't know."

Twenty minutes later, the sun crested, and he fell dormant while holding on to her.

Just before dawn, Wade decided to knock on Rose's door. He didn't like the idea of disturbing her if she wanted privacy, but it was unlike her to spend most of the night in her room. Usually, she would work with either Wade or Philip on developing her telepathy, spend time in the garden with Eleisha, or read in the sanctuary with Seamus, turning the pages for him. If she wished to be alone, Wade did not want to intrude, but he felt she should be informed of the situation.

He knocked on her bedroom door.

"Rose, it's me."

"Come in," she called.

He opened the door to see her sitting in a chair, reading a Dick Francis novel. She wore a loose white dress with a black belt at the waist. But she also wore gloves that came up past her wrists. Recently, she'd manifested a new telepathic power: psychometry. She had to be cautious of touching anything with her bare hands, or she might be flooded with unwanted images of where an object had been or who had been holding it.

Rose wasn't pretty like Eleisha, but Wade always thought of her as a handsome woman. She was tall and looked about thirty years old, with long brown hair sporting a few white streaks. Rather than make her older, the streaks simply made her more exotic. He'd always liked them.

After seeing him in the doorway, she glanced down at her watch.

"Oh . . . ," she said in surprise. "I'd no idea it was so late. I won't even have time to change."

He smiled at her. "Good book?"

"Yes, very good. I forgot the time."

Vampires seldom forgot the impending dawn—they automatically fell dormant the second the sun crested—but she had the windows completely closed off, so he could see how she might have become lost in her novel.

She stood up and started toward the bed. "Thank you for checking in."

"I sent Seamus back to London. I just wanted to let you know."

She stopped. "London. Again?"

"Yes, on the same lead. Another news story appeared tonight, and I'm hoping he'll find something this time."

Her face was impassive. "Let us hope."

Rose was a quiet, driving force behind their operation. She wanted to find every last vampire in hiding and offer him or her a place here.

The first hints of the sun must have peeked up beyond the covered window, because she wavered on her feet, and he rushed in to help her. She raised one hand quickly, stopping him.

"No, it's all right. I can manage."

She dropped down onto the bed, fully clothed. For some reason, her refusal hurt him. He felt rebuffed, as if she didn't want him to touch her for any reason. He backed away, about to tell her good night even though it was morning, but she had already fallen dormant.

Wade closed the door and stood there in the main-floor hallway for a moment. The nights were getting longer, and so he was spending less time awake and alone during the daylight now. He'd long since adjusted his hours to those of his companions, but he never needed to sleep all day as they did.

He knew he should go cook himself something to eat, and then go to bed himself, so he went downstairs to the basement apartment. But instead of turning right to head into the kitchen, he turned left and went down the hallway to undergo a somewhat twisted ritual he performed every morning.

He often had long talks with himself, insisting that he find a way to stop doing this, but he could not. He did the same thing every morning shortly after the sun rose.

Opening the door to Eleisha's room (she never locked it), he walked over to the bed and gazed down to watch her sleeping with Philip—both of them completely dormant, unaware. However, the instant he saw them, he knew something was wrong. She usually slept either curled up against Philip or with her head on his stomach.

This morning, their positions were different. Philip was leaning back against the headboard, gripping Eleisha in both his arms in a tight gesture that looked possessive and protective at the same time.

Wade frowned. What had led to that?

He wished Eleisha would talk to him as she used to. His mind often drifted back to the short period when it had been just the two of them alone, before Philip, before Rose. Philip's entrance had not been unwelcome. Wade was well aware that they needed him, but still . . .

He stood there for a long time, watching them.

Then he walked back out and closed the door.

The next night, Eleisha was in the garden, cutting off some of the last of the fading rosebuds. She had a number of rosebushes that had bloomed into midautumn, but now they were getting ready to go dormant for the winter.

She was so hungry, she could barely hold on to the shears.

Gripping harder, she tried to concentrate. Seamus had not returned, and she was worried he might materialize at any moment, spurring Wade to purchase plane tickets and forcing them all into action. She was not up to a flight to London, followed by an exhaustive search, and she didn't know what to do.

Should she just slip away into the night and go feed by herself?

If her absence were discovered, it would cause a commotion—and not just with Philip. Wade and Rose would be troubled as well, as they had sworn to the same agreement. One of them breaking it might render their pact void, and who knew where that might lead?

Her only other choice was to tell Philip the truth, but this would disappoint him and let him know that she'd suggested the game entirely for his sake, not her own, and then he'd always insist on their previous method of hunting . . . which he found dull and tasteless.

No, she couldn't tell him.

She clipped a lavender rosebud, its dying petals curling outward.

"Eleisha," Wade's voice called from somewhere.

She looked around, feeling weak and wondering what was wrong with her hearing. Then she saw him walking toward her. He'd changed a good deal since last spring, for better and for worse. Although he would never be bulky, his obsession with the weight room had thickened his arms, especially his forearms, and his white-blond hair hung down the back of his neck. His clothes fit him much better now. But his eyes had become harder than those of the Wade she'd first met; they were more guarded, more quietly angry.

"I thought I'd find you out here," he said, coming over and crouching down beside her. "I wanted to see you alone and get a few things straight before Seamus comes back."

She blinked. "Like what?"

"Like no matter what he reports, I'm not staying behind this time."

Eleisha looked at the ground. They hadn't spoken of this very much, and the topic was painful to them both. At the inception of their last mission, she'd decided the situation was too dangerous for Wade to get involved, and she'd gone alone with Philip. The result had been disastrous, and later, Eleisha wondered how things might have turned out had Wade been there to help assess the vampire they'd located.

"I know," she whispered. "I'm sorry about the last time."

"Yes? Well, being sorry doesn't . . ." He trailed off, dipping his head to try to see her face. "Look at me. What's wrong with you?"

She didn't look up.

"Eleisha?" He reached out to touch her shoulder, and suddenly the old Wade seemed to come back, the gentle, concerned Wade she remembered. "Talk to me," he said. "Your skin is almost white."

"I'm hungry," she said as quietly as she could. "I haven't fed in more than a week."

"No, you just went out last night."

"I didn't feed."

Slowly, in halting sentences, she told him what had happened. When she finished, he didn't ask any questions. He didn't need to. That was one thing about Wade. He understood Philip almost as well as she did. Wade didn't need her to explain the dilemma.

"I can't go to London like this and start a search," she whispered.

He crouched there in silence for a few moments. Then he reached over and took her hand, standing and pulling her to her feet. "Come on," he said, starting for the back side of the church.

"Where are we going?"

"Just come on."

Wade led Eleisha into the darkness behind the church and down a short flight of moss-covered stone steps leading to the back door. They were hidden from sight here, and he crouched again, pulling her down with him.

"Lean against the wall," he said, and he positioned himself with his back to the stairs.

She looked at him in confusion, and her face glowed white in the darkness. No wonder she'd been outside in the garden. She probably hadn't wanted Philip to see how white her skin was turning.

"Just feed on me," he said.

Reacting exactly as he expected, she tried to jump up. "No."

But he was ready and gripped her arms, holding her down, surprised by how easy it was. He knew vampires in general were stronger than mortals, especially vampires like Julian and Philip, but he'd always wondered about Eleisha. She kept this aspect of herself a secret, and now he knew why.

He didn't like having to hold her here, but it wasn't difficult.

"Just listen!" he said. "It's all right."

She wore a sky blue flannel shirt over a long skirt—her usual gardening clothes—and the material of her shirt felt soft under his hands. Her expression began to crumble when she realized she couldn't push him away.

"Wade, please don't ask me to—"

"It's all right," he said again. "You can't go out, and I know why you can't tell him. But you *have* to feed before we go to London. I'll just wear a long-sleeved shirt for a while. Nobody else needs to know."

He gave her a few moments to allow his words to sink in. He was right, and she knew it. When she didn't speak again, he let go of her with his left hand and moved his wrist up to her mouth.

"It's all right," he whispered one more time, hoping she'd believe him.

He was ashamed of the excitement building in his

chest. He could finally give her something she needed. She was starving, and she couldn't just walk away.

Slowly, she took his wrist in both her hands. "I'll be careful."

"I don't care."

He shivered when she put her mouth over his skin and bit down. A flash of pain shot up his arm, but he didn't even flinch and pushed his wrist deeper. She was swallowing his blood, drinking him in, and he didn't want her to stop. They huddled in the stairwell, entangled with each other, and he was lost in the moment, almost not able to believe that her mouth was finally pressing against his body.

But he'd forgotten one element of this act, and his small oversight changed things between them forever.

Just a few seconds after she started, his most recent memories began to flow. When a vampire killed while feeding (and he'd experienced this many times while reliving their memories), the victim's entire life poured out. But when feeding like this, Eleisha would see only bits and pieces and shadows, and Wade's most vivid memories of the past weeks involved him standing over Eleisha and Philip while watching them sleep on her bed.

As she swallowed mouthfuls of his blood, she experienced the raw, unexplainable feelings of being "shut out" that he suffered while looking down at them. She felt his internal struggle over trying to stop and being unable to overcome the compulsion.

Panic hit him.

She drew down hard once more, swallowed, and disengaged her teeth, staring at him. Her eyes looked so large in the darkness, but her skin had a hint of color now.

"Wade . . . ?" she stammered.

"It's not how it looks! I just like to check on you."

They both knew that was a lie. She'd been inside his head for only a few moments—but it was enough.

Blood from his wrist dripped onto the lowest stair.

"Eleisha!" Rose called from above. "Are you out here?"

Eleisha's eyes widened farther, but she managed to call back calmly. "Yes, I'm here. Coming, Rose."

She got up and opened the back door, which led into Wade's makeshift gym. "Can you bandage your wrist alone?"

"Yes," he answered stiffly, wondering how she could say anything so mundane after what they'd just been through together.

"Then go. I'll go up and meet Rose."

He moved to slip through the door.

"Wade?"

He paused.

"Nothing," she said.

He walked inside.

chapter three

On the second night of his search, Seamus materialized in an alley near King's Cross Station in London, making certain he was alone in the darkness. After being away from Rose so long, he wasn't up to full strength anymore, but he was still strong enough to search, and he'd finally sensed the hint of an undead signature . . . for a black hole in the fabric of life.

A presence, or perhaps an absence, hit him almost right away, close by, and he blinked out, rematerializing in another alley off Belgrove Street, casting out with his senses again and becoming frustrated with his inability to track down this presence.

He had come looking for this vampire twice before, and he didn't want to fail Wade a third time.

Seamus had spent nearly two hundred years

alone with Rose, never letting her see how a part of him longed for true death, how he'd suffered through the empty nights, one after the next, where nothing ever changed. But another part of him could not bear to leave her all alone. She was his blood and kin, and he endured the endless nights for her sake.

Wade and Eleisha had changed all that, and now he was a part of something much bigger. The underground wouldn't even exist without him. He was their seeker, their searcher, the one who brought everyone together. They could never have found each other without him.

He'd also not realized how hungry he'd been for friendship, and Wade had proven himself a true friend. Eleisha had won Seamus' affections as well, for she was always gentle with Rose.

At first, Seamus had hated Philip, but his feelings were more conflicted now. Since returning from Denver, while Philip had not exactly been kind to Rose, he had not been unkind either, and he'd succeeded in helping hone her telepathy in areas where Wade had not. Yet . . . some of Seamus' instincts still screamed that this new side of Philip was nothing more than a facade to hide the killer he'd always been—always would be. Seamus would never completely trust him.

Although the alley was dark, he could see numerous people walking down the street just past the entrance. This was a busy part of the city, but quite shabby, with many decaying buildings and a large homeless population.

He drifted closer to the entrance, reaching out with his senses and feeling himself growing even weaker. This was the cross he bore in order to be useful to his companions. Shortly after being separated from Rose, he began losing his hold on this world, and the greater the distance, the more rapid the process. All ghosts on this plane were tied to a place or a person. Their spirits remained here due to strong—overwhelming—emotion at the time of death. Seamus was no exception. He'd told Wade that being away from Rose simply weakened him. But this was not the complete truth.

Rose was his only reason for remaining here, and whenever he left her, he could feel himself slipping away and being pulled to the other side. While away from her, he had to constantly fight back, using all his strength to remain.

He'd now been away from her—across an ocean—for more than twenty-four hours, and he was working harder to keep from succumbing and being pulled from this plane to the other side. The effort to remain was agony, but he fought to stay.

He was onto something. He was sure of it.

Last summer when he'd hunted this presence, it had been much fainter, almost imperceptible, but this time he could sense it more clearly—just not as clearly as he'd sensed all vampires in the past.

He focused all his remaining energy on the signature and blinked out again, rematerializing inside a dark, abandoned building just off Euston Road. He could see movement and hear shuffling behind some rotting wooden boxes, and he froze.

But he wasn't prepared for the scream.

A sound like a wailing animal exploded around him just before a figure shot out from behind the boxes. Nothing in this world could hurt Seamus, but he flinched and floated backward anyway.

Then he saw a young man—a creature?—crouched down on all fours across the room. It—he?—hissed sharply, exposing long canine fangs, and Seamus cursed himself for having fully materialized. But he didn't blink out. There was no point now.

The man, hissing and spitting, never stopped moving, shifting about on his hands and the balls of his feet. He was slender, with shocking white skin and black eyes. His blue-black hair was filthy and hung jaggedly around his narrow face. His clothes were in tatters, especially the remnants of his shirt, which exposed the white hairless flesh of his chest and shoulders. His feet were bare.

Seamus looked around, wondering if this place was some kind of "home," and if so, whether he could lead Eleisha back here. But there were no blankets on the floor, no flashlight, no sign at all that anyone had been staying here.

The man hissed at him again, and then he bolted, moving faster than Seamus could see toward a small hole in the wall. Seamus started after him, hoping to learn more, when a large orange cat jumped from the darkness onto a box near Seamus and slashed at him, spitting and snarling in an eerie echo of the man. Again, Seamus pulled away out of instinct rather than any necessary fear, but the action broke his concentration. A sleek gray tabby jumped to the box on his other side, snarling and slashing from the right.

Seamus blinked out, materializing back in the alley on Belgrove. He reached out with his senses again, but he could no longer pinpoint the signature, and the experience in the dark room had further weakened his hold on this plane. He felt himself slipping.

He'd seen enough here. It was time to report. It was time to get back to Rose.

Eleisha sat on the couch, watching *Psycho* with Philip. She could hear Wade in the kitchen helping Rose learn to control her telepathy. He was a patient teacher, and his low voice carried through the archway.

Everything seemed normal.

But it wasn't.

Eleisha kept her expression calm, glad that Philip had become wrapped up in the film quickly. She knew he'd like this one, and he sat riveted during the famous shower scene and the detailed cleanup scene afterward. He even commented on how unusual it was for a film to follow a character for so long—Janet Leigh's, in this case—before the story line completely changed. This was fairly analytical for Philip.

But Eleisha's mind wasn't on the movie. It was on

their impending journey. It was on her having just swallowed blood from Wade's arm. It was on the clear memory of his leaning over her and looking down as she and Philip slept. It was on the loneliness he never expressed.

She had always viewed him as so . . . solid, the rock of their team. Now she would forever see him differently.

She wasn't angry with him; she was worried. She'd picked up enough to see he was fighting a compulsion that consistently left him feeling more and more isolated, yet the thought of his standing over her and Philip while they slept—every morning—made her shiver. Should she start locking the door? Worse, she didn't even know how to help him. If she tried to spend more time with him now, be more intimate with him, he'd interpret it as pity.

"Okay," he said patiently to Rose, "I'm going to push harder. You keep my thoughts out."

Eleisha couldn't believe how calm he sounded, as though the turmoil inside him weren't even there. She couldn't stop thinking about the strength in his hands when he'd pinned her arms, or of him pushing his wrist deeper into her mouth. He was a stranger to her, and yet he was still Wade.

She glanced at Philip. He hadn't mentioned the memory she'd shared with him last night, and she was beginning to think he might not. That act had taken courage on her part, but he seemed to be pretending it never happened. She had hoped for more from him. She wasn't certain what . . . just more.

"Norman should kill his mother," Philip said. "Then he would be free."

"Well . . . keep watching."

Something shimmered through the archway of the kitchen. She tensed.

"Eleisha!" Wade called instantly. "You out there?"

She hit the PAUSE button on the remote and jumped to her feet, moving quickly through the arch to see Seamus standing by the table. He looked exhausted, all his bright colors faded and even more transparent than usual.

"Seamus," Rose said in alarm, "you promised you wouldn't push yourself this hard."

"Did you find anything?" Philip asked, coming in after Eleisha.

Seamus nodded, as if trying to gather the strength to speak. "Yes," he said finally. "Different . . . and I can't always make a pinpoint, but I can get close."

"You think it's a vampire?" Eleisha asked.

He nodded again, floating closer to Rose. "It's a vampire . . . but he's wild, like an animal."

Eleisha just watched him for a few seconds, taking this in. Since returning from Denver, she'd had moments when she wondered if maybe they were all that remained, if they'd already found the few survivors, and what this meant to the future of the underground. But Wade and Seamus had found another, and he needed their help. The world had just shifted.

Her entire focus shifted.

"All right," she said, nodding back at him. "We need to get ready and buy three plane tickets."

"Maybe four," Wade put in.

Eleisha forced herself to look at him. It was the first time she'd looked directly at him since the stairwell. He was wearing a long-sleeved shirt. "What do you mean?"

He didn't meet her eyes. Instead, he turned to Rose. "I think we're going to need Seamus *with* us on this one . . . maybe much of the time, and that won't work unless you're with us, too."

"Wade, no," Eleisha cut in. "You can't ask her to—"

He held up his right hand, and Eleisha paused, watching him warily. Rose had a phobia of travel, and she'd never been on an airplane. They'd only managed to bring her from San Francisco by barricading themselves into a cabin on a train and closing the shutters on the window. Although for Wade's sake, Eleisha had been allowing him to take greater charge of things, to feel more essential, she was still in control here, and she'd shut him down in a heartbeat if he tried to make Rose do something she feared.

"I think I can help you," Wade said, still speaking directly to Rose. "If you let me into your mind, I can take you someplace else, keep you from knowing where you are until we land, even until we reach the hotel if you want me to. Will you try?"

Eleisha's protective instincts surged up, and she got ready to fight him on this if necessary, but Rose's expression did not close up. She seemed to be contemplating his words, and she looked over at Eleisha with hope.

"I so want to help you," she said. "Let me try this."

"Are you sure?" Eleisha asked, still uncertain.

"We're going to need Seamus," Wade stated flatly. "She has to come."

"Yes," Rose answered. "I want to try."

Philip had his arms crossed and was leaning back against the refrigerator, watching Wade with a slightly puzzled expression.

"Good. But we need a few more ground rules," Wade went on. "For one, nobody turns off their cell phone, and everybody answers when it rings—do you understand?"

"You can't bring your gun into London," Philip said quietly, changing the topic.

Eleisha glanced over at the warning tone in his voice, and she didn't like where this was going. Wade seemed to be attempting to put himself in the position of leader—without anyone casting a vote— and Philip didn't take orders from anyone, not even Wade.

Wade frowned. "What?"

"You can't bring a handgun into England. Airport security does random searches of luggage, so if you try to hide it in your suitcase and check it in, someone could still search your bag. You'd be arrested when we hit the ground."

"What about your machete?"

"I can just pack that in a box and send it through with oversized luggage. Julian travels with a sword all the time. But laws there are different for guns." Philip paused, as if something had just occurred to him. "Has anyone here ever been to London?"

His question stopped the conversation. Eleisha already knew the answer was no.

She'd grown up in Wales without ever seeing anything outside of the Cliffbracken estate. After turning her, Julian had put her on a ship bound for America in 1839. She'd seen almost nothing of Europe. Wade had never been out of the country. Rose had been born in Scotland, never gotten far outside her home village, and then lived the existence of a shut-in after coming to America.

"Have you?" Eleisha asked Philip.

"Many times."

Philip was the traveler in their little group, and he'd spent most of his time in Europe. That put him in a unique position here.

But Wade wasn't ready to give up. "I'll book the tickets."

"No, I'll do it," Philip said, just an edge of warning in his voice. "I need to account for the time difference so we can take off in the dark and land in the dark."

Wade opened his mouth, but Eleisha shook her head at him slightly. He closed it.

"We should get packed," she said. She glanced from Philip to Wade. "The only thing that matters now is that we've found another lost one—who needs help." She hesitated. "That's all that matters."

Wade had the good taste to look slightly chagrined, but Philip just walked out of the kitchen. Eleisha's stomach tightened. They were about to embark on a search that had a chance of success only if they worked together and depended upon one another's strengths without question. How was this going to play out with so many rifts cracking the connections between them?

She didn't know.

The following night, Julian had just finished saddling his horse when the air shimmered and Mary appeared beside him at the stable.

"They're in a taxi, on the way to the airport," she said immediately.

For once he wasn't annoyed at her sudden appearance and manner of blurting out words.

"Who's on the mission?"

"All of them."

He put his large hand on the horse's shoulder. "All of them?"

"Yup, even Rose."

Julian digested that information, as he knew Rose suffered from a debilitating phobia of travel, and she always remained behind at the church. Why would they risk bringing her unless they believed they'd found something important . . . an elder?

"What have you learned about the vampire they're seeking?" he asked.

"Nothing. They had a meeting in the kitchen, but I couldn't get close enough to listen. Seamus was there." She frowned. "And if Rose is going to London, he'll be with them all the time. That's going to be a bitch for me."

Julian glanced at her, trying to ignore her crude speech patterns. She was American after all, and allowances must be made. Mary had much greater freedom of movement than other ghosts, as she was not tied to any one person or place; unfortunately, however, Seamus could sense her presence if she got too close, and Julian didn't want Eleisha to know when or if she was being watched.

However, Seamus' doing sweeps of London in search of a vampire could be problematic in other ways. Julian would not be able to book a hotel inside the city.

"You want me to teleport to London and see what I can learn on my own?" she asked.

He put his fist to his mouth for a few seconds, thinking. If Eleisha had found an elder, every move he made would be vital. He had to intercept her quickly once she'd made contact and take matters into his own hands. History could never be allowed to repeat itself, so he had to get closer without getting too close.

"No . . . go to San Francisco. Tell Jasper to book a flight and meet me at the Great Fosters hotel on Stroude Road in Surrey. It's only about nine miles from Heathrow Airport. He should have no trouble."

She brightened. "Okay."

He started to turn away and then stopped. "But tell him to calculate the time zones properly. London is eight hours ahead of California, and he has to land in the dark."

Her transparent forehead wrinkled, and then she said, "Oh . . . yeah, I'll make sure he's careful."

Julian hoped that between the two of them, Mary and Jasper possessed the ability to count to twenty-four. He unsaddled his horse, set it loose in the pasture, and walked back toward the manor.

San Francisco, California

Jasper Nesland tossed the keys of his BMW to a valet, paid his cover charge, and walked into the Cellar nightclub on Sutter Street. Loud music and purple-red lights washed over him before the door even closed. The place was packed, but he still noticed a girl in a short skirt by the wraparound bar flash a smile at him.

Sometimes, he couldn't believe how much his life had changed. Six months ago that girl wouldn't have bothered to spit on him. He walked through the crowd, straight to her.

Jasper wasn't into playing games when he hunted. He didn't like to dance; dancing was for losers who didn't care if they made fools of themselves. And unlike Julian, he never drank red wine or tea, so hanging out at a table with someone seemed equally pointless.

He did, however, get satisfaction from the way flashy girls treated him now that he had money, now that he got his hair cut at L'ShearHair and bought his clothes at Uomo in Union Square.

Money changed everything.

He didn't bother smiling back and just slid up to the bar beside her. She had layered brown hair with blond highlights, and although she wore too much eye makeup, it was artistically applied. But her eyes held no warmth, no light of their own. She was his favorite type.

"You want to dance?" she asked without asking his name.

She wasn't shy.

"No. It's too loud in here. Let's go somewhere else."

He turned on his gift ever so slightly, just a hint. When he'd first learned his gift, he'd hated it, been humiliated by the thought of it, and he would have taken anything else. He'd longed for a gift like Philip's or Julian's. But in the nights that followed, Jasper had come to understand the benefits of his gift: pity.

There was great power in pity once he learned how to use it.

Right now he was making this girl feel sorry that the music was too loud for him and that he wanted to leave. She grabbed her clutch purse off the bar.

"Sure," she said.

He took her hand and led her toward the doors. He'd been inside the nightclub less than ten minutes.

A different valet went to get his car, and he stood

on the curb, enjoying the night breeze blowing across his face.

"What's your name?" she asked.

"Jasper."

"I'm Melanie. You married?"

No girl he'd ever picked up had asked him that before, and he looked at her.

"No. Why?"

She shrugged. "I always seem to end up with married guys."

Well, if you didn't leave bars with guys you just met, that might not happen so much.

The thought passed quickly through his mind, and he didn't say it out loud. The BMW pulled up, and he watched her face. Her eyes flickered once, but she made no comment. He opened the door for her, tipped the valet, and jogged around to the driver's side.

"Where should we go?" she asked once he got in.

"How about the waterfront? Take a walk down by the Cannery? Maybe get some coffee?"

This time, she couldn't stop her face from registering surprise. He'd learned quickly that suggesting things like walks by the waterfront and then having coffee were unexpected to girls who hung out in expensive nightclubs . . . but the suggestion always worked.

"Sure," she said again.

He pulled out into traffic and headed for Jefferson Street. To his relief, she didn't talk much on the way. He found a parking place near the wax museum, and got out, jogging around to open her door. Then he headed toward the water and she followed him—even though she was wearing five-inch stiletto heels.

"I like to look at the boats," he said, moving toward the docks and listening to the sound of the waves. "Sometimes I think about living on one."

That part was true. He'd thought about living on a boat since long before he was turned.

"Yeah?" she asked, but didn't seem too interested. "What do you do?"

What did he do? He followed Julian's orders. That was what he did.

"This way," he said without answering her question, and led her down Pier 45 toward the Fishermen's and Seamen's Chapel. Halfway down, there was a narrow opening between the buildings, and he slipped inside. "Here."

She paused. "What's in there?"

"Just come talk to me for a while. I'm lonely."

He let his gift flow and watched her expression change from one of caution to one of sympathy. She followed him in without another word, and they were alone in the shadows and darkness. In his early hunts, he had sometimes kissed his victims and allowed them to become completely immersed in sympathy for him before he suddenly shut it off and then rejoiced in their fear—rather like revenge for years of rejection. But he didn't do that anymore. He still tended to choose a certain type of girl, but now he wanted no connection whatsoever and no reminders of the past.

As soon as she reached him, he pushed her up against the wall and held her there, but he turned his gift up until her mind was clouded by feelings of pity for his loneliness. He could see she wasn't the type to offer anyone comfort, and yet she still wanted to comfort him. He pressed up against her, smelling her skin. While she was dazed and clouded, he drove his teeth into her neck and started drinking. She bucked once, but he used his strength and his gift to hold her in place, and she barely knew what was happening.

He drew down hard and swallowed quickly over and over, feeling his own body growing stronger.

Her memories were predictable: many nights dancing and drinking in clubs; running up credit card bills until her father threatened her; sex with numerous men at least ten years older than she was—most of whom were already married. He saw a white cat name Percival that she loved, and the wrinkled face of a grandmother she called once a week.

He pulled away. He didn't want to see those last two things.

The girl's throat was a mess, blood running freely down her dress. Within a few seconds, her heart stopped beating, and her head lolled. He listened for any footsteps, and, once certain they were still alone, he picked her up with one arm, carried her out to the rail, and dropped her body into the water. It vanished beneath the waves.

He wiped his face and checked his shirt for blood.

Then he walked back toward his car. He was going home. He'd told this girl he was lonely . . . and he was. But he cared for the company of only one person, a ghost named Mary, and Julian kept her busy in Portland most of the time.

Maybe she could find a way to see him again soon.

Mary materialized inside Jasper's apartment at the Infinity complex, happier than she'd been for a while—grateful Eleisha was following a lead. A new mission for Eleisha meant a mission for Julian . . . and that meant Mary and Jasper would work together.

"Jasper, you here?" she called.

But even before speaking, she knew he must have gone out. She couldn't sense him anywhere.

Floating just inside the front door, she looked around. The place was amazing, with marble-tiled floors and a state-of-the art kitchen of stainless steel appliances. One wall of the living room was a giant window overlooking the bay. The whole room was decorated in black and white.

She noticed a few additions, such as a large-screen TV and a silver DVD rack.

Julian paid for everything here via an account

he'd opened for Jasper with Wells Fargo. The whole situation made Mary uncomfortable—as if Julian had sort of "bought" Jasper—but there wasn't much she could say.

Turning, she could sense an undead presence coming down the hallway, and she floated farther into the room. After a loud click, the door opened and he walked inside.

"Mary," he said, smiling slightly, glad to see her.

He was the only one who was ever glad to see her.

But he looked so different now.

When she'd found him, he'd been a shabby, skinny mess, wearing dirty pants and scuffed athletic shoes. His hair had been a disaster. He'd always slouched back then, with his shoulders pressing inward.

Then Julian turned him.

Some expensive local stylist had taken in the shape of Jasper's face and cut his hair very short, almost into a military cut. The look suited Jasper, defining the bones of his face. Tonight, he wore a loose, button-down black shirt over black jeans. He walked straight, his shoulders back.

Jasper liked his new existence, maybe a little too much, and he'd proven he'd do anything to keep it. Mary had to look out for him, to protect him from himself sometimes.

"I was just thinking about you," he said.

"You were?"

The smallest things like that affected her. He made her wish she were still alive.

"Yeah, I was. . . ." He paused. "Hey, why are you . . . ? Are we on the job?"

She nodded. "He's going to England. We're supposed to meet him at the Great Fosters hotel on Stroude Road in Surrey."

God, what a mouthful.

"You're supposed to fly into Heathrow," she added. "Then take a taxi to the hotel."

Jasper blinked and walked into his bedroom. Mary floated after to see him digging through his dresser drawers. "London?" he said with some hesitation. "I got myself a passport a couple of months ago, after he told me to . . . but did you see where I put it?"

"Um, yeah, I think I saw it with your emergency credit card."

He looked at her briefly and moved to the nightstand, opening a small drawer. His face relaxed. "Here it is. Thanks."

Jasper knew how to handle everything else, and he grabbed a box out of the closet to package his sword. "What's the job?"

"I don't know yet. Seamus found somebody over there. Julian's hoping for an elder, but I haven't learned too much. The vampire's a guy . . . kind of crazy, and he's been attacking people out in the open enough to make the newspapers. Oh, and he can make animals, like dogs and cats, protect him."

"Seriously?"

"Yeah, should be interesting."

While Jasper continued packing, Mary floated over to look into a mirror hanging on his bedroom wall. She put a transparent hand to the top of her head, wanting to grimace.

"What's wrong?" he asked.

No matter what he was doing, he always noticed her. He always put her first.

How could she tell him what she was thinking?

"My hair," she said finally. "I wish I could dye it brown again and grow it back out." She paused, trying not to sound sad. "I wish I could take out the nose stud and wear other clothes, any other clothes."

She would always appear exactly as she'd died.

He took a step toward her, shaking his head. "No. I like your hair. I like the way you look. It's you. Those girls I pick up in bars . . . They're all fake, all the way through to the inside. You're real."

Tragically, this was the most romantic thing anyone had ever said to Mary, but she drank it in and looked back at her spiky magenta hair. He liked it.

She didn't know how to answer him.

"I'll try to book a ticket out for tonight," he said, changing the subject since he may have been a little embarrassed.

Julian's warning flashed into her head.

"Be sure to count the hours," she told him. "London's eight hours ahead, and I think the flight is something like nine or ten hours. You gotta make sure you'll land in the dark."

"What? Oh . . . yeah, okay." He pulled out his cell phone and his wallet. "You'll meet me there?"

"Sure. I'll always meet you."

chapter four

LONDON

As Philip stepped from the taxi out in the Bloomsbury district, right in front of the Montague hotel, he was surprised by an unexpected sense of satisfaction. Eleisha climbed out behind him, staying close to his side and looking around. Instead of a suitcase, she'd brought a backpack, and she shifted its weight on her right shoulder.

"Oh, this is nice, Philip," she said, looking at the front of the hotel and the manicured flower beds along the street. "Better."

Wade and Rose's taxi pulled up to the curb.

Philip was beginning to think Eleisha had seen too many overromanticized British films. They'd landed at Heathrow and taken two cabs to the hotel. But throughout the drive, Eleisha had seemed more and more surprised—and appalled—to find that London was just another big, dirty, crowded city.

Wade got out of the taxi and reached to help Rose step down to the sidewalk. Not for the first time tonight, Philip made a mental note to insist Wade buy himself a more fashionable coat. He was wearing a brown canvas jacket with big pockets, and the bottom hung at an awkward angle below his hips. Seemingly unaware that he resembled a bumpkin, Wade looked around. "Oh, good. Better."

Apparently, he was of the same mind as Eleisha. What had they expected? At least seven million people lived here. Some of it was going to be seedy.

But Philip had handled the hotel reservation. He always stayed here on trips to London, and he knew Eleisha would like their suite.

She walked over to Rose. "Are you all right?" she asked.

"Yes, let's just go inside."

Eleisha took her hand, and they walked to the doors while Philip paid both drivers. True to his word, Wade had managed to keep Rose quiet and calm—almost asleep—the entire trip. Although he wouldn't admit it, Philip did find the prospect of having Seamus entirely at their disposal to be a relief.

A bellhop came to get their luggage. Philip and Wade followed him inside and up to the suite.

"Philip," Rose said, stepping through the door. "It's beautiful."

The suite was split level with one bedroom upstairs and one on the main floor. The color scheme was cream, brown, and light burnt orange. Most of the fabrics were silk, and a crystal chandelier hung over an antique coffee table in the sitting room.

Philip had already decided that he and Eleisha would take the upstairs bedroom, Rose could sleep in the main bedroom, and Wade could sleep on the couch. Wade never minded that, and it was better for them all to stay together.

Eleisha reached down to touch a silk throw pillow, and Philip just watched her, expecting to feel another wave of satisfaction that his greater knowledge of the world was finally useful. But the room was so familiar to him that, without any warning, a memory suddenly surfaced in his mind . . . of a night sometime back in the mid-1980s when he'd brought two prostitutes back here. He'd killed one of them quickly and the other one slowly.

The memory disturbed him—as if he feared Eleisha or Wade might enter his mind and read it—and he pushed it away while he tipped the bellhop and quickly showed the man out.

"I don't think I can start any kind of search tonight," Wade said once the door was closed. His eyes were bloodshot. "I need some sleep."

"I know," Eleisha said. "I feel strange, too. We've been up so long."

At least Wade had the luxury of falling asleep. The rest of them wouldn't go dormant until the sun rose here. But Philip had other plans anyway.

"I need to feed," he said abruptly. "Eleisha, come out with me."

She moved to him, and he studied her. She looked especially pretty tonight, wearing a short denim skirt and a tight-fitting black turtleneck. Some of her hair was pinned up with loose strands hanging past her chin.

"Already?" she asked. "You just fed the other night."

"The woman was small, so I didn't drain her much. But I want to be at full strength before we start anything here."

"Of course." She nodded. "Rose, would you like to come with us?"

This was a polite question, and Philip didn't worry about having extra company along. He knew Rose wouldn't be going anywhere.

"No, I'll stay here with Wade," Rose answered.

Eleisha looked all around the suite. "Seamus? Are you here?"

The air wavered, and Seamus materialized near the door. His colors were bright, especially the blue shades in his plaid. "I'm here."

"Wade's going to sleep for a while, and Philip and I are going out," she said. "I don't think we'll be starting a search until tomorrow night, so you can just stay near Rose."

He nodded his transparent head.

Philip opened the package hiding his machete, strapped the sheathed blade to his belt, and buttoned his coat over the top. He headed for the door, knowing Eleisha would follow. Shortly after they'd first met, she told him she'd follow him anywhere, even to France. But then they'd moved to Portland and started the underground. Tonight, he honestly did want to feed and gain his full strength, but more important, he wanted to show London to Eleisha . . . by himself.

As Eleisha stepped from the subway station out in Covent Garden, she could not help feeling impressed by the sheer organization of the city's underground transportation system. However, she was completely lost in this foreign place, and Philip seemed to know exactly what he was doing and where he was going at every turn.

It was . . . disconcerting.

Staying close to him, she took in the sights around her, finding some pleasure in the old-world charm of this area—more of what she expected. Her first impression of London had not been good, and she was rather glad to be out with Philip now.

An incredible variety of colorful shops and restaurants stretched all around them, along with an overwhelming array of people even this late into the night. Voices speaking in English, French, German, and Swedish floated swiftly past. As she stepped forward into a courtyard area, she heard music and turned to see a young man sitting in a chair out in the open, playing U2's "Sunday Bloody Sunday" at a surprising volume on an acoustic guitar.

"Come on," Philip said. "I want to show you Neal Street. It's so dark there."

The eagerness in his voice caught her attention, and she realized he wanted to do more than just go hunting. Were they sightseeing? This was hardly the time or the right situation.

"Philip . . . I thought you wanted to feed? We left Wade and Rose alone."

He glanced back, and his eyes flickered with something she couldn't quite name. Disappointment? Instantly, she regretted her words. Wade and Rose would be safe at the hotel.

"I'm sorry," she said, moving more quickly to walk beside him. "Show me Neal Street."

His eyes cleared, and he pointed. "That way."

She followed him to a dark street, lit only by the shop windows, and she could see why he liked it here. A busy nightclub graced the entrance, but once they'd walked past, she spotted a more interesting array of choices, including a small store devoted to books on astrology and a tea shop where a lattice-styled window made up the entire front wall.

"This used to be nothing but warehouses," Philip said. "I hunted a good deal down here, and I can still remember when the change began."

Everything but the nightclub was closed at this hour, and Eleisha wondered how Philip was going to hunt down here now. There were no parking garages where he could lure someone into a car. The restrooms at the nightclub would be packed, so they were out of the question.

Something seemed to catch his eye, and walking up to the front of the tea shop, he looked through the lattice window. She followed. Although the place was closed, the inside was well lit, and a large man stood working on a display near the back wall.

Philip suddenly turned to Eleisha and grasped her wrist. He rarely touched her unless they were sleeping, so the action took her back slightly.

"I don't want to play any games tonight," he said. "But I want you to stay with me . . . to stay inside my head while I'm feeding, as you did when you first taught me. I miss that."

She stared at him in the darkness. While she'd been training him how to alter a victim's memory, she'd joined her thoughts to his in order to monitor him—and to take over in case he faltered or failed in the attempt. She always assumed he viewed the act as intrusive. But he missed it?

"Okay," she said uncertainly.

"Now. Come inside my head now."

What was the matter with him? This was hardly like Philip. But she'd do anything he asked, anything to make him happy, and she reached out with her mind. Right away, she could feel him putting up a block against sharing any of his own memories. He just wanted her to see his immediate thoughts.

He knocked on the window lightly.

The man inside turned with an annoyed expression, waved Philip away, and mouthed the word "closed."

Let them in, Philip flashed into the man's head. *They will spend big and leave quickly.*

Eleisha was surprised by his precision and control. He planted the suggestion almost effortlessly. The shopkeeper walked to the door and opened it. Philip turned on his gift.

"Thank you," he said in his thick accent. "We hoped to buy some decent tea before going back to our hotel."

Eleisha had expected him to choose a large man tonight—as he wanted to take in as much blood as possible. But Philip's gift worked differently on most men than it did on women. Men were sort of . . . awed by him, basking in his company as if his aura of attraction would rub off. But Eleisha could feel it sinking under her skin, making her see how perfect Philip was, how much she wanted to touch him. She shook her head hard, fighting to clear it. This was one of the reasons she'd begun hanging back when he hunted. His gift was too strong.

"Come in," the shopkeeper said, locking the door behind them. "I was just tidying up for tomorrow."

The walls inside were covered in shelves and cubbies holding every kind of tea Eleisha could imagine. All around her stood little tables covered with a variety of pots, cups, and strainers. Philip walked straight to the back of the shop and around a dividing wall, out of sight of the window.

"Do you keep the imported oolong back here?" he asked.

The man had hardly noticed Eleisha; he was too focused on Philip. She kept her gift turned off, letting Philip completely run this show.

Stay inside my head, he flashed to her.

She didn't understand why he wanted this, but she stayed inside his mind, still struggling to hold his gift at bay.

The shopkeeper hurried around the divider after Philip. "Yes, top shelf on your right."

Eleisha followed just in time to see Philip reach out with one hand and say, "You're tired. You should sleep." She could feel the power behind his suggestion.

The man dropped like a sack of potatoes, and Philip caught him, lowering him to the floor. Within seconds, Philip had the man's wrist in his mouth and bit hard, drawing down and swallowing. Locked inside Philip, Eleisha could taste the warm, salty fluid and see the images and memories of countless customers coming through the shop, countless nights cleaning and prepping the shop for the next day. Most of the man's days had been almost identical. She saw no wife or children, but a Scottish terrier named Reginald who'd recently died of bone cancer.

Philip kept sucking and drinking, maybe too long, and Eleisha was just on the edge of telling him to stop when he pulled back on his own. He'd consumed a lot of blood, but the man seemed all right. Through Philip's contact, she could hear his heart still beating.

Philip looked at a large glass vase on the counter. "Shatter that," he ordered, "right there." He pointed to the floor beside him.

Eleisha took the vase and dropped it, letting it break into pieces. She watched as Philip used a shard to connect the teeth marks on the man's bloody wrist. Then Philip slipped inside the man's thoughts again, taking him back a few moments earlier. He'd continued working on the display. He'd seen no one. He'd let no one in. Then he knocked the vase off the counter and tripped, cutting himself.

Philip's execution was flawless . . . perfect to the last hint of control and last bit of detail.

He stood up. "Come."

They went to the door, leaving quickly, making sure it was locked behind them, and they moved down the dark street. Eleisha reached out with one hand, grasping Philip's coat and stopping him in the shadows near a china shop.

"Why did you want that?" she whispered. "Why did you want me to stay in your mind?"

He leaned close, his mouth a few inches from her ear, and she could smell the Paul Mitchell gel in his hair. "Because you keep me calm," he whispered back. "You keep the demons away. No one can be closer than the two us of when you're inside my head and we hunt."

She tensed, her fingers still gripping the black wool of his coat. What demons? And what did he mean, "no one could be closer"? Was that Philip's idea of intimacy? He still hadn't said a word about the memory she'd shown him of Robert and Jessenia, and she longed to talk about it.

He didn't seem to want to acknowledge it had ever happened.

Maybe their visions of intimacy possessed a gap they could not bridge.

Julian reached the Great Fosters hotel hours before Jasper, and he went up the suite he'd reserved. While he found the décor here somewhat dated, the service was unparalleled, and the location was perfect, about forty-five minutes outside of London.

Alone, he sat on a dark burgundy couch, staring out the window, and wondering how fast he'd be able to move in once this started. Eleisha had spent far too much time with Robert before Julian had managed to take his head. This time, if she had indeed located an elder—mad or not—the target must be removed quickly.

Unfortunately, the impending chain of events was completely out of his hands.

He didn't care for the unplanned or the unexpected, but there was no choice here. He was forced to wait upon however Eleisha decided to proceed . . . before he could proceed.

He sat there for hours, just thinking, and then a knock sounded on the door.

"It's me," Jasper said from the other side.

Julian got up and opened the door. Jasper walked in with a long box in one hand and a small bag over his left shoulder. He tended to pack light. But every time Julian saw him, he grew more wary of the drastic changes in his servant. Jasper looked like a completely different person from the one Julian had chosen and turned. Worse, he acted like a different person—quiet and confident.

But in truth, Julian worried less about him than he did about Mary. Jasper functioned on a platform of pure greed. Julian understood that. He trusted it.

These days, he wasn't sure at all about Mary's agenda.

As if on cue, the air shimmered, and she materialized into view. "Okay, we're here," she said. "You want me to go into London and track them? Find out where they're staying?"

"There's no need," he said. "They'll be at the Montague."

She blinked. "How do you know that?"

"Because Philip always stays at the Montague."

Mary tilted her head, as if digesting this information. "We're kind of on your home turf this time, aren't we? Yours and Philip's?"

Sometimes, she could be quite perceptive.

He ignored the question. "Just go make sure they're all at the hotel. I doubt they'll begin anything tonight, but make sure. Don't let Seamus sense you." Julian relied almost entirely on the element of surprise. He glanced at Jasper. "Have you fed?"

"Yes. Before I left."

"Good. I'm going out."

As Julian fastened his sword to his belt and then reached for his coat, he noticed how close Mary floated to Jasper while they chatted quietly with each other.

"I'll check the pay-per-view schedule," Jasper was saying. "Maybe when you get back we can watch a movie."

"Okay," Mary answered. "I won't be long."

Julian walked out the door, growing more concerned about both of them.

But as he headed outside, he forgot all about them. These might be the last few hours he had to himself for a while, and he'd always liked hunting in England. He was in the mood for a brutal kill . . . and perhaps the taste of a German tourist.

chapter five

The following night, just past dusk, Eleisha woke up with her cheek pressed into the hollow of Philip's shoulder. The bed beneath her hip was too soft, and she sat up, looking down at his ivory face. He was still dormant.

The hotel room felt completely foreign, and an unwelcome sensation of homesickness passed through her. Climbing off the bed, she was surprised when he didn't move. Normally, he was awake a few seconds before she was. He looked quiet and peaceful with his eyes closed.

Eleisha walked downstairs to find Wade in the sitting room on the couch—alone. He was staring into space, but he jumped slightly at the sight of her.

"The sun is down, but Philip is still asleep," she said, not sure what else to say.

"So is Rose. I think it might be some kind of vampire jet lag."

She moved closer. This was the first time they'd been alone since that raw moment in the dark stairwell of the church. He was still dressed in the same jeans and brown canvas jacket from the night before. Had he slept in his jacket? Eleisha was wearing a pair of gray sweatpants and her favorite Hello Kitty tank top. He looked at her tank top and then glanced away.

Her memories flowed back to their earlier nights together, after they'd first met, when he had been so easy to hurt and he'd talked to her about everything. Suddenly, she wanted to close the growing rift between them, and without warning, she flashed out.

I'm sorry.

They'd made a pact not to use telepathy on each other without permission first, but his eyes flew to her face, and he did not object.

"About what?" he asked aloud.

"Everything. That you've felt so alone. That I didn't notice."

His expression crumbled. He slid off the couch to the floor, and he put his face in his hands. "God, I didn't think you'd see. . . . I was just trying to feed you, and I didn't mean for you to . . ."

She rushed to him, crouching down and grasping his wrists—feeling the bandages on his left one. "It's not your fault. You just always seem so strong . . .

and you seem fine all the time. I should have known. I should have paid more attention."

He let her pull his hands down. His eyes were sad and warm at the same time. How long had it been since she tried talking to someone who responded like this? Philip listened when she told him of the past. He listened, but he never responded.

With Wade, she had only to drop her guard and open up, and he would respond in kind.

"You always do that," he whispered. "You always take everything on yourself. It's not your responsibility to notice."

"No, I've been too focused on Philip, on taking care of him, on making sure he's happy."

"And who takes care of you?" His tone changed, growing harder. "Who makes sure you're happy?"

She stiffened. What did that mean? He turned his wrists around and grabbed her hands, but his grip wasn't tight, as if he'd let go if she tried to pull away.

"Who takes care of you?" he repeated, but his voice was softer this time.

His face was close, and she looked at his mouth. What would he make of the memory she'd shown Philip?

"What memory?" he asked.

She jerked away, feeling his mind searching on the edge of her thoughts. "Wade!" She put up a mental block and pushed him out.

He didn't apologize. "What memory?"

His light brown eyes glowed softly, and she

couldn't believe how *right* it felt to be speaking with him this openly. She scooted close to him again. "Something I saw from Robert."

Just for an instant, the academic in Wade surfaced. "You showed Philip a memory you saw in Robert?"

She nodded. "It was easy, just like showing him one of my own." She paused. "But he didn't like it, and he doesn't want to talk about it."

He took her hand again. "Show it to me."

"I can't. It's too . . . Wade, I can't."

"Do you know how long it's been since you shared a memory with me?" he asked, his voice urgent now. "How long it's been since you shared anything with me?"

Her empathy for him wavered, and she felt as if she were standing on the edge of a cliff. A part of her was desperate for his insight, his open manner of thought and discussion. But something about this felt wrong.

"Show it to me," he whispered gently.

Still hesitant, she gripped down on his fingers and closed her eyes, dropping her block and reaching out into his mind.

For the first time in months, Philip woke up alone.

He was groggy and disoriented, but he was also aware that Eleisha was not curled up against him or sleeping on his shoulder. He reached out and touched nothing. Then he sat up.

"Eleisha?"

The bedroom was empty. He always woke before she did. Where was she?

Springing to his feet, he didn't bother grabbing his shirt off the chair and hurried down the stairs. At the sight of her dark blond head and Wade's white-blond head by the couch, a moment of intense relief passed through him.

But it lasted only a few seconds.

He stepped toward the couch and got a clearer look. A sharp emotion, something he couldn't name, rushed in and replaced his relief.

He'd seen Wade and Eleisha in mental contact before—mainly back when they all lived in Seattle—but it had looked nothing like this. When the two of them joined telepathically to work on their skills or to share memories, they normally sat cross-legged, facing each other, their faces calm and collected.

Now Wade was on the floor with his back against the couch. Eleisha was still in her nightclothes, and he'd pulled her small body up against himself, gripping her hand so hard that three of her fingers were turning red.

Their expressions were rapidly flickering and flinching with emotion, and Wade's breath came in ragged gasps.

The sharp unnamable emotion inside Philip expanded, and he was hit by an impulse to grab Eleisha and pull her away. He stepped toward them.

"Philip?"

The voice broke through his haze, but he snarled anyway, seeing Rose in the doorway to her bedroom. Her eyes widened as they dropped down to Eleisha and Wade on the floor, and she seemed to understand what Philip had been about to do.

"Don't," she said, hurrying forward. "Just stay back." When she reached them, she crouched down. "Eleisha!" she said, her voice resonating. "Come out of it. Now."

Wade gasped loudly as Eleisha blinked and then opened her eyes.

"No!" Wade cried, gripping down on her hand. "Wait."

But Eleisha was looking up in confusion at Rose . . . and then at Philip.

Every muscle in Philip's body was tight, and this time he didn't stop. Striding over, he took Eleisha's arm to pull her up.

"Let go," he told Wade.

Wade released her hand, but he was shaking and sucking in air. His eyes were wild and lost. Too many questions roared through Philip's mind, and he wanted to shout, to ask what in the hell they'd been doing. But he couldn't. His mouth couldn't form such words, and he just stood there, holding Eleisha on her feet. She clung to him to steady herself.

"I'm sorry," she managed to choke. "We got lost in a memory."

For once, her soft voice did not move him. She said she was sorry too much. And *what* memory would cause Wade to breathe like that? Philip was angry, but he didn't exactly know why, and he didn't know the proper response. He did know that every response or possible reaction passing through his head was wrong—and violent.

The three of them had shared memories and thoughts countless times.

Why was this different?

"That was very bad timing," Rose said, making light of the whole scene. "You both know better than to share memories on a mission unless it's necessary. What on earth were you thinking?" Her voice took on a matter-of-fact quality, which Philip suspected was intentional, as if the whole event had simply been another practice exercise. "Wade, you should order something to eat," she went on, "and Eleisha, get into the shower. Your hair is a mess. The search begins tonight, and I'll call on Seamus once you're all ready."

Her businesslike manner broke through the tension in the room, and Wade climbed to his feet, still trembling. When he looked over at Eleisha clinging to Philip, his eyes flickered slightly, but he nodded to Rose and walked toward the desk phone.

Eleisha let go and stood on her own for a few seconds before stepping away. "I'll get in the shower." She turned back to Philip. "I am sorry."

She did look sorry, but this only made him feel worse. Maybe she told him she was sorry too often, but she'd never once apologized for sharing memories with Wade.

She'd never needed to.

* * *

About an hour and a half later, Wade stood in the shadows outside the British Museum, waiting to see what Seamus might be able to sense. Eleisha and Philip stood a few feet away, but no one spoke. Due to Rose's cavalier handling of the "incident" back in the hotel suite, they'd all been able to get past it and move on with tonight's mission.

Wade wasn't sure whether to be grateful or not.

The air shimmered, and Seamus appeared behind a tree along the quiet street.

"I have something," he said instantly. "Not far. In the Russell Square gardens."

Wade tried to clear his head and get focused. Over and over, he just kept seeing the memory Eleisha had shown him.

"Where in the gardens?" he asked. "East or west end?"

Eleisha and Philip listened carefully.

"I can't tell," Seamus answered, sounding frustrated. "He's not like one of you. His signature isn't so clear."

"I wonder why?" Eleisha asked. She'd pulled her hair up into a ponytail, and she was wearing straight-legged jeans and a short wool coat. But she didn't seem to expect anyone to answer her question. "How should we play this?" she asked Wade.

They'd already decided not to even try making verbal contact and to lean completely on telepathy for now. But beyond that . . . they hadn't been in a position yet to make a more structured plan.

Telepathically, they all had different strengths. Wade was best at mind reading. Eleisha was best at pushing commands into someone else's mind, even the mind of another vampire—to the point of using this ability as a weapon. Philip had amazing control over what he did and did not show to other telepaths, even when they were lost inside his memories.

Wade thought for a moment. "Seamus, just try to get us as close as possible. I'll do a scan and see if I can home in on his thoughts. Once I've got him, Eleisha, you link with me, follow the path, and then try to get control of him. Can you do that?"

She nodded. "That's good, Wade." She turned to Philip. "You . . . just be ready to put him down if I fail. Try not to hurt him, but do what you have to. We have to get him off the street."

So far, Philip had spoken a total of two words all night. "Then what do we do?" he asked. "Bring him back to the suite?"

"Of course," she answered, sounding surprised. "What did you think? If he's as wild as Seamus says, he won't be able to fly back to Portland yet. We'll have to lock him up somewhere until Wade can assess the best way to help him."

"At the Montague?" Philip asked.

This did sound a bit absurd, and Wade realized they probably should have discussed the situation more before this point. Everything had just felt so . . . off balance lately, and they hardly constituted a crack professional team yet. So far, they'd only managed to locate a total of three vampires, and Julian had beheaded two of those before they'd even reached the church.

"If the Montague doesn't work, we'll make a change and stay somewhere else," Eleisha said, "but every vampire we find is going to be different, and every situation will be different." She paused and then asked Philip, "Can you put him down without wounding him?"

"Yes," he bit off.

Her expression softened. She started to reach out for him but drew her hand back. "I'll try to make sure it doesn't come to that." She turned to Seamus. "Okay . . . meet us at the gardens."

He nodded and vanished.

Philip started walking. "This way."

He had not reacted at all to Eleisha's gesture of reaching for him, as a mortal man might, and Wade struggled with the knowledge that *this* was the true problem—even though Eleisha did not know it yet. Almost as soon as Wade had come out of the memory she'd shown him, or as soon as he could think clearly again, he'd understood the situation.

For the first time in her existence, she was experiencing an almost-normal life. She was in a relationship and sleeping in the same bed with a man. From what Wade now knew, vampires in the distant past had overcome certain obstacles of being undead. They had wanted romantic attachments. Whether Eleisha understood this or not, she was following a normal path . . . even for a vampire.

And Philip would never, ever be able to reciprocate. He was incapable. Wade had been inside Philip's mind enough to know this.

If Wade wanted to, he could exploit this enough to make a radical change in their trio.

But he wouldn't.

He couldn't.

The three of them needed one another if the underground was to succeed. And to Wade's surprise, the underground was still more important to him. Finding vampires who were a danger to the public was important to him. After accomplishing this, the next part of his job was to help train them to feed without killing.

He valued this job.

It made him useful.

Mary was up on the roof of the museum, looking down.

In some ways, she was enjoying herself here in London. Julian kept to his room in the suite much of the time, while she and Jasper had the run of the main living area.

But now she was wondering how this whole hunt was going to play out if Seamus stayed so close all the time. Mary had several advantages over him. For one, he was tied to Rose, and she wasn't tied to anything. She could go anywhere she pleased and stay as long as she liked—while he got weaker the farther he traveled from Rose.

However, at the moment, Rose was in a hotel just

up the street, and he looked as strong as ever. The blue in his plaid was positively glowing.

If Mary got any closer, he'd sense her, and Julian really wanted to maintain the element of surprise. Sure, they'd suspect he was around somewhere— but they weren't supposed to *know* anything.

That left her in an awkward position.

She couldn't hear a word they said from this distance, but . . . she could see them clearly, and their body language caught her attention. Something was wrong. Philip looked as stiff as a board, and Wade kept fidgeting as though uncomfortable. Eleisha stood there with her arms crossed.

They seemed deep in conversation with Seamus, and Mary was frustrated she could not hear them. Then Seamus vanished, and Philip started walking.

Mary floated off the roof and followed.

Eleisha was torn between feeling miserable inside and settling into the quiet focus of locating a lost member of her own kind. She never should have shown Wade that memory.

But it was done and over, and she couldn't go back in time and change anything.

Philip just looked so . . . tight.

Everything about him looked ready to snap, and she didn't know how to make him feel better. Worse, she really needed him at the top of his game here, as she had no idea what they were moments away from facing.

Only a few people wandered down the sidewalks at night here, and then Eleisha followed Philip from the street down a narrow path into the Russell Square gardens. Flowers and trees soon surrounded them, and several squirrels dashed past, darting for the trunks of the trees. A large fountain gushed water up ahead.

"Veer left," Seamus said, "away from the fountain.

She looked around but didn't see him. Philip veered left, moving into the darkness of more clustered trees. A few moments later, Wade stopped.

"Wait."

He closed his eyes. Wade had been born a telepath, and his ability to pick up thoughts exceeded hers.

But within seconds he gasped loudly. "Eleisha!"

Instantly, she closed her eyes and reached her thoughts into his, nearly dropping to her knees. Flashes of wild fear and savage impulses hit her too fast to absorb. She stumbled once and then fought to get control of the mental onslaught. The thoughts were cold and ugly and driven by pure instinct. She separated Wade's mind from the source he'd located, feeling just a hint of clarity on the other end.

Something knew they were here.

It could see them.

It was terrified.

It began to run.

Wait! She flashed, using all her internal power of

suggestion but trying not to hit Wade with the same command. She could feel the mind on the other end of her thoughts nearly burst into emotions beyond panic as its body jerked to a halt.

"Eleisha?" Philip asked, his tone concerned.

But she couldn't see him. She could barely hear him, and she fought to hold on to her target's mind.

We won't hurt you, she flashed.

The sound of wailing came in answer . . . and screaming exploded from the darkness ahead. Anyone within a half mile would hear it. Eleisha opened her eyes and bolted forward, but Philip was already moving. She ran after him, leaving Wade behind, and she skidded to a halt between two trees at the sight of something crouched on the ground, still screaming.

It looked up, and she froze.

It was a young man . . . or might once have been. His eyes were black and void of reason. His filthy black hair hung in crusted pieces around a stark white face. His feet were bare and his shirt was rotting off his body, exposing a glowing, hairless chest. His yellow teeth were pointed, and red flakes of dried blood clung to the side of his mouth.

A whooshing sound caught her attention, and she broke her gaze long enough to see that Philip had pulled his machete and was stepping forward with a hard, shocked expression on his face.

"Philip, wait!" she shouted.

But this action broke her mental connection, and the vampire crouched on the ground stopped screaming. He darted away on all fours.

"Don't let him get away!" Wade choked from behind her, stumbling into view. "Eleisha, try to stop him again!"

Philip broke into a run as Eleisha reached out to reestablish a connection, but then two gray squirrels, leaping from the trees, landed on Philip, squealing and biting him. The sudden attack caused him to trip, and he hit the ground on his knees. One squirrel bit and clawed savagely at his face. The other raced over his shoulder, biting his neck. Black blood squirted, and Eleisha forgot everything else as she ran to help him.

Before she reached him, Philip had gripped the squirrel that was on his face by the tail and had thrown it. Eleisha grabbed the other one and tossed it away, whirling to watch it in case it came running back.

It did not, dashing into the trees instead.

Philip's face was gouged and bleeding, but he jumped back to his feet. "Where is he?" he shouted. "Seamus! Where did he go?"

"Philip, stop," Eleisha said. "Let me see your face."

He shoved her away and ran forward, gripping his machete and searching the trees. "Seamus!" he yelled again.

The air shimmered, and Seamus appeared beside Eleisha. "He's gone. I've lost him, and I can't sense a signature." He looked down at her with his transparent eyes. "Should I widen the circle? Keep looking?"

Wade reached their other side, panting and trembling slightly. "I don't think so. Philip's hurt."

"Seamus!" Philip shouted, apparently having heard them from the trees. He strode back. "You start searching now!"

"Philip," Eleisha said quietly. "He's gone, and you're bleeding. You need to stop."

Black-red fluid was running from the deep slashes on his face and throat, flowing onto his coat.

He flipped the machete to hold it point down. "Didn't you see him?" His tone was more urgent than anything she'd ever heard from him before. "He's not just wild. He's . . ." He trailed off, and his amber eyes shifted back and forth as they did whenever he searched for a correct response or word. "Feral," Philip finished. "He is *feral*."

The force behind the word confused her, and she didn't know why he was this upset. Seamus had warned them, and the newspaper stories had openly used the term "wild man."

Eleisha reached out, touching his arm. "We'll find him soon." The sight of this new vampire had disturbed her, too, but they'd been foolish to rush in so blindly, so unprepared. She'd simply not realized the extent of the situation and had believed she'd be able to speak to him—at least to a point— telepathically. What could have happened to him to drive him into such a tragic state? "But we need to talk about our next move, and you're hurt. Put the machete away and come with me."

Why had he pulled it in the first place? Maybe as

a threat? Gently gripping the sleeve of his coat, she took a step back in the direction of the hotel. For a few seconds, he stood firm, and then he let her pull him along.

Julian grew restless in the bedroom of his suite, but there was little to do besides wait for a cue from Mary. Jasper seemed equally bored, out in the sitting room, awaiting orders for something—anything—to do. But Julian could not move in just yet. Timing was everything.

The air by the window of Julian's room wavered and Mary materialized. For once, she did not start babbling immediately. Instead, she pursed her mouth, as if wondering how to begin.

"What?" he asked.

"They found him . . . at least for a few minutes," she said, and again seemed to be mulling her words.

"What do you mean, 'for a few minutes'?"

"Well, I think he might be more than they bargained for. He seems fruit bat crazy . . . like a reject from the loony bin who missed his meds, if you know what I mean?"

He did not know what she meant. He seldom did.

"So they lost him?"

"Yeah, he set two squirrels on Philip, and they cut up his face and throat pretty good. I think that Armani coat is ruined." Her transparent mouth curved up into a smile. "It's kind of funny."

"What?"

"Well . . . super tough, badass Philip gets attacked

by a pair of squirrels? Oh, come on, don't you think that's funny?"

Julian was not amused.

"Mary," he began slowly, trying to maintain control, "what did you learn about the vampire himself? What did he look like?"

"Young when he was turned, early twenties. Really white skin. Black hair and eyes, kind of thin. Ring any bells?"

It did not.

"Did he strike you as newly turned or older?"

She shrugged. "Couldn't tell. I saw him for only a few seconds. Then Seamus popped in, and I had to pull back. But Eleisha won't give up. I'll find out more. Don't worry."

Julian paced. Well, this was something. If the vampire was as mad as Mary suggested, even if he was an elder, he was hardly in danger of preaching the four laws just yet.

"Where is he now?" Julian asked.

She pursed her mouth again. "That's the weird part. I don't know. He's hard to track. Seamus keeps losing him, too."

What could cause that?

"All right, then just go back. Stay as close as you can and learn as much as you can."

"Sure." She looked at the bedroom door. "Is Jasper out there? I want to tell him what's going on before I take off again."

She vanished before he could speak, but her last sentence left him unsettled.

*   *   *

Shortly before dawn, Philip sat on the bed in their suite watching Eleisha change into her nightclothes and brush out her hair. They'd all decided to wait until tomorrow before making another attempt to trap the wild vampire and had spent the remainder of the night discussing possible plans and running ideas past Rose, who possessed the gift of wisdom and offered various bits of advice. But Philip hadn't taken part in this discussion. He'd barely been able to listen.

Relieved to finally be alone in this room with Eleisha, he got up and moved to the mirror, looking at the flat, neat gauze she'd taped earlier to his face and throat. Since he had fed—and fed well—only last night, his body should be healing quickly. He reached up toward the bandage over his cheek.

"Not yet," she said. "Leave it on while you sleep today."

He ignored her and peeled it off, wanting to see the damage. The gouges had stopped bleeding, but the marks were still ugly. Eleisha put her brush down and moved to join him.

"Oh," she said. "The worst ones are closing up. Do they still hurt?"

"No."

"Don't worry. They'll heal soon, and you'll look like yourself again."

She completely misread him. Normally, he would be worrying about his appearance, as it was so integrally tied to his gift, but tonight a ravaged face was the least of his troubles.

The vampire they'd located was feral, and Eleisha was going to see more of this creature, see what it was capable of . . . and Robert had once shown her his memories. How many images had Robert shown her? Philip hated the word "feral." He hated even thinking it. At one time, long ago, he had heard that word spoken in relation to himself. He hadn't known what it meant then, but he did now, and Robert had seen him at his worst.

What if he'd shown that memory to Eleisha?

This creature Eleisha had located was beyond help, beyond reason. Philip wanted nothing . . . nothing in their world that might remind Eleisha of what he himself had once been. There were large sections of his existence that he wanted to erase completely and pretend never happened.

"You should rest," she said quietly.

She had not spoken of the scene from just past dusk when he'd found her locked in a memory with Wade. Had she been showing him something, or had it been the other way around? A small part of him wanted to know, but the larger part did not.

He certainly wasn't capable of asking her, and he was coming to terms with some of his limitations.

She was here. She was tending his wounds. She was worried about him. That was all that mattered now.

He'd decide how to handle the feral vampire to-morrow.

Feeling slightly more settled, he pulled his shirt over his head and dropped it on top of his suitcase.

Then he went to the bed, leaning into the pillows up against the headboard. She seemed almost relieved that he didn't want to talk about anything that happened tonight. She just came over and curled up beside him, resting her head on his stomach before closing her eyes.

For him, that was enough.

chapter six

That night, Eleisha woke up and raised her head quickly. Philip was awake, but lying still, just watching her. His body must have adjusted to the time difference. His face looked better— the gouges were down to red marks now. His throat was still bandaged.

"How is your throat?" she asked.

By way of answer, he reached and pulled off the gauze, lifting his head so she could see.

"Better," she said. "You should be healed in a few more days. Do you need to feed?"

"No."

Eleisha couldn't help wondering how Wade was doing. He'd been shaken by his experience inside the vampire's head the night before, and again, she'd been so focused on Philip, she hadn't had the opportunity to catch Wade alone and ask if he was all right.

She climbed off the bed and moved toward her backpack. "Do you want the shower first?"

Before he could answer, the air shimmered and Seamus appeared. He glanced at Philip, who was still lying on the bed, and then at Eleisha in her nightclothes. For some reason—and she wasn't sure why—his observance made her uncomfortable.

"I have a signature," he said. "Down by Westminster Bridge."

"Already?" she asked. "The sun just set."

"He's awake. How fast can you get dressed?"

Philip was already off the bed, grabbing a shirt. "Go tell Wade," he said.

Not long after waking that night, Julian was out in the sitting room of the suite, watching Jasper practice with his sword. Julian offered a suggestion now and then. They'd moved the furniture back to make more room, and he was surprised at the improvement in Jasper's skill since midsummer. Apparently, Jasper had found a Chinese martial arts instructor willing to engage in a private nighttime class.

"Don't ever try to take a head one-handed," Julian put in. "Always use both hands."

Jasper nodded and continued practicing a block and thrust move. Julian was half-tempted to get his own sword and offer more detailed instruction in several moves his own master had taught him, but he had been his master's social equal . . . and Jasper was lower than one of Julian's housemaids. He could not reconcile himself to blurring these lines.

The air wavered, and Mary appeared. He was surprised to see her so early in the evening.

"Seamus picked up a signature down by Westminster Bridge," she said. "Eleisha's already on the move, and I think they might have a better plan this time."

"What plan?"

She shook her head. "I didn't hear everything, but I was floating up over their heads when they came out, and Seamus was already gone. All I heard was 'Westminster Bridge' and 'three-way split' and that they're going to bring this vampire back to their hotel and lock him up when they catch him. So I figure they're going to split up and try to cut him off from three directions?"

Jasper froze with his sword in midair. "You want me to go? See if I can slip in and take him out first?"

Julian didn't answer.

He put his fist to his mouth, thinking. If this vampire was difficult for Mary to track, and Eleisha planned to lock him up in the hotel, several opportunities presented themselves. Once the vampire was trapped inside a room, Seamus would stop doing any active searches, allowing Julian to get much closer without so much risk of detection. He could use both Mary and Jasper to cause a distraction, something to keep Philip and Eleisha's attention. Then he could go in through a window, take his prey by surprise, kill him, and be back outside before anyone knew what was happening.

After this, it was still possible Seamus might locate him or Jasper, but by then, it would be too late. If Eleisha's group trapped this "wild" vampire quickly, in the early hours of the evening, this could all be over tonight.

"No," he finally told Jasper. "We wait." Jasper's face fell, but Julian turned to Mary. "Let me know as soon as they've got him."

Wade headed south by himself down the Victoria Embankment. The night was cold, and he had his canvas jacket buttoned up to his collarbone.

He, Eleisha, and Philip had decided to split up this time and try to trap the vampire between them, using one another's positions to keep him from escaping. Philip hadn't liked this plan at first, but then he'd seemed to change his mind and openly agreed.

So . . . at the moment, Philip was much farther down the embankment, walking north toward the bridge, and Eleisha had hidden herself between them in the shadows around Westminster Hall. Seamus had placed the vampire somewhere between them—and the men were supposed to use their presence to try to drive him toward the middle as near to Eleisha as possible, and out of sight of the general populace.

Then Wade would reach out telepathically again, and Eleisha would link but not bother trying to communicate this time. She would just hold the vampire with a mental command so Philip could take over physically, knocking him senseless long enough to lock him up at the hotel.

This plan was risky for Wade—in case the vampire bolted toward him—but Wade thought he could defend himself telepathically and get the vampire running in Eleisha's direction, or at least he hoped so . . . and, in essence, this plan had been his idea.

He was determined to make it work.

The gurgling water of the river Thames flowed past him below, and he walked faster.

Philip headed north up the Victoria Embankment, already doing mental scans on his own. Though his long coat was bloodstained, he wore it over his sheathed machete, but since the wool was black, someone would have to look closely in the darkness to notice the stains.

At first, this plan of Wade's had struck him as ridiculous and far too dangerous for either of his companions. But then . . . he realized it would give him some time on his own during the search.

He had no intention of letting this feral vampire anywhere near Eleisha or Wade, and his ability to home in telepathically was more advanced than he'd ever let on. He was going to track down this creature, kill it himself, and then claim self-defense.

As long as he was otherwise alone when he sliced that vampire's head off, no one could question his word.

* * *

Eleisha hid outside in the shadows between the main building and the smaller east wing of Westminster Hall. She stood poised, even tense, expecting to hear in her head at any moment Wade's telepathic voice telling her to follow his connection.

Like Philip, she had been uncertain of this plan at first, and she hadn't liked the idea of the three of them splitting up. But from her few seconds of contact the night before, she knew this vampire could see and feel that they were different from mortals—or at least he could on a purely instinctive level. By coming at him from three directions, they might be able to keep him confused and panicked enough for Eleisha to get a mental hold on him before he started sending animals to attack them.

She'd never even heard of this ability and was curious to find out how it had developed.

Tonight, she wore the same jeans and short wool coat from last night, along with a pair of canvas sneakers. She wanted to be able to move freely and run at top speed if necessary.

She might not be as strong, but she was fast.

London was a busy city, and she hoped Philip and Wade would be able to drive their target back here to her and away from all the people walking up and down the embankment.

The space where she stood was dark and quiet.

Wade should be contacting her any moment now.

Then suddenly, she heard Seamus' voice in her ear. "Eleisha, the vampire is close to you. . . . He is very close."

She went rigid. She couldn't see Seamus, but, deciding she could not wait for Wade or Philip, she reached out telepathically to create a link to protect herself. Unfortunately, even though Seamus had warned her the vampire was close, she was not ready for immediate contact and stumbled forward when a barrage of madness hit her again.

The images were rapid and primal and drenched in fear. She fought to get control of the comingled thoughts and send a command, but she'd never been mentally tangled in anything like this before, and the permeation of fear was overwhelming.

Something flew straight at her from the darkness, and she tried to duck away, losing any mental connection. Incredibly strong hands grabbed her and threw her against the wall. She hit, striking her head hard against the bricks, and bounced off, falling to the ground. Looking up, she could see the vampire's white face and black hair as he came at her again, hissing and spitting.

But Seamus fully materialized beside her in all his transparent glory. As the vampire charged, Seamus snarled back and took a swing. Of course, he couldn't make contact, but he'd used this move before, and it always worked. Just the sight of his fist coming was enough to make anyone flinch.

The vampire spun away.

Everything was happening too fast.

Eleisha pushed herself up, struggling to clear her

dazed head, reestablish contact, and send a command, but to her shock, the vampire just kept spinning all the way around, darting under Seamus' arm and scrambling toward her.

She managed to fire off only one mental scream.

Philip!

Then she was pinned to the ground and a blinding, searing pain struck at her throat.

Philip heard the scream explode inside his head, and he was running before it faded, ignoring the startled faces of the people around him. Soon they became a blur.

He knew exactly where Eleisha had been stationed, and he jumped a low stone fence, running toward the isolated shadows of the inner side of the east wing of the hall.

Seamus was shouting from somewhere ahead. "Get away from her!"

Philip ran toward the sound. Skidding to slow himself, he came upon a scene that took a few seconds to absorb.

The feral vampire had Eleisha pinned to the ground, and he was tearing at her throat with his teeth. Her light-colored hair was soaked in blood. Seamus was still shouting, and, without coming to a full stop, Philip opened his coat and jerked the machete from its sheath.

He moved straight in, and the vampire had only an instant to look up, his white face smeared red.

Philip kicked him hard in the side, tossing him away from Eleisha, and then moving after him with the blade level.

"Philip, no!" Wade shouted as the sound of his running footsteps mingled with his voice.

Philip ignored him and kept walking. He was taking this creature's head off right now.

But the feral vampire somehow landed on all fours. His black eyes flashed to Philip, and then he whirled to dart away.

Philip rushed after him, only one goal driving him.

Stop!

Every muscle in his body jerked to a halt as the command pierced his mind. He'd never felt anything like it. Rage and despair followed as the vampire disappeared into the night.

His muscles began to ease, and some control of his body returned. He turned his head to see Eleisha on her hands and knees on the ground, dark blood running down her throat as she stared at him with wild eyes.

"What were you going to do?" she managed to choke, putting one hand to her torn throat.

"Did you stop me?" he nearly shouted back. He couldn't believe it.

"Were you going to kill him?" she asked.

"Wade, she's hurt," Seamus called.

"I'm here," Wade called back, running up and dropping beside Eleisha.

Philip was having trouble following the words

and activity, but then he realized he could move again. The vampire was gone.

"Seamus, start tracking," he ordered. "And don't tell me you can't find him this time!"

Seamus didn't move. His eyes dropped to Philip's blade.

Wade tore off the bottom of his own shirt and began tying it around Eleisha's throat, but she stopped his hand and struggled up to her feet, staring at Philip. He was ready for her. It was time he dropped any pretense of some "rescue mission."

From now on, they were doing things his way.

Mary floated over the roof of the east wing, and Seamus seemed far too occupied to sense for her.

She'd watched the whole scene play out and couldn't help being impressed by how he'd waited until the last second to materialize and then used both the element of surprise and a hard swing to startle that crazy vamp.

She used both those tricks herself a few times—but he was a whole lot more intimidating.

She'd grown alarmed, however, when the vampire started biting Eleisha. Julian would be more than mad if Mary let Eleisha get her head ripped off, but he wanted her to stay out of sight, too. In a moment of indecision she almost popped down to the scene. Thank God Philip had come running in when he did.

But now . . . the tension meter on the ground was shooting up. Bleeding or not, Eleisha was squaring

off against Philip, with her right hand on her throat
and her left hand in a fist.

Mary floated a little closer to listen.

"What were you going to do?" Eleisha asked again.
Her throat was torn open, and she was in pain, but
she knew Philip too well, and she'd seen that look in
his eyes before. "We didn't come all this way so you
could kill him."

He took one more look into the darkness where
the wild vampire had escaped, and then he strode
back to her, leaning down so he could put his face
directly in front of hers. He used this aggressive
stance to intimidate others sometimes, but she didn't
back up an inch.

"It's over," he stated flatly, and then he half turned
to Wade. "Look at her throat! You want to bring that
thing home? You want it around Rose?"

To Eleisha's shock, Wade's expression wavered,
almost as if he agreed with Philip. What was happening?

"You both say you're trying to protect mortals? To
teach vampires the old laws?" Philip rushed on. In
his anger, he seemed to have overcome his difficulty
finding words, and they spilled out of his mouth.
"But you will never teach that *thing* to feed without
killing. You'll never even teach it how to speak. It
has to be put down. It is feral!"

Eleisha grew quiet inside, noting how he'd
switched to using "it" to describe this vampire. He
had never shown any interest in the old laws. Her

throat was beginning to feel as if it were on fire, and she could feel her blood leaking out, but this moment was crucial, and again, she didn't back up.

"So were you," she said softly.

He winced as if she'd slapped him, taking a few moments for those words to sink in.

"I was not like him," he answered in clipped words.

"No, you were worse. I saw you."

His face looked like chiseled stone as she said this, and a wealth of unspoken knowledge passed between them. She knew his past existence embarrassed him—more than embarrassed him—and that he'd shown her only selected pieces of his memories. But he also now knew that Robert had shared memories with Eleisha, and she'd seen images of Philip shortly after he'd been turned . . . when he was savage and half-naked and couldn't even speak.

The two of them understood each other quite well, but Eleisha was growing weaker with each word.

Wade was looking between them in confusion until Eleisha stumbled and fell forward to one knee. Philip reached her first, picking her up off the ground and holding her in an angry grip against his chest.

"We need to get her back to the hotel," Wade said quietly.

"Take off your jacket. Try to cover her up," Philip said.

"My jacket . . . no." Wade hesitated, and Eleisha

began losing track of the conversation. "Just stick to backstreets and go in through a side door," Wade was saying. "Even if I covered her, you can't just carry her through the lobby like that."

Philip started walking, and she tried to hold on to his neck.

She needed him to listen. "Don't kill him," she whispered in his ear. "Please, please, Philip, give him a chance."

He didn't answer.

Julian looked at Mary expectantly when she materialized in the sitting room in the Great Fosters' suite.

"Do they have him?" Julian asked. "Is he locked up at the Montague?"

She tilted her head and answered slowly. "No . . . but if you want this crazy vamp dead, you may not even need to go outside."

"And why is that?"

"'Cause I think Philip is going to kill him for you."

chapter seven

Eleisha lay on her bed in the upstairs room of the suite. Rose had cut her out of the bloody shirt rather than trying to pull it over her head, and had then bandaged her throat tightly.

Seamus had vanished as they'd started back for the hotel, and he'd not reappeared. Philip paced the bedroom, just waiting for him to return. Wade and Rose were both watching him with equal measures of discomfort, and Eleisha wanted to read their minds.

She was weak and light-headed, but she drew on any inner reserves of strength she had, knowing she would have to take action tonight. Once Philip set his mind, he was like a freight train barreling forward, and she didn't know how to stop him.

To make matters worse, Wade had a tendency to

project what he was feeling, and she was almost certain he agreed with Philip. She could not fight both of them at once.

Wade came over and sat down on the bed, studying her face. "You're so pale," he said quietly. "Do you need me to . . . ?"

"No."

His offer was clear, but she couldn't allow him to feed her again so soon. Dressed only in a pair of jeans and a white bra, for some reason, she didn't even feel self-conscious. Maybe there were bigger things to worry about than modesty.

His eyes drifted up to the headboard, as if he were someplace else. "How did you manage to get a command off to stop Philip, but not that vampire?" he asked.

Philip stopped pacing long enough to listen to her answer.

"I don't know," she whispered. "I tried making contact with . . . him, and I got lost. You felt him last night. He's so afraid, and the emotions come so fast. And then everything around me started happening too fast."

She was embarrassed about what had happened tonight, about her failure to send even one command, about screaming telepathically for Philip, and then about what she'd said to him afterward. She wanted to go back in time and do the whole night over again. If she'd succeeded from the beginning, they'd have this poor creature they'd found safely locked up by now. But her explanation to Wade wasn't helping to change his mind—or Philip's—about "putting down" the feral vampire.

So she stopped talking.

"Where's Seamus?" Philip asked in frustration.

Rose glanced at him, but her concern was different from Wade's, and Eleisha suspected that Rose was her only ally here.

"This bandage is loose," Eleisha said. "Rose, could you check it?"

Wade stood up to make room as Rose hurried over.

Eleisha flashed to her, *Get them downstairs. Don't let Philip leave.*

Rose didn't blink or make any response as she checked the bandage. Then she said, "Yes, I see. Don't worry. All fixed."

Eleisha nodded.

"She's tired," Rose said. "Let's leave her to rest for a while."

Wade was easy to manipulate in this manner. No matter what he was trying to turn himself into, he was kind by nature. "Of course," he said, his tone sounding almost guilty, as if he alone had been tiring her out.

But Philip did not function on a platform of kindness, and he stopped pacing to watch her for a long moment. His face was expressionless, and she had no idea what he was thinking. Finally, he said, "I'll be downstairs until Seamus gets back. Then I'll be out."

She nodded, having no intention of arguing with him further. It wouldn't do any good.

Rose glanced at Eleisha once, and then followed both men down the stairs. Eleisha waited a few moments, hoping Rose would try to engage one of them in conversation—to cover any sound and offer distraction.

As voices soon floated up the stairs, she thanked Rose internally, and then slipped off the bed, moving silently toward their luggage. First, she pulled on her black turtleneck, using the snug neck to cover her bandages. Then she took out the remaining contents from her backpack.

Turning to Philip's suitcase, she refilled the backpack with a pair of his jeans, his Ralph Lauren sweater, socks, shoes, soap, and a bottle of shampoo. She also stuffed in a towel from the bathroom, her hairbrush, wallet, cell phone, and a small street map of London.

Still feeling light-headed, she wasn't thrilled at the prospect of going out the window, nor of abandoning Philip and going off on her own again, as she had on their last mission. But he really wasn't giving her any choice.

After putting on a pair of canvas sneakers, she slung the backpack and slipped out the window, climbing down to the street.

Downstairs, in the sitting room, Wade found himself politely going through the motions of explaining the night's events to Rose. But his mind was elsewhere.

Since the earliest stages of the underground, he'd never felt so torn—so indecisive. He honestly wasn't certain what to do, but he had no intention of showing this internal struggle to the others.

Philip was still pacing, growing more agitated by the moment that Seamus had not returned yet, as he wanted nothing more than to go hunting immediately and take this new vampire's head.

However, out of sheer common sense, Wade did not disagree with him. During his graduate studies, he'd once accompanied his mentor, Dr. Van Tassel, to an institution for the criminally insane. What he'd felt there was comparable to what he'd read inside this feral vampire's mind. Even after a brief connection, Wade was convinced there was no hope this creature could exist inside a community, much less learn to hunt without killing. At present, he was a danger to society, and the police would not be able to catch him.

That left Philip.

On the other hand, Wade knew Eleisha would never give up, and if Philip destroyed the very thing they'd come to help, and Wade didn't even try to stop him, would she ever forgive either of them? Would Rose?

They'd all made a pact to find lost vampires and bring them in and train them to exist as their elders had done before Julian—quietly with no drain on mortal society. That was their purpose, and Wade needed a purpose.

From Eleisha's point of view, they hadn't even *tried* to help this vampire yet.

She was not wrong either.

Suddenly, Philip let out an anguished sound and slammed his hand into the door frame. "Where is Seamus?" he snarled at Rose. "Call him! He should have found something by now!"

Rose stood poised with her usual graceful dignity. She wore a long chocolate brown dress that matched her hair, and Wade could not but admire how she had not even flinched at Philip's outburst. "If I call him away just as he's sensed something," she said, "he may not be able to pick up the trail again, and you will lose more time. Do you still want me to bring him here now?"

Without answering, he snarled again and turned away.

For once, Wade hoped that Seamus would not pick up a signature and not return any time soon. Wade needed more time to decide what to do.

Eleisha walked down Euston Road, turning off and heading into the British Library. She didn't know London well enough to locate a decent underground parking lot in a hurry, but she'd seen the library on the map, and all its nooks, crannies, and alcoves struck her as useful.

Upon arriving, however, she was disappointed to

find it closed; the Portland library stayed open much later.

The vast brick courtyard spread out behind her.

"It's closed," someone said. "Been closed for hours."

The accent was Irish, and she turned to see a man sitting alone on a black iron bench, half hidden by the shadows. He was about thirty-five, with long hair and a brightly colored knit cap on his head. A backpack, a guitar, and a bottle of whiskey rested beside him, but he neither looked nor sounded drunk. Except for him, the courtyard was deserted.

He lit an unfiltered cigarette as she walked toward him.

Under normal circumstances, she'd never consider feeding on someone and leaving an unconscious person outside in the dark. But these were not normal circumstances.

His brows pulled together as she drew closer. "You all right?" he asked.

She must have been absolutely white by now, and so she didn't bother answering, and simply turned on her gift, letting the aura flow outward in strong waves.

"I'm lost," she said. "I'm supposed to meet my sister in Argyle Square. Do you know how to get there?"

His expression shifted like a light switch. He dropped the cigarette onto the bricks and nearly jumped to his feet. She turned up the power, clouding his mind until he saw her only as a small, helpless young woman who needed him. There was a deep overhang to the right of the library's front doors.

"Come over here and help me read this map," she said, pulling back into the darkness of the overhang, so hungry by now she was fighting not to lunge at him.

"Your map?" he asked. "You don't need a map. I can take you to Argyle Square."

He still sounded fairly lucid considering how much she was blurring his thoughts.

"Just take a look," she said, moving farther back.

He followed her, and she got him as close to the black shadows of the building as possible before linking into his mind.

She crouched down. "Here, come here with me."

He crouched down beside her, his eyes drinking in her face.

"You're tired. You need to sleep," she said, driving the suggestion telepathically at the same time.

He nearly fell into her lap and she caught him, but she was too weak to hold him up, so she laid him on the brick floor. Taking his wrist quickly, she bit down into a vein, tasting the warm, much-needed fluid as it flowed out. She was starving and sucked in mouthfuls of his blood. His arm was covered in light brown hair. He smelled of whiskey, cigarette smoke, and the hint of strong coffee. His memories were happy, filled with walking, traveling, and singing in pubs and clubs. But the images moved quickly by as she was drinking too fast, trying to replace the blood she'd lost, and then she felt his heartbeat begin to slow.

Instantly, she pulled her teeth out, reeling at her own actions of allowing hunger to let her take so much of his life force. She felt his pulse, panicked that she'd fed too much. Though his heartbeat was slow, it was steady, and her own body felt so much better. The pain in her throat began fading. He was strong, and he'd passed his strength into her.

She felt more like herself again.

Standing, she hurried back to the bench, gathering up his things and bringing them into the alcove. She'd noted the corner of the bench was sharp, and she was too frazzled to come up with an elaborate memory replacement, so she reached back inside his head, taking him back to a few moments before she'd arrived. He'd met no one and seen no one. He had tripped over his guitar as he'd stood up, cutting his wrist on the sharp edge of the bench. He'd managed to gather his things and make it back here to the overhang before passing out.

This was a shabby replacement, and she knew it, but it would have to do. She hated the thought of just leaving him here, but she'd hidden him as well as she could, and now she had to start searching on her own before Philip discovered she was gone.

Slinging her own backpack, she paused long enough to whisper, "Thank you," to the musician, and then she hurried across the courtyard.

But she'd taken only a few steps when the air

shimmered, and Seamus materialized in her path. He crossed his transparent arms and looked her up and down.

"What are you doing?"

She could ask the same of him, but she dropped her eyes, focusing on the empty sheath at his hip.

"I can't just let this vampire be killed," she said, deciding to go for straight honesty. "And you heard what Philip said."

"I heard him." Seamus paused. "That's why I haven't gone back to the hotel."

Eleisha looked up to his face, with hope rising. Maybe Rose wasn't her only ally.

"Will you help me?" she asked.

The transparent skin over his cheekbones tightened and he said, "Rose would agree with you, but I think Wade's in agreement with Philip."

"What about you?"

He seemed caught in indecision, and then his voice took on a similar tone to Wade's. "Even if you find this mad creature, what will you do?" He pointed to her throat. "I won't help you if you're just going to let him overwhelm you again."

"I won't," she promised. "If I can get a sight line, I won't even try to make contact. I'll just drive a command in to make him freeze. Once he's frozen, I can hold him."

Seamus blinked, and Eleisha stepped closer. "You know where he is, don't you?" she said.

He watched her for a few seconds. "He's not far.

In an abandoned building up past King's Cross Station."

"Will you show me?"

He nodded.

"And you won't tell Philip or Wade?"

Again, he hesitated. "Not yet . . . but you had better be able to stop him if he rushes you."

"I will."

She had no doubt. If she failed, there would be no one to save him, and somehow, she had a feeling this vampire had been lost for a very long time.

Philip felt as if he might explode from the inside at any moment. He couldn't stop picturing Eleisha lying on the bed upstairs with her white face and bandaged throat. He never should have let things go this far.

The instant Seamus returned with a location, Philip was leaving the hotel on his own.

As of yet, Wade hadn't challenged him—he hadn't said much of anything besides recounting the events—but Wade had been more openly assertive in recent months, and Philip wasn't ready to either trust his support or place him in danger.

That feral vampire would die tonight. Philip didn't care whether Eleisha forgave him or not. He was beginning to suspect she needed him as much as he needed her and that she would not send him away no matter what he did.

But the entire idea of the underground was begin-

ning to seem absurd to him. Yes, he understood the
need for laws. He understood the need for secrecy
and for being able to live in one place for years and
years without depopulating the area. Those con-
cepts made sense.

But two of the four vampires they'd located so far
had been damaged beyond help, and both of them
had tried to kill Eleisha.

He'd gone along with this for her sake so far—
and for Wade's. They both needed a purpose. But
maybe this was the wrong purpose, and it was time
for him to pull the plug. Besides, Eleisha and Wade
had been acting . . . strangely since they arrived here
in London. He didn't like it, and he wanted them all
to be able to go home.

Tilting his head to one side, he listened for the
sound of Eleisha turning on the bed or making even
the slightest noise from upstairs. She wouldn't be
able to sleep until dawn, and he suddenly wondered
about Rose's suggestion to just leave Eleisha up
there alone. That wasn't like Rose.

Also, he knew Eleisha needed blood, and she'd
refused to feed on Wade, but he'd expected her to
refuse. She would never feed on Wade. Even while
he was pacing, Philip had considered calling a hotel
servant in here, letting her feed, and replacing a
memory. But he was too focused on the prospect of
Seamus returning at any second, and he wanted to
be poised to run. Anything else was too much of a
distraction. He'd find a way to feed Eleisha as soon
as that feral vampire was headless dust.

He heard nothing from upstairs, not even the sheets rustling.

Walking to the bottom of the stairs, he looked up. "Eleisha?"

To his surprise, Rose hurried over, stepped past him, and stood in his way. "Philip, she needs to rest."

Alarm bells went off inside his head. "Get out of the way."

When she didn't move, Wade came to join them. "Rose?" he asked, sounding worried. "What are you doing?"

Eleisha, Philip flashed.

No one answered, and he felt no connection. With one hand, he moved Rose aside and took the stairs two at a time.

"Eleisha!"

The bedroom was empty. Her backpack was gone. The window was open.

Again. She'd done it again.

He roared. "Seamus! You come here now!" Then he whirled to glare down the stairs. "Where is she, Rose? Where?"

Rose gazed up at him calmly. "I don't know."

He ran back down the stairs for the door, but this time, Wade tried to stop him.

"Wait, Philip. You won't help by running blindly through London. Let me try to call her cell phone. Let Rose try to call Seamus. We need a better idea where she is."

But Philip ignored him and kept going straight

for the door. If Eleisha didn't want to be found, she wouldn't give them any help.

And anyway, right now he wasn't looking for her.

Eleisha followed the directions Seamus had given her, up Euston Road and past King's Cross Station. This area was busy and quite run-down. Faded graffiti covered many of the buildings, and beer cans and cigarette butts rolled down the streets. People heading for the station walked swiftly, and they did not make eye contact.

When she reached the point where Euston split into two different streets, she veered to the left, up Pentonville, and when she arrived at a collection of plywood-covered abandoned buildings, she stopped.

"Don't go in there, darlin'," a gravelly voice said. "He'll set the cats on you."

Half turning, she saw a grizzled, one-legged old man about a half block away. He sat, leaning against the rotting plywood boards of what appeared to have once been a police station. Rusty chains hung across the doors.

Eleisha walked over to him. Crouching down, she dug into her backpack. "You need some money?" she asked.

"You American or Canadian?"

Technically, she was Welsh, but she wasn't sure that mattered anymore. "Neither." Pulling out her wallet, she handed him a ten-pound note. "Who'll set the cats on me?"

The old man blinked at the money in surprise. "Him . . . himself."

Eleisha wondered whether the police had bothered questioning the homeless population around here after the first attack occurred. "But he doesn't bother you as long as you don't go inside?"

"No, I save scraps for Molly and Silverpants sometimes, so he don't bother me none."

"Molly and Silverpants?"

He blinked again. "The cats."

Absorbing this, Eleisha found it to be a good sign. It suggested the vampire was still sane enough to understand the old man was useful—a good sign indeed. In addition, the old man had expressed concern over Eleisha's being attacked by the cats . . . but not over her having her throat ripped open, suggesting he'd never seen the vampire try to feed.

She smiled and stood up. "Don't worry about me. I can take care of myself."

So far on this venture, she'd not managed to prove that yet, but she was about to. Slipping in between the cracks of two decaying structures, she moved out of sight of the street.

She did not reach out telepathically but relied upon Seamus to warn her of danger. He'd promised he'd stay close. Without warning, he materialized beside her and pointed down.

"There," he mouthed silently. He'd already promised he would not materialize inside unless she called for him. Even then, he couldn't do much to help her, but she wanted as few "invaders" inside as possible.

Following his finger, she saw a small hole—barely large enough for herself—in the rotting boards. She didn't need to bother asking whether the vampire was inside. Seamus would not forgo the sound of the speech otherwise.

She set down the backpack and steeled herself.

There was only one way to do this.

Clearing her mind, she dropped down and darted through the hole, coming up into darkness and the musty smell of decay . . . and she heard a screaming wail before she hopped up to all fours.

Even in the darkness, she could see his twisted white face across from her as he screamed and hissed. He seemed shocked, so he hadn't sensed her outside and she'd caught him off guard.

He charged.

Stop! she fired, driving the command directly into his mind.

The sudden halt caused him to hit the ground face-first, but she held him there, using every ounce of telepathic strength she could. He did not try to push her out. Perhaps he did not know how.

A huge orange cat jumped up onto a box and hissed at her once, but it did not seem to know what to do and kept watching the vampire, as if waiting. A sleek gray tabby hopped up next, looking equally confused.

Eleisha ignored them, focusing entirely on holding the vampire as he writhed and choked in panic.

Without allowing herself to read his thoughts, she began sending her thoughts in simple, calming messages.

I won't hurt you.

Here to help you.

I am like you.

Keep you safe.

I am Eleisha.

She kept this up, repeating several phrases over and over until he ceased to writhe and just stared out at her through his black eyes. Still, she kept a hard mental hold on him, ready to freeze him again if he charged.

Here, she got her first truly clear look at him. His white face was slender with high cheekbones, but so much of him was obscured by years of filth, and only the remnants of a tattered shirt remained on the top half of his body. His grimy hands were small and delicate, almost like a woman's.

He pushed himself partially up, and she tensed, ready to freeze him again, but he did not rush her. He opened his mouth, curling it into a snarling shape without releasing sound and exposing pointed yellow teeth. Even without reading his mind, she could feel the waves of fear and confusion pouring off him.

She repeated for the sixth time, *I won't hurt you. Keep you safe.*

Bracing herself, she knew it was time to connect to his thoughts. Nothing was certain here until she knew whether any thoughts she sent got through to him—if he at least understood the emotions if not the words.

Both the cats were still watching them in puzzled caution, giving Eleisha an idea to try before she opened her mind to him. She pointed to the cats.

Molly and Silverpants.

She had no idea whether the vampire knew these names, or whether they were simply something the old man outside had come up with, but she needed to try.

The vampire's eyes flickered ever so slightly, and then Eleisha opened herself to his thoughts, preparing for the onslaught of images as they hit her. But urgency and a myriad of driving emotions were not so manic this time. They came quickly: fear, confusion, anger at being invaded . . . but they were not as intense as before.

Then she flashed again, *I am Eleisha.*

He was aware that something had changed, and she was reading him now. She could feel it in his shift of thoughts.

What is your name? she flashed.

Images flooded his mind . . . and she watched them pass by: a rocky beach; the front of a faded building in an old fishing village; the round face of a man with thinning red hair; image after image of trees, wildlife, and dark forests.

What is your name? she repeated.

Maxim.

The word surfaced with an emotion of surprise,

like something buried so long it had been completely forgotten.

He pushed himself up to all fours, his eyes shifting back and forth in a kind of excitement. Eleisha
kept a close watch on him, knowing he could break
down again and rush her at any second.

Keeping her voice soft, she said, "Maxim?"

He froze, and the moment was crucial. The sound
of a voice was very different from a telepathic joining. But he didn't attack her. He just studied her
face.

Maxim, he sent back amidst his jumbled thoughts.

Without knowing why, Eleisha began to communicate with a series of pictures. She started with her
memories of the church: the rose garden, Wade's office, the downstairs living room, and the sanctuary.
Then she moved to images of her companions in
normal nightly activities: drinking tea at the table,
reading aloud, playing cards, working in the garden. . . .

She could feel his fascination, like a hunger, begin
to grow as he watched everything she showed him.

Now you, she flashed. *Show me.*

She had no idea if he would understand, but he'd
already shown her a few images of his past—
whether he'd meant to or not.

Some part of him did understand, and he sent
back more mental pictures of the fishing village, of
the man with the thinning red hair . . . and then an
aged stone house set among a mass of dark trees. He

showed her what appeared to be a small library inside the house.

He seemed to get stuck there, and he let out a frustrated hiss, as if trying to make his mind work.

But Eleisha couldn't help being startled when the images ceased, and he began slamming the heel of his palm into his forehead.

"No!" she said aloud, moving to him. "Don't do that."

He stopped, and his eyes flew to her face in warning, but he didn't attack. She kept her thoughts clear and ready to freeze him if need be. She had made the mistake of trusting unfamiliar vampires before, and that would not happen again. He leaned his white face closer to hers, and she tried not to wince at the stench coming from his mouth and body.

"Maxim," she said softly, sending the same images of the fishing village back into his mind.

She was certain of one thing now. He was not a newly created vampire, but someone who might predate herself. His memories, even the memory of his own name, had been locked away for many years. The attacks in London had started only a few months ago. Where had he been?

Now that she'd started this, he seemed desperate to pull up his own past, but he was unable. Yet every memory that surfaced, no matter how vague, seemed to bring him slightly closer to attempting communication with her.

His memories were intact. They were just buried beneath layer upon layer of years without access.

She did not know why, and she needed to know. Grimacing, she pushed her thoughts deeper into his mind.

Let me in, she flashed.

She hadn't wanted to do this so soon, but she had to get closer to his being able to offer real communication before Philip found them. She had to make progress . . . and she had to do it quickly. If she could just get Maxim to begin at any solid point in his life, she could focus the memories into a chronological stream from which he could not break.

I'm going to touch you. Don't flinch.

Reaching out slowly, she still did not know if he understood her, but when she touched his hand, he did not jerk it away.

Maxim, go back. Back to the beginning.

She felt him trying, struggling.

The world went dark, and then she was lost inside his past.

chapter eight

Maxim

Maxim Patrick Carey was born in Hastings, England, in 1805. Hastings was a fishing town then, and there was nothing Maxim hated more than fish.

Except perhaps his life.

Until reaching the age of ten, he was fully convinced that someone had slipped into his parents' home the night he was born, taken their baby, and replaced it with him. He believed he was a displaced spirit. He did not belong.

There was much evidence to support this theory. His papa was wide and muscular with dark blond, curly hair. His mama was stocky with dark blond straight hair. His two brothers and three sisters were all stout, with dark blond hair and gray eyes.

Maxim was small and wiry, with thick blue-black

hair. His eyes were so dark brown they often appeared black, especially at night. His hands were slender, and his skin was pale. By the time he was ten, the local boys called him "pretty," and sometimes they hit or kicked him. Seeing the cruelty in their faces, he was afraid, but he tried to keep his fear hidden and to take the pain they inflicted. He had no other defense against them.

His papa existed in a state of almost-constant, seething anger. Papa did not shout or beat his family, but rather he looked at the lot of them, including Maxim's mama, with a kind of disappointed disgust. In his youth, he'd wished to be the captain of a sea vessel; however, he'd then been "trapped"—due to the impending birth of Maxim's eldest brother—and forced into life as a fisherman to support a family.

Papa's dissatisfaction with his own fate was like a poison drifting through the family's small quarters near the docks.

However, some of his sentiments were not unjustified. Mama was neither a cook nor a housekeeper. She preferred to sit with other women and visit much of the time. As a result, Maxim's home was a cluttered, untended place; his clothes were dirty, and he often had to fend for himself when it came to meals.

Papa complained about being surrounded by "filthy" children, and Mama pretended not to hear him. She pretended that nothing was wrong and that all was right in their household. Maxim's brothers and sisters accepted her premise.

Maxim did not.

He found his family dull and witless. He was like a dark pebble thrown among a pile of tan stones. But for as much of a stranger as he felt among these people, they certainly did not disagree. His two elder brothers used any opportunity to kick him under the table or elbow him hard in the chest. He feared being alone with either of them.

"You think you're better than us," his elder sister, Edith, accused.

He didn't argue. He did think he was better, and they hated him for it. As a child, Maxim didn't know what he truly wanted. He knew only that he envied other children with clean homes and clean clothes and papas who cheerfully brought home bread and cheese to share.

Of his parents, Mama was the one given to intermittent bouts of kindness.

One night, as the family began preparing for bed, the crusty dishes from a supper of near-sour milk and two-day-old bread still littered the table. The threadbare rug was soiled by filth and crumbs, and both of Maxim's younger sisters were covered in grime. Papa glared daggers of blame at everyone before striding off to bed alone.

The other siblings began slinking away, and Maxim was so filled with despair, he could not keep silent. "I don't belong here," he told Mama.

She looked up from her chair by the low fire, drinking ale from a tin cup.

"What do you mean?"

He was surprised she responded to such words. That wasn't like anyone in his family. Except for Papa, they all pretended everything was fine. But then . . . Papa never did anything to try to improve the situation. He just placed blame.

"I think your baby was taken and someone put me in its place," Maxim said. "I don't belong here."

"Why do you say that?"

Pent-up anguish poured from his mouth. "I don't look like any of you. I'm not *like* any of you!"

She watched him for a little while, and then stood up. "Come here."

Hesitantly, he followed her to a small chest she kept in the kitchen. Opening it, she took out a miniature portrait of a dark-haired lady.

"Look closer," she said.

He did, seeing a small woman with pale skin, fine features, and blue-black hair.

"This was my mother," Mama said without any feeling. "You look just like her. I named you after her father."

Something inside him crumbled. He'd been wrong. He wasn't a changeling after all . . . and this *was* his family.

Mama looked at him. "She was just like you, too, always wanting something better, thinking she was better than everyone else. She looked at me, at my hair and face, as if I were dirt."

"What happened to her?"

"She drank . . . wine at first, gin later. Fell down a flight of stairs when I was seventeen."

For the first time in his life, Maxim was moved by something Mama said. Even though she had just devastated him, he realized she'd been trying to make him feel better, to feel that he belonged. He wanted to say something, do something, for her in the moment, but he had no idea what that might be.

In the year that followed, he slowly came to terms with the fact that he indeed was a member of the Carey family, and that as soon as he turned twelve, he would be out on a fishing boat with Papa and his brothers, and there was nothing he could do about it.

Other men seemed to hate him, and he'd learned to fear them. The prospect of a life among them—netting and gutting fish—was like a death sentence.

Then, in 1816, a miracle happened, and the vicar of the local rectory died of a massive stroke. Besides resulting in his being excused from Sunday services for a few weeks, this event meant little to Maxim until the old vicar's replacement arrived.

But when Maxim saw Alistair Brandon up on the pulpit at the Sunday morning service, he knew something in the world had shifted. For one, Vicar Brandon smiled at the people in his congregation, and the smile reached his light blue eyes. He had a round face and thinning red hair even though he was young—almost too young to be a vicar. This was the first time Maxim had ever looked upon another man without feeling fear. Its very absence affected him.

Vicar Brandon's voice was clear and deep, and instead of making "his flock" feel guilty about a week's worth of past sins, he gave a sermon on the virtues of avoiding the pitfalls of undue greed, and instead of a Bible, he held up a book called *The Iliad* written by a man named Homer, and he began speaking of something called the Trojan War. Maxim was on the edge of his church pew.

Apparently, in the story, Achilles was asked to give up a war prize—a girl—and he didn't want to, and this made him behave badly.

"Most people see Achilles as a hero, a brave warrior," Vicar Brandon went on, pushing back a few strands of red hair, "but he was plagued by greed and arrogance, and he neglected the needs of his men, leaving Odysseus to tend to such duties. Succumbing to the call of greed can bring out the worst in the very best of us, and we must ever guard against it."

Just then, Maxim noticed that his two elder brothers were nodding off to sleep, and his father was frowning at the new vicar in disapproval. How could his brothers possibly fall asleep during such a story?

After church, most of the adults murmured to one another in quiet voices, but on the way out, as Papa tentatively shook Vicar Brandon's hand and introduced himself, Maxim stared up, and Vicar Brandon looked down at him. Their eyes locked, and a jolt passed through Maxim. He did not know what it meant, although he did know it had nothing to do with fear. The vicar quickly looked away and nodded politely to Papa.

At supper that night, Papa asked, "Does the new vicar have a wife?"

Mama shook her head. She always knew the gossip. "Not yet. He'll be a catch for some girl."

But Papa's frown deepened.

For the following five days, Maxim pestered Mama a good deal to send him on errands that might take him past the rectory. He hung outside the rectory garden as long as he could, not certain what he was hoping for . . . but only that he was hoping for something.

On the fifth day, a side door of the rectory opened, and Vicar Brandon stepped out. He wore a plain shirt and trousers, and he carried a hoe in his right hand. He stopped upon seeing Maxim.

"Well, hello," he said. But his voice sounded different now, almost cautious. Had he felt the jolt back at the church door, too?

Maxim didn't answer. He didn't know how and just stood outside the gate as Vicar Brandon approached.

"Can I do something for you?" the vicar asked. "Do you need something?"

Feeling as if he were about to burst, Maxim had the sense that this meeting was critical and that he had to say the right thing or the moment would vanish forever.

"What happened to Achilles?" he asked.

By way of answer, the vicar's face broke into an open smile, the first one ever aimed directly at

Maxim. He wanted to smile back but didn't know how.

"You come inside, and I'll show you the book," Vicar Brandon said. "Can you read?"

"Yes . . . some."

Mama had taught him his letters, but his family had no need for books.

Maxim spent the next hour sitting beside Vicar Brandon, listening to him read sections of the precious, faded copy of *The Iliad*, all about a Trojan horse and a fierce battle with a man named Hector. It was the best hour of Maxim's life. He nearly wept when it ended and he had to go home.

Two nights later, lying in his bed, he heard his parents engaged in an open fight—something they rarely did.

"No!" Papa roared. "Something ain't right about him. You tell him no."

Maxim wondered whom his father meant, but he didn't expect to find out, because whenever Papa took that tone, Mama would fall silent in a hurry. To Maxim's surprise, she shouted back.

"That boy don't belong on a fishing boat, and you know it! He'll be less than useless to you, and I think . . . I think it might kill him."

"So it's good enough for me but not for the boy?"

"No, I didn't mean . . . Please, give him a chance. He could make something of himself. The vicar ain't even asking for money. He says the boy is gifted. Please."

Maxim nearly gasped. They were talking about the vicar and him. He didn't sleep much that night.

The next day, Mama took him aside. "Vicar Brandon's made an offer to be your teacher. He says he needs help there at the rectory, and if you'll run errands for him and do some of the gardening, he'll pay you a small wage and give you lessons for a few hours a day."

A few hours a day? Every day?

Lessons *and* a small wage? Maxim's twelfth birthday was rushing toward him, and it seemed he was being given a reprieve from becoming a fisherman. He could hardly believe it. At first, he thought his brothers would be green with envy—and they might even make him suffer for his good luck. But instead, they appeared relieved that he would not be joining them on the boat. Perhaps his presence made them as uncomfortable as theirs made him.

While Papa still expressed silent displeasure at the situation, the only one to openly object was Edith, Maxim's sister. Stunned by the news, she cried, "No! He already thinks he's so much better than us."

He looked with disdain at her lank hair, doughy face, and stout figure. Then he forgot about her. Nothing was going to stop him from taking Vicar Brandon's offer.

In the following years, a new world opened up for Maxim. Under the vicar's tutelage, he studied history, literature, philosophy, and theology, literature being his favorite. He learned that Vicar Brandon was the third son of a family "of name," and that he had studied at a grand university called Oxford. Maxim never tired of hearing stories about the university and the professors there.

Such men must command great respect.

But he also loved the quiet of the rectory. He loved its cleanliness and its order—so different from his filthy home bursting at the seams with people. Whenever possible, he arrived early enough to share oatmeal and apples with Vicar Brandon for breakfast, marveling at the taste of fresh milk laced with honey. In the afternoons, the vicar always put out a lunch of ham or cheese and fresh bread. The two of them planted a strawberry patch in the garden.

About the time Maxim turned eighteen, he heard rumblings at home and could sense his father gearing up to insist that he finally take his place among the fishermen. The small wage he earned at the rectory could hardly make up for the additional help of one more man on the boat—even if that man was Maxim.

"Papa's going to take me away," he told Vicar Brandon, unable to keep the fear from his voice. "He's going to force me onto the boat."

"Don't worry. I'll take care of it."

And a second miracle occurred. To Maxim's astonishment, a number of families in Hastings suddenly began offering him part-time work tutoring their young sons. Within a few weeks, he was earning good money, most of which he handed over to Papa, and any talk of the fishing boat ceased.

But the families he worked for were . . . *better* than his own, and although he took great care with his personal hygiene, his clothes were still those of a fisherman—or at least those of someone from a fisherman's family—and the shame was surprisingly sharp. He felt caught between two worlds.

Without Maxim saying a word, Brandon gave him enough money to buy his first tailored suit—dark gray with a black shirt. The colors suited him, contrasting with his pale skin. Looking in the mirror at the tailor's shop, he finally saw himself as a tutor, a teacher, who belonged among the better families of Hastings.

He looked different. He was different.

In addition, although he would never be tall, he'd gained some height and felt comfortable in his slender body. He wore his hair a bit longer than was fashionable, with thick bangs hanging over one eye, and while the vast majority of men disliked other men who were "pretty," Maxim found that women had no such objections.

When he walked down the street near his home, the girls would follow him with their eyes. He enjoyed their admiration, but they were just fishermen's girls—like his sisters—so he never spoke to them.

The following year, he met Opal Radisson when her parents engaged him to tutor her younger brother. The Radissons lived in a fine house a good distance from the docks, and the first time he saw her, she was standing near the bottom of a staircase with a large vase of roses behind her. Nearly as tall as he and quite slender, she was wearing a peach muslin dress. Her chestnut hair hung in curls to the small of her back with her bangs pulled up at the crown. She was beautiful.

As they looked at each other, he could see she found him beautiful, too, but this was the first time he'd returned any girl's admiration. It was an uncomfortable feeling. He wasn't certain what to do.

She solved the problem for him.

When he'd finished tutoring her younger brother that morning, he was forced to walk through the parlor to reach the front door. He heard music before even entering the parlor, and he tensed upon seeing Opal behind the piano.

Without stopping her playing, she looked up. The lightest shadow of freckles covered her milky skin. "Do you like Mozart?"

"I don't know," he answered honestly. It never bothered Maxim to admit ignorance on a topic. Such admissions usually led to further education. "Vicar Brandon was never a student of music."

"Then come and listen. I'll play some Bach for you, and you can decide what you like."

He walked over to stand behind her, and he was still standing there when Mrs. Radisson walked in a half hour later and froze at the sight of them. Maxim looked at her calmly, as if he belonged there, and she smiled slightly, taking a closer look at the cut of his suit. After all, Vicar Brandon had recommended him. Surely he must be a respectable young man.

Two days later, he was invited to tea.

He had no idea how to behave "at tea," but Opal and her mother managed everything, and all he had to do was sit and eat and discuss the Christian merits of Daniel Defoe's novel *Robinson Crusoe*—a book Maxim had always found rather dry, but which Opal seemed to find fascinating.

Right in the middle of things, Mrs. Radisson suddenly asked, "Mr. Carey, what does your father do?"

The question caught him so off guard that he answered, "He owns a number of fishing vessels."

This seemed a good answer, somewhere between the truth and a lie. His father owned one, small decaying boat from which he barely carved a living . . . but he did own it. Mrs. Radisson nodded in approval.

After tea was finished, he felt he'd conducted himself well, but in truth, he was beginning to fantasize about what Opal's slender body looked like beneath her dress . . . what her skin would feel like against his hands.

Their friendship continued in this vein of his visiting with her at home (in the company of her mother) for several months. As of yet, he'd spoken to her father only once—and briefly at that. Mr. Radisson was one of the wealthiest merchants in Hastings. He owned six trading ships and spent much of his time either at his office or at the Mistletoe Coffeehouse near the south docks, where he made many a deal.

Maxim did not understand merchants any more than he understood fishermen.

Then, one day, just as he was about to leave the Radissons' house, Opal picked up a basket of jam jars by the front door.

"Mother," she called, "may I walk to the rectory with Maxim? I know you wanted to send the vicar some of your new jam."

Families like the Radissons did not attend the same church as families like the Careys, but the upper-class families sometimes sent gifts to various members of the local clergy.

Mrs. Radisson walked quickly into the foyer, her forehead wrinkling. "Oh . . . I was going to send Nancy with those later."

Nancy was one of their servants.

"I'd rather take them myself, if it's all right," Opal said. Her voice sounded like music to Maxim, and he watched the delicate hollow of her throat as she breathed.

"Of course," Mrs. Radisson answered, somewhat nervously. "Mr. Carey, would you invite your mother to tea next Thursday afternoon? I have been remiss in not asking her before."

His mother?

The ground felt as if it were slipping beneath his feet. He could just imagine the result of Mama's coming here for tea. Not only would he lose his friendship with Opal, he'd probably also lose his position.

"I would be honored," he answered. "I'll give her the invitation this evening."

Mrs. Radisson smiled at him openly and handed him her card. "Please give her this."

He slipped it into his pocket and opened the door for Opal. Then, for the first time, they found themselves alone, walking down the open street. The sensation was quite liberating. He wondered what it would be like to be her husband, taking walks together on summer afternoons, listening to her play the piano in the evenings, drinking tea in their own tastefully decorated parlor. . . .

"Oh, Maxim, look at these climbing roses."

She stepped ahead of him to touch a mass of yellow roses clinging to a wrought-iron fence, and as she moved, his eyes dropped to her hips. A rush of desire hit him so hard, he stopped walking. He couldn't stop picturing himself running his hands down her bare sides.

"They're lovely," he managed to say.

Upon arriving at the rectory, he opened the main doors to let her in.

"Brandon?" he called. In recent years, he and his mentor had grown more informal, but he found the vicar preferred to be called by his surname.

This place felt like home, and Maxim often wished it were his home. He was proud of his deep connection to the scholarly vicar and this peaceful place.

No one answered.

"Is he not here?" Opal asked.

And then, Maxim realized that he and Opal were truly alone now, behind closed doors.

"You can put the jam in the kitchen," he said.

She followed him to Brandon's small kitchen in the back of the rectory. Maxim watched her set the basket on the table. Then she turned toward him slowly.

Without thinking, he crossed the short distance between them and took her by the waist, pressing his lips against hers. She responded, kissing him back, but when he slipped his tongue inside her mouth, she gasped and drew away, staring at him with wide eyes.

He was shaking slightly, fighting himself not to grab her and kiss her again.

"I . . . I should go home," she said.

"I'll walk you," he said hoarsely.

A few days later, Brandon was not behaving like himself. Maxim had no idea what was wrong, but his mentor seemed unable to focus on anything that afternoon. Then finally, Brandon put away the copy of Voltaire's *Candide* they'd been trying to discuss, and he took out a volume of Shakespeare's plays. Maxim hoped they might pursue a discussion of *Macbeth*. It was a favorite of them both, and they often debated that play when nothing else could pique their interest.

"Maxim . . . ," Brandon began, then trailed off. He did not appear to be thinking of *Macbeth* at all.

"What's wrong?" Maxim asked.

"I want you to read *Henry V* by Thursday evening. I know we've never studied that play, but there's a reason."

Maxim nearly winced at the mention of Thursday. As of yet, he'd not decided how to make excuses for his mother's not coming to tea at the Radissons'. Of course, he hadn't even mentioned the invitation to Mama, but now he had to think of some plausible excuse to give Opal's mother.

"Did you hear me?" Brandon asked.

"Hear you? Yes, *Henry V*. I'll read it."

"Don't discuss it with anyone. Just read it and then meet me at Carp's Pub for a drink at eight o'clock."

"The pub?"

To the best of his knowledge, Brandon had never stepped inside a pub.

"Yes!" Brandon answered sharply. Then he closed his eyes. "There is someone I want you to meet, one of my teachers from Oxford. He's German, but he speaks a number of languages. When he questions you, don't try to agree with him to be polite, and don't argue just to impress him. Tell him exactly what you think." He opened his eyes again. "It's important, Maxim. Read the play."

Wordlessly, Maxim took the book from his hand.

By the time eight o'clock on Thursday night had arrived, Maxim had grown more curious about this impending meeting. He'd managed to plead that his mother was "indisposed" and gracefully avoid the afternoon tea. Mrs. Radisson had been disappointed—perhaps even mildly distressed—by his excuse, and he knew it was just a stopgap, but for today, he'd avoided disaster.

So when he walked through the door of Carp's Pub that evening, his thoughts turned to the prospect of a scholarly discussion with one of Brandon's old teachers.

Perhaps his expectations were colored by some preconceived idea of an Oxford professor, but unconsciously, he expected to find a short, rotund, balding man wearing a black robe and thick spectacles.

"Maxim," Brandon called from a table near the bar. "Over here."

Maxim walked slowly, with his eyes locked on Brandon's companion, and for the second time in his life, he felt a jolt.

"This is Adalrik," Brandon said, standing.

Even while still seated, Adalrik appeared unusually tall. He was somewhere between fifty-five and sixty years old, with a narrow, handsome face, and long steel gray hair tied back at the nape of his neck. He wore a finely tailored suit.

Maxim could not help noting that Brandon did not include any kind of title in Adalrik's name—nor did he specify whether Adalrik was the man's Christian or surname.

Adalrik intently studied Maxim's face before saying, "My God."

"I tried to tell you," Brandon answered.

Maxim shifted uncomfortably, as they spoke of him as though he weren't there. Then he sat down.

"What will you drink?" Adalrik asked.

Maxim had never heard a German accent before, and he rather liked the sound.

"What are you having?" he asked.

"Red wine."

"That will be fine."

Brandon sat quietly with a mug of dark ale, and once the pleasantries were over and more drinks were ordered, Adalrik leaned forward and asked, "Did you read the play?"

"Yes."

Suddenly, Maxim felt eleven years old again and that this was the same crucial moment when he'd asked Brandon about Achilles.

Adalrik sat back again, sipping his wine. His eyes were an unusual shade of very light brown. "The accepted interpretation of King Henry V in Shakespeare's play is steeped in awe. He's viewed as the finest and most virtuous of English kings. He defeated the French in the face of great odds and was hailed by the English as a hero." He paused. "Do you agree?"

For a few seconds, Maxim said nothing, thinking on Brandon's instructions not to try to impress Adalrik, but simply to express his own opinion.

"No," he answered.

Adalrik raised his brows. "Why not?"

"Because he had no justification for invading France, and he goes to the bishops only so they can provide him with some propped-up justification. He invades France because . . . because he wants to. I don't find that heroic." Maxim placed both hands on the table. "Then he executes his friends Cambridge, Scroop, and Grey for treason without giving them any chance to explain themselves . . . and I think he must have once loved Scroop, because he said, 'Thou knewst the very bottom of my soul.' So they must have been close. A hero doesn't murder a beloved friend without at least giving him a chance to explain himself."

Maxim let his thoughts roll through the play, which he could still see clearly in his mind. He remembered almost everything he read.

"Henry tells his soldiers they can't raid any farms or villages for food during the invasion out of compassion for the French," he went on, "but then he doesn't find any way to feed the soldiers himself, and he hangs Bardolph for stealing a plate from a church to buy food." His mind's eye was moving faster, but this time backward through the play. "At the gates of Harfleur, he tells the townspeople that if they don't surrender to him, he'll send his men in to rape their daughters and bash their old men's heads against the walls and—"

"Stop," Adalrik ordered.

Maxim froze midsentence, worried he had committed some breach. But Adalrik turned to Brandon. "Is this him speaking or is it you?"

"It's all him."

Adalrik stood up. The pub was becoming crowded

by this time, with a dull buzz of voices all around them. "It's been a pleasure, Maxim, and at my age, I don't say that often."

He turned abruptly and walked out the front door, leaving Maxim sitting in confusion.

"Did I do something wrong?"

"No," Brandon answered quietly. "You didn't do anything wrong."

"He's not really one of your professors from Oxford, is he?"

Brandon's eyes grew sad. "Not exactly. He's the one who got me admitted to Oxford, prepped me for the oral exams. I wasn't sure how to explain him to you." He leaned forward, gripping his ale mug tightly. "He made me an offer once . . . that I could not accept. He was disappointed, and it's weighed on me ever since."

"What offer?"

"For a much different life than I wished." His mouth formed the hint of a smile. "When I was young, I longed for education, but after that, I decided I wanted a quiet life in a place like this . . . with perhaps a few students to keep my mind sharp."

"Why did I have to tell him what I thought of the play?"

Brandon shook his head and would say no more.

Maxim was alone at the rectory in the early afternoon, trying to get a fire restarted in the kitchen. Old Mrs. Tillard was dying, and Brandon had gone to comfort the family. Maxim had accidentally let the fire go out, and now the blackened logs smoldered before him. An autumn chill had set in upon Hastings, and the room was cold.

A knock sounded.

He stood quickly, heading to the door to tell the visitor that Brandon was not in. But he opened it to see Opal standing on the other side. She wore a dress of cream silk that made her hair look even more vibrant, and he drew in a sharp breath. Since he'd kissed her, she'd been a little uneasy around him.

"I'm alone," he said instantly, politely warning her that she'd best not come inside. "Brandon's at the Tillards'."

"I know," she answered. "Mr. Jacobson delivered our milk a little while ago, and he told Mother. I made an excuse to slip out. I thought you might be here."

Maxim tensed with a kind of hope. She'd come here on purpose, knowing he was alone? He stepped aside and let her in, closing the door softly behind her.

"Maxim," she breathed, turning to him. "I'm so sorry about before . . . I haven't been able to stop thinking about you . . . to stop thinking about—"

He needed no more encouragement and took the back of her head in his hand, pressing his mouth upon hers. This time, she responded with force, kissing him back and opening her mouth.

The room didn't feel cold anymore, and his mind filled with images of her lying beneath him. He didn't even try to stop himself. Still kissing her, he pulled her through the kitchen into Brandon's room and pushed her down onto the bed. She didn't protest but ran her hands up his back, kissing him harder.

Later, he barely remembered the next few moments, but everything seemed to happen quickly. Breathing harder, he moved his hands to her breasts. Then he pushed her skirts up and pulled his trousers open. When he entered her, she cried out once, but he didn't stop, and then she was moving with him until something inside him exploded, and he was gasping into the pillow beneath his face.

He almost couldn't believe what had just happened.

Opal Radisson had given herself to him.

On Brandon's bed.

"Maxim," she whispered, "we must be married soon."

He raised his head, looking down at her anxious face, knowing she needed to hear the correct thing. "Yes," he said.

What was the procedure?

"Should I speak to your father?" he asked, the thought filling him with dread. Mr. Radisson might be wealthy, but he had the look and manner of any man who worked near the docks. Maxim couldn't help his fear of such men. They were a foreign species.

"No, let me," she whispered. "He listens to me."

While Maxim believed this to be somewhat unorthodox, he had no experience in such matters, and her response filled him with relief.

He gazed at the pale skin of her throat, and then leaned closer to kiss her again.

The next day, he finished his tutoring session with Opal's younger brother, and he headed through the house toward the front door, wondering if he'd have a chance to see her for a few moments. His whole body still tingled from their afternoon together the day before.

However, she was not waiting for him in the parlor.

Instead, Mr. Radisson stood in the foyer, his muscular arms crossed. Though he was well dressed, his face bore several white scars, and he wore his hair cropped short like a fisherman.

"Mr. Carey," he said, "would you come into my study?"

Fear flooded Maxim's stomach, but he kept his face still. The study was decorated sparsely, with a large desk, a braided rug, and several paintings of ships. Mr. Radisson closed the door.

"I've met Vicar Brandon at the coffeehouse a few times," he said, "and he seems a good sort to me. Educated, but not lookin' down his nose at honest workingmen. That's why I hired you. I want my son educated but not overly proud."

Maxim had not expected this topic.

"Yes, sir," he responded.

"So Brandon's shoring you up to take your exams

for the church? To be a clergyman like him? Then you'll find yourself a parish?"

These questions threw Maxim, as he and Brandon had never discussed any such thing, but then he realized that Opal must have already spoken to her father. Mr. Radisson was simply asking what profession he was choosing and how he planned to support Opal. Maxim had no desire to become a clergyman, but he had to say something. He certainly couldn't afford his own household on his tutoring salary.

"Yes, sir."

Mr. Radisson nodded. "That's not what I'd hoped for my Opal, but she's a few years older than you, and it's past time she married."

Was she older? He'd just turned twenty, and he'd never asked her age.

"Seems she's got her heart set on you," Mr. Radisson went on, "and I'd almost despaired of her accepting anyone. Once you've been ordained and found yourself a parish, I'll give my permission."

Maxim took a step back. What Mr. Radisson was suggesting could take years, and he did not think Opal had any intention of waiting that long, not after what had happened yesterday. . . . But more important, Maxim had given no thought to becoming a clergyman. He wasn't even sure what he did want—except to learn more and read more.

"We'll need to meet your family," Mr. Radisson said, "and speak of these things together. I'm assuming your father has no objections to your going

into the church, and he'll pay all the costs for your
ordination?"

"I . . . no, he has no objections."

"Good. My wife tells me your father owns fishing vessels, but that your mother's not been well?
Try to bring 'em round next Friday evening for
supper, and we'll talk more then." He held out his
hand, shaking his head slightly as he looked at
Maxim's face. "Not at all what I had in mind for
my Opal, but she's always had her own way of
doing things."

Maxim forced himself to keep steady, and he
shook Mr. Radisson's hand. Then he fled the house.

By the time he reached the rectory, his fear had blos-
somed into full-blown panic. What had he done to
himself?

He was trapped.

The Radissons could never be allowed to meet his
family. Whatever would they think? Oh God, what
would Opal think? His lie about Papa's business
hadn't seemed so dangerous when he'd told it, but
now . . .

And becoming an ordained clergyman was costly.
He didn't know how costly, but he was well aware
that most vicars like Brandon were second or third
sons from "the better" families.

He ran through the door of the rectory's kitchen
and stood against the wall, panting. Once word of
his deception got out, no one would ever hire him as
a tutor.

Squeezing his hands into fists, he could think of no way out.

"There you are," Brandon said, coming through the door. He looked so pale and serious that Maxim almost forgot about himself for a moment—almost.

"What's wrong?" Maxim asked.

"Come and sit down," Brandon answered, motioning to a kitchen bench. "We need to talk."

Maxim longed to pour out his whole story, but of course he couldn't. Even Brandon wouldn't understand *this*. So he sat, waiting to hear what his mentor had to say.

"Maxim, if you could, would you wish to attend a university?"

This was a day of shocking questions. Really, it was cruel of Brandon. They both knew such a thing was not possible.

"Why would you ask me that?" he almost spat.

"Because Adalrik has offered to make you his protégé, to prepare you for oral entrance exams, assist with your admission, and pay all your costs."

Maxim's mouth fell open, and Brandon raised one hand. "I know it sounds eccentric, but he's done it before . . . for me and others. He's rich and alone, and this is the only thing that gives him pleasure."

Speech was still beyond Maxim, but he tried to close his mouth.

"You're a long way from being ready for a place like Oxford. Preparation will take years, and you'll need to live with Adalrik up near Shrewsbury while you study."

"Doesn't he live in Germany?" Maxim finally found his voice.

"Yes, his home is in Hamburg, but he sometimes lives in England, and right now there are some issues going on inside his . . . family, which make him prefer to be here." Brandon's eyes grew sad again. "Losing you will feel like a hole inside of me, but you could go so far, Maxim. Shall I tell him yes or no?"

"When would I leave?"

"Right away. He's arranged a hired carriage for tonight. I know that doesn't give you much time to bid your family good-bye, but he's anxious to head back north."

The escape hatch loomed before Maxim.

"Tell him yes," he whispered.

Maxim did not go home to tell his family good-bye. He had a little money saved, which he kept at the rectory, so he went to a shop and purchased a traveling bag and a few personal items such as a comb, razor, and spare pair of stockings. Then he went back to wait with Brandon.

He was already wearing his only suit.

An hour past sunset, Adalrik arrived at the rectory in a covered carriage drawn by two matching horses, and Maxim said good-bye to Brandon. The moment was awkward, as Maxim had never told anyone good-bye.

"I'll write," he said weakly.

"Go on," Brandon answered, his voice hoarse.

There were many things to say, and neither was capable of speaking the words.

Inside the carriage, Maxim pushed all thoughts of Opal away as he sat down across from Adalrik.

"Move along," Adalrik called up to the driver, knocking one hand lightly against the ceiling.

Tonight, his long hair hung loose over a black cloak, and his eyes were bright in the darkness as he studied Maxim. "Brandon has told me all your strengths and faults," he said. "That you remember everything you read, and you analyze subtext better than anyone he's ever known."

Maxim warmed under this praise.

"He also tells me you are cold by nature," Adalrik went on, "and that you have almost no understanding of true human relationships, only those in literature. He says you fear most men, but you've learned to hide it well, and that you'll say anything necessary to get through a moment in which you feel threatened, then worry about the consequences later."

Maxim sat straight, stung. Brandon had said those things? About him?

Adalrik looked out the window. "Do not concern yourself. I take no exception to any of those qualities. You and I will suit each other well."

Over the course of the following year, Maxim entered an alien world for which Brandon could never have prepared him—although at times, Maxim wished he'd at least tried. Brandon had called Adalrik "eccentric," but this description did not begin to cover the reality.

At the end of the long journey from Hastings, Maxim found himself living in a three-hundred-year-old, isolated stone house more than an hour from the nearest village.

Adalrik did not employ any live-in servants. He engaged a charwoman to come clean twice a week, but he never saw her himself because he slept all day behind a heavy locked door, and he forbade Maxim to ever try to enter that room during daylight hours.

He also insisted that Maxim sleep during the day and live by night.

They had no cook, but within the first week, Maxim realized that Adalrik did not eat. Every Saturday morning, a man from Shrewsbury came to deliver food for Maxim: ham, cooked chickens, bread, fresh vegetables, preserved fruit, tea, and milk. By the following Friday, the bread was stale and the milk had turned—even though Maxim kept it outside—but he soon grew accustomed to the schedule, and he'd long been accustomed to laying out meals for himself.

Boxes of new clothes for Maxim sometimes arrived with the food delivery: fine suits, shirts, shoes, and even a black wool coat.

Although Maxim was well dressed now, he and Adalrik did not travel into Shrewsbury, although occasionally Adalrik would go out and vanish for hours. They did not entertain any company. They lived alone and apart from everything else.

At first, the bizarre state of affairs caused dark and anxious thoughts for Maxim. Why did Adalrik never eat? Why did he slip away before sunrise and emerge from his room only after sunset? In addition, Maxim could not remember much of his life before Brandon, and he found the absence of his mentor had created a painful hollow he could not fill. He had never *missed* anyone before and was not sure how to stop this unwanted feeling of loneliness.

But there were compensations, and slowly, over time, Maxim thought less and less on his previous existence, and after a while, he came to not even notice Adalrik's strange behaviors. When one lives in close quarters with another for months on end, life begins to take on a reality of its own.

Maxim's true education began.

They spent much of their time in the library. Adalrik's collection of books was astonishing, and he bemoaned Maxim's limited grasp of Latin. Apparently, Brandon had been quite lax in this essential subject.

Maxim studied Latin, Greek, and Italian. Adalrik was a superior teacher, and soon Maxim read these languages fluently. Together, they pored over the works of Augustine, Erasmus, and Thomas Cromwell. They read Socrates, Plato, and Aristotle. They read Machiavelli.

Maxim's favorite nights came later, when Adalrik

would reward him with literature. They discussed Sophocles, Euripides, Chaucer, Molière, Voltaire, and Milton.

Although he never pinpointed when it actually happened, Maxim's attachment and gratitude to Brandon gave way to something deeper in what he felt for Adalrik. Brandon had made him feel loved. Adalrik made him feel . . . valued.

It was better to be valued than to be loved.

Adalrik also made him feel safe.

They lived in their own private hideaway with no one but each other and their books. The squalid home of Maxim's youth, along with Opal Radisson and her parents, became nothing but vague memories.

Adalrik kept two horses in the stable, which he tended himself, and he also taught Maxim to ride. This had been frightening at first, but Adalrik said, "A gentleman must know how to ride."

So Maxim learned.

After a while, Adalrik began to tell him about Germany and France and Italy. Maxim had never traveled, and the idea had always seemed daunting, but he would be safe with Adalrik. The prospect now appealed to him.

"Will we see such places?" he asked.

"Yes."

"When?"

"Soon."

Only one event could spoil their evenings: the arrival of a letter on Saturdays.

Every Saturday night, Adalrik would check to see if any letters had arrived along with the food delivery. Sometimes, he would read them and either put them away or begin writing a response. But sometimes, after he had read a letter, his face would take on a stricken expression, and he would fall into a depressed state—with no interest in discussing Milton.

"What is it?" Maxim would ask.

"There is trouble among my . . . family."

But this was the most he would say.

One Saturday night, just after the New Year of 1826, a letter arrived that caused Adalrik to cry out in anguish and sink into a chair.

"What's wrong?" Maxim begged. "Tell me."

"A death. A death in my family."

When Adalrik looked up from the white page of paper, his eyes shifted back and forth as if he were trying to make a decision. He stood and picked up a fat candle. "Come with me."

They walked out into what had once been a dining hall, to stand before a large mirror hanging on the wall.

"Look," Adalrik said, holding up the candle.

Maxim gazed into the mirror at his twenty-one-year-old face and blue-black hair.

"I have known many would-be scholars over the years," Adalrik said softly. "Some were beautiful and some were brilliant. But I have never known both qualities to be so completely joined in a person until you." He put his free hand to his face with a

sad smile. "I was beautiful once, too. It was a different kind of beauty from yours, but I was beautiful
nonetheless, and I was offered a gift too late in my
life."

He moved closer, holding the candle aside. "I
wanted to wait a few a more years, but there are . . .
things happening among my family that have convinced me that we will have to leave this place soon
and hide ourselves. I cannot tell you more or take
you with me unless you have joined us."

His family? Was Adalrik offering to adopt him?

"You will be like me," Adalrik went on. "You
won't eat food, and you'll be forced to take cover
during daylight hours. But you won't age another
day, and you will wear that face forever. Is this not a
fair exchange?"

Maxim found his mentor's words to be some kind
of heated fantasy, like Goethe's *Faust*—probably
brought on by the death of his family member.

"Sir . . . ," he began. He had no idea how to comfort anyone in mourning.

"Look at me," Adalrik said harshly. "I am in ear-
nest, but we do not have much time, and I need your
consent."

Then Maxim remembered something Brandon
told him the year before: *He made me an offer I could
not accept, and it has weighed on me.*

Maxim looked back in the mirror. Could he really
keep this face forever? Could he study and travel
with Adalrik, growing more educated, more cul-
tured each year, and yet keep this beauty?

"Is it true?" he asked.

"Yes, but you must consent," Adalrik repeated.

"I do," he answered.

Relief passed over Adalrik's face in a messy display of emotion, and Maxim glanced away.

"Come back to the library," Adalrik said.

Maxim followed him back, and they both sat on a low couch. What was about to happen? Did Adalrik possess some potion gleaned from an ancient Latin text?

He could not have been more stunned when Adalrik's right hand suddenly shot out and gripped the back of his head. In all their time together, they had never once touched each other. The hand was incredibly strong, and Maxim couldn't move, and his former fear of men came rushing back.

"Don't be afraid," Adalrik said. "This is the only way."

The room grew hazy, and an unfamiliar feeling began washing over Maxim . . . of complete trust. He trusted Adalrik absolutely with his body and his soul, and he relaxed in his mentor's grip.

Then Adalrik pulled him close and bit down hard on his throat. The pain was blinding, and Maxim cried out. But the feeling of trust passed through him in stronger waves, and he ceased struggling, even while aware on some level that Adalrik was drinking his blood, swallowing it by the mouthful.

This went on and on until he could hear his heart slowing, and the library seemed far away.

Adalrik pulled his teeth from Maxim's throat and

used them to tear open his own wrist, which he pressed into Maxim's mouth.

"Drink," he ordered. "Now."

With blood smeared all over his face, he neither looked nor sounded like the calm German scholar of Maxim's nights. He was hard and savage. Maxim began swallowing, and the intense pain in his throat began to fade. He drank and drank, and then the world went dark.

He woke up lying on the same couch and opened his eyes to see Adalrik packing some of the smaller volumes.

"Maxim," Adalrik said instantly, dropping the books and moving to his side. "How do you feel?"

The memory of what had occurred between them should have driven Maxim to shout in rage and horror. But it did not.

How did he feel?

The candle's light looked brighter. He could hear a spider crawling up the wall.

"Your throat is almost healed," Adalrik said, "but not so much as I expected. You'll need to feed tonight."

He looked like himself again, his eyes calm and concerned, his face clean. What did he mean by "feed"?

"This should all be so different," Adalrik said, his voice heavy with regret. "But I need to teach you quickly, and we must leave this place as soon as possible. It is too well-known to others like us."

"Like us?"

"Just come with me. I'll get the horses saddled."

When they stepped outside, Maxim realized it was early evening, so it could not be the same night. Had he slept so long? He did not even remember which direction they traveled. He remembered only riding into a village and seeing other people for the first time in a year—besides the charwoman and the deliveryman.

They dismounted, climbing down onto a cobbled street.

"When I tell you," Adalrik said, "I want you to reach into my mind with your thoughts and follow everything I do. . . . No, no, don't look at me like that. Just do as I say." He looked around quickly and then led Maxim to the mouth of an alley. "Move farther inside and sit on the ground near that stack of crates. Pretend to be unconscious."

Maxim just stood there. He missed the library. He missed their books and quiet evenings. The man before him didn't seem like Adalrik at all.

"Do it!" Adalrik ordered quietly.

Maxim moved into the alley and sat against the wall. Looking out, he saw a portly man wearing an apron emerge from an inn across the street.

"Can you help me, friend?" Adalrik called. "My son can't hold his ale, and I cannot lift him by myself."

Once again, Maxim was overwhelmed by the strong sense of trust. Adalrik could be trusted absolutely. The portly man hurried over and smiled as he peered inside the alley.

"Oh, look at that," he said, shaking his head. "I'll help you."

As he moved close to Maxim, Adalrik suddenly said, "Better stop there, friend. You are tired. You need to sleep."

The man collapsed, but Adalrik somehow caught him, lowering him to the ground. "Now," he said to Maxim, "come inside my head."

This seemed like madness to Maxim, but he reached out with his mind.

Good. Pick up his wrist and drink. But be careful. You cannot take too much.

The words appeared in his mind as if Adalrik had spoken them. The thought of biting the portly man's wrist was repugnant, and Maxim feared that at any moment, someone might walk into the alley and see them.

Hurry.

An ache inside him, beyond hunger, drove him to pick up the man's wrist and bite down, and then warm fluid flowing down his throat was the sweetest thing he'd ever tasted. He began gulping. As he did, images flowed through his mind of the man serving meals and sweeping floors with laughing patrons all around him. He saw a memory of the man throwing a loud drunk out a door. He saw a small wriggling spaniel name Sheba who slept at the foot of the man's bed. . . .

That's enough! Pull out, but stay with me.

Again, Adalrik spoke inside his head. Maxim jerked his head away from the man's wrist, even though he didn't want to stop. But he felt strong, whole again. Then he could feel Adalrik inside the man's mind, taking him back a few moments to when he'd emerged from the inn. He had seen no one at the mouth of the alley, but he'd heard two dogs fighting and come to stop them. Once inside the alley, he'd slipped, tripping against the crates, cutting his wrist on a loose nail, bleeding, and falling unconscious.

Adalrik cut the connection between both the man and Maxim.

"That is how it's done," he said aloud.

Fear filled Maxim's stomach. "We can't leave him alive. He will tell someone. They will come after us."

Adalrik flinched. "He will not remember us, and you cannot kill to feed. Do you understand? You can never kill to feed. That is the first law."

Maxim stared at the unconscious innkeeper. He did not understand, and although he'd never committed an act of violence in his life, every instinct inside him screamed that this man must be forever silenced.

Adalrik's voice echoed in his ears.

That is the first law.

chapter nine

A gurgling sound broke Eleisha's concentration, and something on the edge of her awareness caused her to open her eyes. Suddenly, she was back in the small, abandoned building, lying on the floor and looking into Maxim's contorted features.

He was in agony, with dark blood flowing from his eyes down into the dirt.

"Maxim!" Forgetting how unpredictable and dangerous he could be, she sat up and grabbed his hands. "Come out of it!"

She'd pushed him too far; she had kept the memories inside too long. He'd forgotten all these events long ago, and she'd forced him to remember at much too fast a pace. He was in shock.

And yet she longed to keep going. What could

have possibly happened to turn a young scholar into . . . into this creature on the ground before her?

His filthy face was close to hers, and she wanted to clean his tears away—if that was what they were? Tears? Was he crying blood?

"Maxim," she whispered, "you're back here again. Come out of it."

His black eyes focused on hers, and then moved down to her hands holding his. Without warning, he snarled and reared up, pinning her to the floor. He didn't try to bite her, but he snarled again, directly in her face.

"Stop!" a voice with a Scottish accent roared.

Maxim and Eleisha both looked over to see Seamus standing beside them. How long had he been there? Maxim let go of her and darted toward the tiny escape hole, but Eleisha somehow scrambled up and moved faster, blocking his way.

Wait. He won't hurt you. He can't hurt you.

She did not fire the first word as a command— hoping she could move beyond force by this point— but simply as telepathic communication.

Maxim stopped, watching her, and something in his expression was different. He seemed to actually see her now, to distinguish her from the mass of threats he constantly saw and felt from all around. He just crouched there on all fours.

"It's all right," she said aloud, crouching down herself, but holding both hands up. "No one will hurt you." Her words did not seem to register or cause a reaction, and she wondered whether she'd need to lean entirely upon telepathy for a while.

No, he'd have to start using language soon. He'd known how to speak once, and she'd just made those memories resurface for him in glorious living color. She simply needed to keep speaking to him and try to make him trust her.

Her gift was useless here, as he was not remotely susceptible to feeling protective, but her mind still reeled from the memories she'd seen. What a strange young man he'd been. What an unusual life he'd led before being turned. What had happened after?

How could she gain his trust?

A thought occurred to her. Perhaps someone else—someone with a different gift—might have better luck?

"Seamus, are you still there?" she asked without taking her eyes off Maxim.

"Yes."

"I can't do this alone. I need Rose. I want you to help her get away from Philip and Wade and bring her here." He didn't answer, and this time she glanced away from Maxim. "Seamus, can you do this?"

He seemed locked in indecision. Finally, he nodded. "I'll try. But I'll not risk her angering Philip. You're the only one safe from him."

Eleisha rocked backward. Trying not to let her awareness stray from Maxim, she said, "Philip would never hurt Rose."

How could Seamus even think that? But from the

doubtful look on his transparent face, clearly he did. "I'll get her," he said.

"If you can, have her pick up a toothbrush and a hand mirror."

Seamus vanished, leaving Eleisha alone with Maxim, who watched her with his glittering eyes while tears of blood began to dry on his white cheeks.

"I'm sorry I did that to you," Eleisha said. "Can you understand me? Do you understand what you saw? That was you. That was your life."

He just kept on staring at her. Then his thin lips began moving, and hope began to grow inside Eleisha. She didn't press him.

"Braaaaa," he gurgled, as if trying to form a word. "Braaaaaan."

Slipping inside his mind, she saw a round face with kind blue eyes.

"Brandon," she said for him.

His expression melted into sorrow. "Braaaaandeen."

Somehow she was not surprised that Adalrik's name did not come first. Maxim was much more affected by the memory of Brandon. Perhaps in the end, it was better to be loved than to be valued after all.

Rose sat alone in her room at the suite, with the door closed, laboring over the consequences of her actions and wondering whether she'd done the right thing. She couldn't push away the sight of Eleisha's torn throat . . . and the knowledge that she'd helped Eleisha slip off on her own to locate the same vampire who'd injured her in the first place.

Had she done the right thing?

If only Philip weren't so determined to destroy this lost soul they'd found. If only he'd give Eleisha a chance. If that had been the case, Rose would never have even considered letting Eleisha go off alone— much less helping her to do it.

The air shimmered, and Seamus materialized.

"Oh, thank God . . . ," she began, but he put his finger to his lips.

"Quietly," he whispered. "Don't let Wade hear."

"Have you found the vampire?"

"Yes, Eleisha's with him. No, don't worry. She's safe. But she needs you." He glanced at the door. "Listen to me carefully, and do exactly as I say."

Philip stormed back into the hotel suite, ready to explode. He'd searched the streets of London for hours in vain, using his own telepathy to try to pick up any hint of the feral vampire, and then finally realized he was getting nowhere.

He needed Seamus.

The very thought of needing anyone else's help was enough to drive him toward the edge, but to need someone's help this badly pushed him near madness.

"Is he here?" Philip asked loudly as he walked into the sitting room, not caring if other hotel guests could hear him. "Has he come back yet?"

Rose was not in sight, but Wade sat on the couch, going over some city maps. He looked up. "No."

"Has Eleisha called?"

He knew this was a pointless question, but he had to ask.

"No, and she's not answering. I think she turned her phone off." Wade spoke these last words bitterly.

Philip's whole body tightened. If Seamus had not returned and Wade had not managed to contact Eleisha, the only thing left to do was pace the room again, and he did not think he could stand that for even five minutes.

Rose's bedroom door opened, and she walked out with a composed facial expression. How long had she been alone in there? Something was wrong. Philip didn't know what, but he was no fool, and she had her gloved hands clasped together. She did that only when she was nervous.

"What's wrong?" he asked instantly.

She hesitated. "Philip, I know this isn't a good time, but I need to feed. It's been too long."

This was the last thing he'd expected her to say, and she caught him off guard.

"When Seamus returns, he'll come directly to me wherever I am," Rose continued, "so we won't lose any time."

To his shame, the thought of doing anything, anything at all, in this moment appealed to Philip. He could take Rose out to feed, and Seamus would come directly if he located a signature.

"But if Seamus comes to you," Wade said, sounding confused, "you'll pull him off the search for the vampire and tell him to look for Eleisha? Right? We have to find her."

"Yes," Rose answered. "Of course."

"Then I'll come, too," Wade said, standing up.

"No, you should wait here in case she comes back," Rose said. "We'll phone you if Seamus finds anything."

Wade frowned but did not argue.

Good, Philip thought. He had no intention of phoning Wade, and he had no intention of pulling Seamus off his current search. He knew of only one way to protect Eleisha, and that was to remove the threat. He didn't care if Rose watched him take the feral vampire's head. At this point, he didn't care if Eleisha watched him.

"Come on," he told Rose, heading for the door.

She followed him out of the hotel and into the night. "Where shall we go?" she asked. "Eleisha says you know the city well."

How could she sound so calm when Eleisha was missing? As if they were simply two tourists going out on the town? Her manner made him angry, and he kept walking without bothering to answer.

He headed south, toward the Tube station on New Oxford Street, wondering if Rose might simply be able to lure someone off into the many shadowed nooks and crannies of the station itself.

"Rose," a deep voice said.

Philip froze at the Scottish accent, casting his gaze

around wildly until he spotted the yellow in Seamus' plaid from the mouth of an alley. He ran over.

"Where is it?" he demanded, no longer thinking of the feral vampire as a "he."

"Near Leicester Square," Seamus answered.

"Is Eleisha there?"

"No, I've not sensed her."

Relief flooded Philip as Rose hurried up behind him. This was so much better than he'd hoped that he didn't even shout his anger at Seamus for taking so long.

Philip knew Leicester Square well, and Eleisha was nowhere near the vampire. He had only one problem now, and he glanced back at Rose, expecting her to tell him to phone Wade immediately, but she did not.

"Go," she said. "I'll be all right."

He blinked in surprise. Perhaps he'd misjudged her, and she understood this situation better than he'd realized. After all, she'd seen Eleisha's throat, too. Maybe she did understand what he had to do now.

Without another word, he turned and ran after Seamus, who vanished in and out, depending on whether they were in a populated street or a deserted alley. They ran on and on.

"This way," Seamus said, appearing in a nearly black alley, and then moving southwest.

Just as Philip stepped out onto Monmouth, Seamus disappeared, but Philip did not worry. The street was busy even this late at night. He strode quickly toward Leicester Square, looking about for a shadowed, empty space where he might reconnect with Seamus. All his rage at the ghost was gone now. Once he'd taken this vampire's head, he could turn to finding Eleisha.

Everything would be all right.

He moved in the darkness behind a pub, seeing no one about. "Seamus?" he called quietly. "I'm here. Where to next?"

Nothing happened.

Philip waited. Seamus did not materialize. At first, Philip still wasn't concerned, but the minutes continued to pass.

"Seamus?" he called again.

Anxiety began tickling the back of his mind, and he stepped back out onto the street, casting about with his thoughts, trying to connect with the vampire on his own.

He found nothing.

Nothing at all.

Anxiety turned to fear, and he started running back toward Oxford Street where he'd left Rose. He could feel alarm emanating from the people he ran past, but he didn't slow down, and he skidded to a stop near the alley where Seamus had first appeared.

"Rose!" he called.

She was nowhere in sight. Flipping open his cell phone, Philip hit the button to dial Wade.

"Do you have a signature?" Wade asked on the other end without even a greeting. "Where are you?"

"Has Rose come back?" Philip asked. "Put her on."

"Rose?" Wade asked. "What do you mean? Isn't she with you?"

Philip's hand dropped, and he closed the phone, not knowing what to think . . . not knowing what to feel.

Eleisha explored the interior of the small decaying building. Maxim followed her as she moved about—and so did both the cats. Eleisha talked to him the whole time, about anything she could think of, and although he did not try to speak again, she had the distinct sense that he was listening to her.

This place Maxim inhabited consisted of two rooms: a larger open area and a smaller one. Spiderwebs hung from all the corners. The open area was littered with stacks and stacks of dusty wooden crates, some still filled with old paperwork, as if someone had begun moving once and given up before everything was out. In the very back of the smaller area, she found the remnants of a bathroom. "Oh, look," she said. "The sink is intact."

But when she turned on the faucet, a spitting sound, followed by rusty water, came from the spigot. Maxim jumped backward, snarling at the sound. Molly and Silverpants echoed him, their fur standing on end.

"Don't be afraid," Eleisha said, turning off the water, but still ready to make him freeze if he bolted. Now that she had him, she was not letting him out of here.

Eleisha?

Rose's voice sounded inside her head.

Blessing Seamus' name, Eleisha flashed back, *Where are you?*

I'm just outside the opening. Should I come in?

Turn your gift on first . . . as high as you can.

Just the thought of having help from Rose made Eleisha feel better, more confident in their chance of success, but she kept her focus sharp, ready to stop Maxim if he charged at Rose.

She slipped into his head.

A friend is coming inside. She will not hurt you. She's come to help.

His expression shifted to panic, and she knew he'd understood some of what she'd just related.

Long, brown hair with white streaks came through the hole near the ground, and in spite of the bizarre circumstances, Eleisha could not help thinking how strange it was to see Rose crawling through a hole into an abandoned building and hiking her long skirt with one hand. Both her gloves were soiled.

Maxim dropped onto all fours again, moving nervously on the balls of his feet from one side to the other, nearly dancing in agitation, but a feeling of calm spread through Eleisha as Rose stood up and smiled gently.

"It's all right," she said.

When she spoke, Maxim stopped shifting, and Eleisha could hear the power of Rose's words, hear her wisdom, and could know indeed that everything was all right. Shaking her head, Eleisha tried to focus again, to shake off the strength of Rose's gift, but she found herself in a haze of awe at Rose's wisdom.

"Turn it down a little," she said. "I can't think straight."

The feeling faded, but thankfully, Maxim still watched Rose in wonder.

"Oh my God," Rose whispered, staring back at him.

Eleisha suddenly remembered this was the first time Rose had seen Maxim. His appearance could be quite shocking at first.

"Don't get too close yet," Eleisha warned. "He startles easily, but he's getting better by the hour."

"Look at the state of him."

"I know." Eleisha hesitated, not sure how to broach her next idea. "That may be part of the problem where Philip's concerned." She wished Rose could see some of Maxim's memories right now, but they had no time. "I brought some clothes and soap . . . a towel. I thought the first thing we should try to do is improve his appearance. He seems to react to how others react to him."

Rose was still absorbing the situation, but she held up a small drugstore bag. "I bought a toothbrush and a mirror."

"Good." Then a hint of worry struck Eleisha. "But you gave Philip the slip? He has no idea where you are?"

"None," Rose said with resolution. "Seamus led

him toward the south side of the city, then teleported back and brought me here."

Well, that was something. They needed to get Maxim clean, dressed, and a great deal more coherent before Philip or Wade saw him again.

However, good intentions were cheap. Achieving them was another matter. Eleisha took off her coat and dropped it on a crate.

"Um . . . okay, Rose, you keep him here for a few minutes. There's a sink in the back, but I need to run the water for a few minutes to get it clean. Don't try to touch him or move toward him. Just talk to him and keep your gift on."

This was not going to be easy.

She grabbed the backpack with the clothes and shampoo, and she hurried to the sink, turning on the faucet and letting it spit until the air pockets were cleaned out and the brown water began turning clear.

Turning the faucet off, she went back to Maxim and Rose.

"See if you can coax him to follow. Don't worry. I won't let him rush at you if he panics."

Rose nodded and smiled at Maxim. "Come with me," she said. "Come this way." She stepped toward the sink, and Eleisha remained poised and ready, but the strength of Rose's gift flowed out, and Maxim followed her like a child all the way to the sink.

Eleisha stepped around him. She took the mirror

from Rose's shopping bag and held it up for Maxim to see. "Look in here. This is you. This is what you look like to other people."

· She remembered Adalrik showing Maxim his beautiful, slender face in the dining room mirror, and how they'd both studied it. Maxim's eyes lowered into the mirror in confusion, and then his teeth snapped together. He jumped backward.

"No," Eleisha repeated, holding the mirror up and moving after him. "You need to see this."

"Look in the mirror, Maxim," Rose said gently. "See yourself."

The power of her gift drifted through the small space, and this time, he focused on the reflection looking back at him. Something flickered in his face . . . first shock and then sorrow. A small noise came from the back of his throat.

Eleisha knew he was ready.

Okay, she flashed to Rose, *we're going to have to do this next part the hard way, and you'll need to do most of the work. Get ready.*

She hated to damage whatever trust she'd established with Maxim, but she just didn't see any other way. He'd never let them undress him and wash his hair. Not even Rose's gift would get him to allow that.

Freeze!

She drove the command into his brain so hard that every muscle in his body tensed. His face contorted as he tried to fight, but otherwise, he was completely rigid. Eleisha focused all her strength on holding him there.

Rose did not waste any time or need any instructions. She instantly peeled the tattered remains of his shirt from his body, and then she unfastened his pants, pulling them down.

Lift your leg, Eleisha commanded.

Maxim did, and Rose got his pant leg off.

Now the other one.

He wasn't wearing underwear, and his body was crusted with filth. Rose took off her gloves, got the washcloth wet, and soaped it up.

"Try to get him closer to the water," she said.

Step forward and lean down, Eleisha ordered.

Fear and confusion poured from his mind, but he could not help acting upon her commands, and he seemed to have no mental defenses at all. Apparently, Adalrik had never taught him how to block another telepath. How was that possible? That was always the first thing Eleisha taught.

However, at the moment, she wasn't complaining.

Within seconds, Rose was soaping him up and scrubbing him, and Eleisha couldn't help but admire the ease with which her friend handled this task. In life, Rose had been a midwife, and the human body was no mystery to her—although how many naked men she'd seen was uncertain.

Eleisha, however, had seen naked men before, but only a few. In both her mortal life and after she'd been turned, she'd cared for Julian's father, including helping him to bathe. She'd seen Philip naked a number of times, but only when he stepped from the shower or changed his clothes.

Rose washed Maxim and then rinsed him with her hands as if such an act were second nature. She washed his hair with shampoo, scrubbing his scalp with her fingers while his eyes stared wide with panic, and he continued trying to fight Eleisha's control.

Rose dried him thoroughly with a towel and then said, "Perhaps we should wait to brush his teeth. I think he's had enough."

"No," Eleisha managed to get out, still holding him with her mind. "I don't want to put him through this again for a while. Do it now."

With a small frown, Rose picked up the toothbrush. "Don't let him bite me."

Eleisha kept Maxim leaning over the sink, and she held him there hard. Although she agreed with Rose that he'd had enough, his teeth were so yellow (even brown) in places that no matter what else they did for his appearance, his teeth would give him away.

Rose parted his lips with her fingers and began brushing. This was by far the most difficult task she'd attempted.

Open your mouth, Eleisha drove into his mind.

He did, but his eyes widened even more.

This went on for a while until Rose said finally, "That's all I can do with a brush. I'm going to get him dressed."

Eleisha did not object as her strength was beginning to wane. Holding him like this was growing more and more difficult.

Following the same pattern they'd used to get his clothes off, Rose put a pair of Philip's jeans on Maxim and then pushed his arms into the sleeves of the sweater before pulling it over his head. The clothes were too large, but at least he was dressed. She combed his hair until it hung in long, damp, clean layers around his face.

While he did not yet fully resemble the beautiful young man in his memories, he did look much improved and good enough to walk around in public.

"These shoes will never work," Rose was saying as she slipped on her gloves. "They're too big, and we'll have to roll up the bottoms of these jeans."

But Eleisha was beginning to tremble from effort, and she was only half listening. "Turn your gift back on. I'm going to let him go."

Rose tensed, stepping away, and Eleisha released him. The instant he realized his muscles were working, he darted across the room until Rose called.

"Maxim."

The sound of her voice and the power of her gift caused him to stop and look back at her. He was still traumatized by the personal invasion they'd just inflicted upon him, but Rose picked up the mirror and walked over, holding it out for him. "Now look again."

He looked down, taking in the reflection, and he touched his damp hair. Eleisha took this as a good sign—a normal response. That was what anyone would do.

But then Maxim looked over at Eleisha and back to Rose, and his expression changed to sorrow and confusion again.

"Braaaaaandeeen?" he croaked.

Rose jumped slightly. "He's speaking! What is he trying to say?"

Pity washed through Eleisha. Poor Maxim. He'd forgotten everything for so long, and she was forcing him to remember. Perhaps he had no idea how much time had passed.

"He's asking for Brandon," she answered softly. "Someone who loved him. Someone who took care of him."

Mary had no trouble zoning in on two clear signatures—and on one faint signature. She materialized just off Pentonville Road and looked at the graffiti-covered, abandoned building.

Had Philip located the crazy vampire so soon? Perhaps this would all be over tonight. She wasn't quite sure how she felt about that. It seemed almost . . . anticlimactic. Afterward, Julian would go back to Wales and order Jasper back to San Francisco, and Mary would simply be waiting for the next vampire Eleisha and Wade managed to find.

It was rather a disappointing adventure on the whole.

Mary often enjoyed this part of the hunt, and although, of course, it would please Julian to have it finished so quickly and easily, without even having to show himself, she wasn't looking forward to just hanging around the church, watching and waiting again.

Maybe . . . maybe she could talk Julian into letting her and Jasper stay in London for a little while? Didn't they deserve a reward of some kind? Jasper hadn't done anything this time around, but there'd been nothing for him to do. That wasn't his fault. And Mary had worked her ass off.

Yes, she'd tell Julian he'd better give them a little vacation. After all, he needed her, and although they never talked about it, they were both well aware he was blind without her.

She floated a little closer to the abandoned building, making sure she kept to the shadows. Nothing seemed to be happening in there—no noise, no crashing sounds at all . . . no screaming.

And since she was picking up two strong vampire signatures, that meant if Philip was inside, he wasn't alone. Would Eleisha or Rose just let him take this crazy vampire's head? That didn't seem likely, not after some of the things Eleisha had said to Philip back at Westminster Hall.

Frustrated, Mary realized she had to find out who was in there and what was going on. But how? Could she blink herself inside and somehow stay hidden? Probably not.

"What are you doing here? What do you want with us?"

Mary froze at the deep voice and the heavy accent. Slowly, she half turned to see a six-foot, transparent Scottish Highlander standing right beside her.

He didn't look happy.

Seamus had waited outside the abandoned building. He knew the sight of him agitated Maxim, but he remained poised and ready, in case Rose called him. As he was still torn over whether they were doing the right thing, it bothered him to pick sides against Wade, but in truth, Wade hadn't voiced a side yet. He simply hadn't disagreed with Philip.

Having Rose along on this journey had been an unexpected relief, and Seamus had remained at full strength most of the time. She was handling the journey far better than he'd anticipated, following him through the dark streets of London without question until they'd reached Eleisha here. Perhaps her belief in the mission was overriding her phobias.

So he'd remained outside and waited . . . until the air wavered near the low, open hole leading inside, and he watched the magenta-haired girl materialize. He froze, just observing her for a few moments. This was the first clear look he'd ever had. The only other time he'd seen her was in an outdoor parking lot in San Francisco when she'd attempted to terrify Eleisha. In turn, Seamus had scared her off that night, and he'd tried to follow when she blinked out, but he'd lost her signature too quickly.

Now he studied her profile. She was younger than he'd first thought, maybe sixteen. Her face was sharp . . . intelligent. But whenever she showed up, violent trouble always followed.

This time, if she blinked out, he wasn't going to lose her.

He dematerialized and popped back in only a few steps away.

"What are you doing here? What do you want with us?"

Her transparent body tensed, and then she turned to look at him. Her eyes widened.

"Oh jeez!"

She vanished instantly, but he'd locked onto the particular "hole in the world" her presence created, and he followed.

Mary was so panicked that she teleported all the way to a parking lot at Heathrow Airport. How could she have been so stupid? She'd been so focused on the vamps inside the building, she'd forgotten to sense for Seamus.

To her horror, the second she appeared in a dark corner of the parking lot, he materialized a few feet away. She honestly didn't know if he could hurt her or not, but she couldn't go anywhere near Julian until she'd lost him.

"You stop," he ordered. "Tell me what you want from us."

Wow, he was big. He looked like something from a painting in a museum.

Her mind raced. She could go anywhere, and he was tied to Rose. That was his weakness. But his colors were bright, and he didn't seem to be weakening one bit.

How could she lose him? Maybe distract him for a few seconds and then vanish?

He was standing farther into the light than she was, and a family pulling rolling suitcases was now walking their way.

"Ghost!" Mary screamed. "Ahhhhhhhhhhhhhh! There's a ghost!"

She couldn't help a moment of glee when his expression switched to surprise, and he jerked his head toward the family.

A little girl saw him and began to scream.

"Daddy! Daddy!"

"Hah!" Mary taunted Seamus, and popped out.

She rushed back toward King's Cross Station and rematerialized in the darkness behind the British Library, fairly certain she'd lost him but wanting to make sure.

The air shimmered.

"Oh, for God's sake," she moaned.

He appeared directly in front of her. "Stop this!" he said. "You tell me who you are and what you want!"

She blinked out, and this time, she could think of only one thing that might keep him busy long enough to lose his hold on her signature. Her cover was blown anyway, and she had nothing left to lose.

In a flash, she materialized inside the abandoned building, quickly taking in the entire scene. Eleisha and Rose were both crouched on the floor, and they

seemed to be trying to talk to the crazy vampire—
who looked substantially better. He was still paper
white, but at least his hair was clean and he was
dressed.

Eleisha looked over at Mary and stood up in
alarm. She was so pretty. Mary would have given
anything to look like that back in life. But now
wasn't the time for regrets. Mary waited only long
enough for the first hint of Seamus rematerializing,
and then she screamed again—loud.

"Ahhhhhhhhhhhhhhhhhhhhh!"

She charged the crazy vamp on the floor and
watched him shrink in terror as he took in the sight
of her magenta hair, nose stud, and transparent
form. Hissing and spitting, he darted, trying to get
past Rose—who was closest to the exit hole.

"Maxim!" Eleisha shouted, moving after him.

And the whole room exploded into confusion. A
huge furry orange cat jumped on Eleisha's back, and
a gray tabby leapt up on a box, spitting louder than
Maxim. Rose somehow managed to keep herself between Maxim and the escape hole, and she seemed
to be trying to say something, but in all the chaos,
she was too startled to get much out.

Maxim charged at her.

"Rose!" Seamus yelled, blinking over in front of
her, trying to herd Maxim away by waving his
arms.

There it was: the perfect moment.

Mary couldn't help smiling as she blinked out.

*   *   *

Eleisha had the presence of mind to ignore the en-raged cat clawing at her back and to focus every ounce of energy she had left on Maxim.

Freeze!

His slender body jerked to a halt, but his eyes glowed with anger this time. Maybe he was getting tired of having his brain invaded. The cat on her back stopped at the same moment, its mind seem-ingly connected to Maxim's—something Eleisha had counted on.

But her back hurt, and she had a bad feeling her shirt had been shredded.

Seamus immediately began turning around, cast-ing his gaze everywhere. "Oh no."

He blinked out.

"Seamus!" Rose called.

What was going on? Eleisha kept a tight hold on Maxim until he calmed slightly, and then she moved over to him. "I'm going to let you go. Stay here with us. Everything is okay."

She released her mental hold, and he raised his lips to form a snarl, but he didn't bolt again. Actu-ally, the snarl was another good sign. He'd figured out that she was the one freezing him, and he was offering an objection.

Another quite normal response.

"Noooo," he croaked.

She blinked, not sure whether to be glad. He was clearly telling her not to do that again. So his first word was to ask for a long-dead vicar, and his sec-ond word was "no."

Not that she blamed him.

"Oh, Eleisha . . . your back is bleeding," Rose said.

As Eleisha craned her neck to look, Seamus popped back into the room, his face a mask of fury.

"Damn it! I lost her."

He rarely swore, but Eleisha was running out of patience. "What is happening?"

"She was outside in the alley," he answered bitterly, "looking down toward the hole. When she blinked out, I followed, and I kept following no matter what. She must have been desperate and came back here, trying to throw me off." He paused, and his voice softened. "She's a quick thinker." Then his tone hardened again. "But she knows where you are now . . . where Maxim is, and the last time she showed up, Robert lost his head."

Eleisha just stared at him, trying to take all this in at once. He was right. If the girl ghost was here, Julian wouldn't be far behind.

"We need Philip," she said quietly.

"No," Rose said, moving closer. "Not yet. Eleisha, you didn't see him after you left us at the hotel. He'll kill Maxim."

"But . . . Maxim's getting better. He looks better, and he's trying to talk. That should count for something."

"Not with Philip," Seamus put in. "I think you'll need to get a lot further to even give him pause—maybe even to give Wade pause."

A cold feeling crept up Eleisha's neck, making her forget about the scratches. "How much further?"

Both Rose and Seamus glanced away, and finally Seamus answered, "I think he'll need to be able to feed without killing for either one of them to give him a chance. That's the whole goal here, is it not? I think that's what it will take."

"To feed without . . . ?" Eleisha's mouth fell open. "I don't know how long that might take. I don't even know what his gift is yet."

"Well, we can't stay here," Rose said, "not if that ghost is on her way to Julian. We don't even know how close he might be."

The decaying walls seemed to be closing in. "Okay," Eleisha said, fighting to think. "But I have to at least call Wade and tell him the girl ghost is in London. We have to warn them that Julian's here somewhere. Then we'll move Maxim. I don't know where, but we need to move him quickly."

To her shame, she was afraid of attempting this without Philip.

"You cannot stay inside the city," Seamus said, his accent sounding thicker.

"What do you mean?" Eleisha asked.

"You'll need to get much farther away, some-where she won't find you."

"Where?"

He tilted his head. "I have an idea. When I was here last summer, I widened my search quite a dis-tance, and I saw a place that might work. Do you trust me?"

Eleisha nodded. She might not know the inner workings of Seamus' mind, but she did trust him.

However, his next question was much more difficult to answer.

"Can you get Maxim to the Paddington train station?" he asked.

By the time Mary returned to the Great Fosters hotel, she wasn't smiling anymore. This was going to be a bad scene, and she knew it.

The one thing Julian had told her was to stay off Seamus' radar . . . and she'd failed.

But if Mary had learned anything from her time with Julian so far, it was to rip the Band-Aid off as quickly as possible, deal with his anger, and look for ways to move on.

She blinked into the suite to see Jasper sitting on the couch, holding his sword, and looking miserable. Poor Jasper. He'd been practically locked in this room since arriving in England, and he hated being cooped up.

Julian walked out of his bedroom, wearing black slacks and a white shirt. His pale feet were bare.

"Well?" he asked coldly. "Is the vampire dead? Did Philip kill him?"

If Mary had still been alive, she would have swallowed hard. "Not exactly . . . I screwed up. Don't be mad. But I really screwed up."

She always told Julian not to be mad. It never worked.

Jasper got to his feet, moving closer to Mary, and Julian stiffened.

"I picked up two strong signatures," she said,

"and a weak one in some old abandoned building on the north end of the city. I was trying to think of a way to see what was going on without being spotted, and . . . Seamus caught me."

"He saw you?" Julian's voice had no inflection. "Clearly?"

Oh boy. This was about to get worse. "Um, yeah, he saw me. I blinked out right away, but he kept following! No matter where I went, no matter what I did, he was on my tail."

Julian's face seemed to grow even paler, and she could see the rage building.

"I couldn't shake him," she rushed on, "so I popped in right on top of Eleisha and Rose and that crazy vamp, and I got them all scrambling long enough to distract Seamus, and then I blinked out. I figured by that point that losing him was more important than anything else."

She stopped. Again, had she been alive, she would have taken a deep breath.

Julian still stood stiffly. "Let me understand," he began. "Seamus has not only seen you, but so have Eleisha and Rose? The vampire they located is still intact, and Philip is nowhere near him?"

That pretty well sized things up, but Mary had been planning for this, with a distraction in mind. "I don't think Philip even knows where they are."

That did the trick.

"What do you mean?" Julian asked instantly.

"Well, he wasn't there, and I didn't sense another

vamp anywhere close by, and he'd never let Eleisha near that crazy guy on her own, so she must've given him the slip. She's been all for saving the new vamp, and Philip's been for killing him. Rose is on Eleisha's side, and Seamus always sides with Rose. I think their group has split up."

For the moment, Julian's rage was on hold, and he put his fist to his mouth. "Then where is Philip? Where is Wade, for that matter?"

Mary shook her head. "I don't know. But I can check their hotel. . . . I was thinking that now the cat's out of the bag, about me I mean, maybe I could find a way to sort of *lead* Philip to where they are? With a little help, he can still take care of this problem for you."

Jasper had been silent through this entire exchange. He stood with his legs slightly bent, almost as if he'd need to protect Mary. She was touched by the gesture, even though Julian could not hurt her physically. But she didn't like for Julian to make her feel like an idiot, especially not when she was the one out there doing all the work.

"All right," Julian said slowly. "You find a way to lead Philip to this . . . abandoned building, but don't let him know you're trying to help him. Make him chase you if you can." His eyes looked like dark glass. "But don't fail me. You've been stupid tonight, careless, and don't think I don't know you're trying to cover your mistakes by offering a new plan."

"None of this is her fault!" Jasper said angrily. "You

try spying on five different people, and keep your eyes open for another ghost and see how you do."

Mary tensed when Julian turned on Jasper. Julian might not be able to hurt her, but he'd kicked Jasper into a pulp once or twice. What was Jasper thinking? Wasn't he the one always expounding on how he had to obey Julian because Julian paid the bills? Now who was being an idiot?

"No, Julian's right," she blurted out, stepping between them. "This is my fault. I'll fix it." She looked at Julian. "I'll fix it," she insisted.

But when she blinked out again, he was still watching Jasper.

Wade sat in the hotel room, waiting for Philip to burst back in the door at any moment. He wasn't certain what was going on just yet—but he had his suspicions. It now appeared that Philip had lost both Rose and Seamus.

His cell phone rang.

The room had been so quiet, he jumped at the sound, and then grabbed for the phone, seeing Eleisha's name on the caller ID.

"Where are you?" he nearly shouted into the phone.

"Wade, listen to me," she said. "I'm with Rose. We're fine, but that girl ghost of Julian's is here in London. That means he's here. You have to be careful. Tell Philip."

"Where are you?"

She hung up, leaving him looking at his cell

phone with his mouth open. How could she be doing this?

The door flew open, and Philip strode inside.

"Is Rose here? Is she back yet?" Philip asked, looking around. His hair was a disheveled mess, and his coat was open, exposing the sheathed machete.

Wade fought hard to keep his emotions under control. He decided not to tell Philip about Eleisha's warning just yet. Philip was near the edge of losing control, and one of them had to keep thinking clearly.

But whenever he closed his eyes, even for a second, all he could see on the back of his eyelids was the image of Eleisha's torn throat, and all he could think was that he had no idea where to find her . . . and that he'd heard her voice seconds ago, and she'd told him nothing. She didn't trust him.

"Has Rose or Seamus come back?" Philip asked insistently.

"No," Wade managed to say.

"Then where are they?"

"You need to quiet down," Wade said, but his own advice sounded foolish. "What happened?"

Where is Eleisha? Wade thought to himself.

That question kept pounding in his head, and he tried not to project it.

Philip opened his mouth as if trying to speak, but the muscles of his jaw were so tight and his eyes were so wild, he couldn't seem to form words. Taking two strides, he grabbed Wade's shoulder and flashed a barrage of images, starting with Seamus appearing and then ending with Philip running back and not finding Rose where he'd left her.

"They ditched you," Wade choked, his suspicions confirmed.

"What?"

"Don't you understand? That was intentional. All of it!"

With the images still reeling in his mind, Wade came to terms with their tightly knit group having broken into two factions . . . and that he'd been left behind with Philip.

chapter ten

R ose gripped the arm of her seat as the train lurched forward, beginning its journey north to Oxford. She'd never traveled on a train without having first secured a private cabin with a locking door, but that was not possible tonight.

Maxim sat across from her, with Eleisha beside him. Although his eyes shifted back and forth, and he, too, gripped the arms of his seat, he was silent and still for the most part. Eleisha was inside his head, using every method she knew to mentally take him from this place and keep him somewhere in a calmer world—as Wade had done for Rose on the flight to London.

Unfortunately, with Eleisha focused completely on Maxim, this left Rose to fend for herself, and as the train picked up speed, she trembled at being completely exposed under harsh overhead lights, trapped both out in the open and yet still in a place from which she had no escape.

Thankfully, there were few other travelers at this hour.

Maxim's hand twitched and his nostrils flared in a moment of fear. Perhaps Eleisha's focus had slipped. Rose forgot her own fears and reached out to touch his hand.

"Don't worry, Maxim. We are here. You are safe."

He still looked a bit like a patient from a lunatic asylum. With no other choice, Eleisha had stuffed newspapers into Philip's shoes and managed to tie them onto Maxim's feet. They were somewhat ridiculous, but he could not have boarded the train barefoot.

Then she'd put on her wool coat to cover the slashes on her back. In essence, the three of them appeared normal enough not to gain unwanted attention, and the trip to Oxford was just more than an hour. Rose felt certain she could hold on for that long.

When she stroked Maxim's arm, he calmed slightly, and so she kept it up.

It was far too dark to see anything out the window, and sixty-two minutes later, she was surprised when the train pulled into Oxford Station. She'd hardly had time to suffer in fear the entire way. Taking care of Maxim and helping Eleisha to calm him had kept her from thinking about herself.

However, getting him on the train in the first place had not been easy, and Eleisha had already expended far too much mental energy for one night. She was beginning to look weak . . . and now they had to get him off.

"You stay here," Rose said, standing. "I'll get us a taxi and come back for you as quickly as I can."

Keeping one hand on Maxim, Eleisha looked up with a mix of gratitude and uncertainty.

"Are you sure?"

"Yes, I'll be right back. We don't want him standing out in the darkness while one of us hails a cab. It's better to do the whole transition in one rush."

Without waiting for the thank-you she knew would follow, Rose hurried off the train and through the station, shocked at how her need to care for others was overcoming her crippling fear of travel.

Seamus had given them clear instructions to take a train to Oxford, and then take a taxi to Caufield Cemetery, located up above the Farmoor Reservoir. This was one of the few heavily forested areas remaining in south central England. Once they were alone among the trees, Seamus would materialize and lead them the rest of the way.

Rose gritted her teeth and hurried on. Everyone had a part to play here.

The least she could do was arrange for a cab.

Sitting on the couch in the hotel suite, Philip could not name the emotion pressing down on his chest. The last time he'd been separated from Eleisha, back in Denver, he'd suffered from an unwanted mix of guilt and fear—as he'd been to blame for the chain of events that had played out.

This time, he was not to blame.

This time, he was in the right, and Eleisha had disregarded him, manipulated him, and then abandoned him in order to follow her own decisions, as if he had no voice in this group at all.

Maybe he didn't.

The possibility pressed down against his chest.

Wade sat on the floor, reviewing maps of London. "Okay, most of the sightings have been in the central north area of the city, and Seamus definitely tried leading you south as far as he could, attempting to throw you off. So I say we focus our search between Russell Square and King's Cross Station."

His tone was so matter-of-fact.

"Eleisha doesn't want our help," Philip answered, his voice sounding strange to his own ears, like some pathetic mortal's. "And you said that Rose and Seamus 'ditched' us."

Wade's eyes flashed up. "Snap out of it! Don't you understand? If Eleisha has Seamus on her side, he could track down that vampire tonight. Do you want Rose and Eleisha facing that *thing* alone? Do you want them facing Julian alone?"

No . . . Philip did not want that. Not at all. He stood up. Wade had told him of Eleisha's phone call, and it only made him feel worse. Now she was the target for two enemies.

Wade nodded, growing calmer and pointing back

to the map. "We'll start in Russell Square and move north doing mental sweeps, but I think we should stay together."

Philip nodded back, even though Wade wasn't looking at him. Of course, they had to go out searching. Of course, they had to take action right away. Why had he wanted to sit on the couch and do nothing? Eleisha somehow always managed to expose emotions he'd never known he possessed.

But he didn't like the ones he was feeling tonight.

Buttoning his coat, he followed Wade out the door.

Mary hovered in the shadows near the Montague hotel, wondering how she might lure Philip and Wade outside without being conspicuous. If she popped into the hotel suite, the whole ruse would be too obvious. But, then again, they might just follow her no matter what. They didn't seem to have any other leads.

The dilemma was cheerfully solved for her when the hotel lobby doors opened and Wade walked out, followed by Philip. Oh good—they'd finally decided to do something. Philip's bloodstained coat was buttoned, which meant he was wearing his machete, but only someone who'd seen what happened to him would know the dark patches on his black coat were blood. Mary watched them head toward Russell Square, and she blinked out, rematerializing in the trees up ahead of them.

She could tell from the look on Wade's face that

he was doing mental sweeps, trying to pick up thoughts from either one of his companions or the crazy vamp.

Mary shook her head. She'd been trying to convince Julian for months that Wade was fully telepathic—stronger than Philip in that regard—but Julian just couldn't seem to believe this of a mortal. Arrogance was Julian's biggest weakness, and sometimes she wished he could see that.

Just as Wade and Philip were coming to the north end of the square, she fully materialized near a tree by the main path, but with her back turned.

At a gasp from Wade, she whirled around, looking at him and Philip in surprise, as if she'd been waiting and watching for something, and they'd just stumbled upon her.

Philip almost couldn't believe the sight. He'd never seen this ghost before, but Eleisha had once described her in detail, right down to the nose stud. She was so different from Seamus, so slender and so . . . modern.

Even after listening to the descriptions of her, she'd never quite seemed real to him—even after hearing of the phone call tonight. Yet, there she was.

And if she was in London, Julian was not far behind.

The girl ghost made a gasping sound, as if horrified they'd seen her, and she rushed forward in a blur. Without a word, Philip bolted after her, and Wade flew into motion, doing a fair job of keeping up.

She vanished as they emerged onto Woburn Place.

"Which way?" Wade called, looking up and down.

Turning north, Philip caught a flash of magenta far up the street near the mouth of an alley. "There!"

They ran, once again not caring whom they jostled or startled on the street. Did no one in London ever go to bed? But as they skidded to a stop near the alley, an unexpected sight awaited them. The girl ghost was blinking in and out in the same exact spot, and her expression was desperate.

"She's having trouble," Wade said. "I don't think she can teleport."

"Where's Julian?" Philip demanded of the girl.

In answer, she blinked out, and this time she vanished. He bolted back out onto Woburn, swiveling his head left and right, until he caught another magenta flash up near Euston Road. "Come on!"

This was the most fun Mary could remember in a long time. Both Wade and Philip had been completely duped by her show of distress and horror, not to mention her last-minute trick of faking difficulty in teleporting.

They were running after her like a pair of dogs.

Once they both skidded out onto Euston, she vanished, giving them just a hint or two of a sighting until she reached Pentonville, and she floated over to the abandoned building. If she could get them this far, Wade could pinpoint Eleisha's location inside in a heartbeat.

But this time, she kept her eyes and her senses wide-open for Seamus.

And that was her first clue that something was wrong. She didn't sense anyone—anyone at all—inside.

Philip was coming up fast, and she blinked out, materializing inside the decaying main room and looking around for the things she'd noted earlier: the backpack, spare shoes, wet towel, etc. She floated all the way to the back.

Everything was gone.

The place was empty except for Maxim's tattered clothes on the floor near the sink. Even the cats were gone. All of Mary's glee dissipated. Julian was going to have an aneurysm.

Then he was going to blame her.

Half turning, she could sense Philip right outside. She blinked herself away.

As Wade came around the corner of some decaying, graffiti-covered buildings, he glanced down at a one-legged old man who sat leaned up against a wall while feeding a can of tuna to two cats.

But he didn't do more than glance, because Philip was already well ahead of him.

"Where is she?" Wade called.

Philip had stopped completely, and by the time Wade reached him, he'd crouched down, leaning toward a hole at the bottom of an especially shabby outer wall.

"What are you doing?" Wade demanded. "We'll lose the girl!"

But Philip didn't budge. Instead, he made a sniffing noise, as if forcing his long-dead lungs to take in air.

"Eleisha has been here," he said.

"What?"

Instead of answering, Philip crawled through the hole. It was a tight fit, but he got through. With little choice, Wade followed, emerging inside a large spiderweb-infested room filled with dust and wooden crates.

Philip's voice held no emotion. "She was here a long time, for hours. I can smell her everywhere."

It never occurred to Wade to doubt Philip. He'd not realized Philip's sense of smell was so developed, but they'd never been in this position before.

"Why did that ghost lead us here?" Philip asked, almost to himself.

"I don't know."

Slowly, Wade moved toward the back of the dusty room, bypassing the crates, and he spotted the sink.

"Philip . . . ?"

Wade's eyes dropped down to the tattered remnants of clothing on the floor and the dried remains of soapy water staining the area all around. He walked closer. The sink was still wet.

"They cleaned him up," he whispered.

The implications of this were staggering. For one . . . if they had managed this feat, they must have had some cooperation from the vampire, which suggested he was not entirely beyond reach. And two . . . why would Eleisha and Rose clean him up and then leave? Why not try to work with him here, locked away from all other eyes? This was an ideal place for such an attempt.

"Some of my clothes were missing," Philip said, looking down at the rags.

"What?"

"Tonight, at the suite. I noticed some of my clothes and our shampoo and my leather shoes were missing."

Rose had been carrying only a small purse when she left with Philip, so that meant Eleisha had been thinking far ahead before she'd ever slipped out the hotel window.

Wade grimaced. "I don't know what she's planning or what she'll do, except that she's staying about five steps ahead of us."

Philip closed his eyes in what appeared to be a mix of anger and despair, and Wade could not help echoing the sentiments. Eleisha was always saying how much she needed them, but that was a lie. She didn't need either one of them.

And Wade had a sinking feeling that until she contacted them, they would both be wandering in the dark.

Eleisha climbed out of the taxi, with Maxim and Rose coming after. Then she found herself standing at the outer edge of a forest, with a narrow street in front of her, and Caufield Cemetery behind her. In the distance, at the edge of the large graveyard, she could see a small shed and a cottage, but nothing else. They were basically out in the middle of nowhere—in the wee hours before morning. But this was where Seamus had told them to stop. If the cab driver found their destination questionable, he didn't say anything, and she tipped him thirty percent.

He drove away.

Eleisha looked around, fighting the urge to ask Rose, "Now what?" But she managed to keep silent. Maxim, however, turned around to look at the trees, and the tension in his face relaxed visibly. But then he stepped forward and stumbled on the oversized shoes. Eleisha moved to help him.

"You don't need those anymore," she said, untying them and taking them off.

He pointed to the forest.

She slipped into his mind, seeing images of him running through the trees . . . and digging in the dirt. He wanted to go.

"Not yet," she said. "Soon." And she braced herself to freeze him again if he bolted. That had been her overriding goal on this entire journey from London—not to lose Maxim.

Rose was not so comforted by the dark trees, and she crossed her arms, glancing around anxiously. Eleisha was proud of her, though. She'd overcome her own fears and provided much-needed assistance tonight.

"This way," Seamus said.

Eleisha turned quickly to see his transparent form standing near a hidden, overgrown path into the forest. True to his word, he'd popped in to play their guide. She motioned to Maxim with her right hand.

"Come on. Follow me."

This was the first time she'd simply asked him to follow—without driving in a mental command—and she wondered if he understood her, or if he'd agree even if he did understand. But to her relief, he stepped after her, moving much more easily in bare feet, and Rose brought up the rear. Seamus floated down the path with his feet just about an inch off the ground, and they traveled down the path, through the dense trees, for about ten minutes before emerging into a second, smaller graveyard, this one much older, with headstones dating back to the early 1700s. There were weeds growing over all the graves, and the fence was decayed and broken. No one seemed to have been here in many years.

"There," Seamus said, pointing.

Eleisha came around a thick oak tree and saw a small shack beyond the graveyard. While the shack was somewhat decrepit, the roof was intact, and it boasted a few windows. She hurried over—keeping one eye on Maxim—and opened the door. The main room was dusty, but she could see chairs and a broken table. A bedroom was visible at the back. The walls were thick, and the few windows could be covered.

"Oh, Seamus, this is good." She turned. "Rose, come inside. I think we can make this work."

Rose didn't waste any time walking through the door, but Maxim hesitated, cocking his head and pointing back at the trees. "Theeere," he tried to say.

"No, not there," Eleisha told him. "We need to sleep in here. It will be safe. I'll show you."

Although pleased at his attempt to communicate with words, she noticed that he looked even whiter now. His slender face was glowing in the darkness. How long had it been since he'd fed?

Cautiously, he examined the door frame, and she suddenly realized she'd never seen him inside a building except for the little home he'd made in London. She took a few steps back and motioned him forward.

"It's all right."

Looking upward, he moved in after her, but his body was tight, as if he expected an attack at any moment. Then to her surprise, he pointed at the window and shook his head.

"Oh, Rose, he's worried about the windows. That's another good sign."

Maxim could not be completely mad if he was rationalizing concerns about things like windows when dawn was not far off. But Rose didn't answer. She only stood near the wall with her arms crossed and her eyes closed. Now that they had reached their destination, some of her armor was beginning to weaken and break down. Eleisha brought her a chair.

"Sit here."

As Rose sank down, Eleisha moved into the bedroom. It didn't have any windows at all but was completely enclosed by four walls. She grabbed two dusty blankets and hurried back out to the main room, covering both windows completely.

"See?" she asked Maxim. "Safe now."

He studied the blankets, sniffing one of them. From what Eleisha could guess, this had once been the home of a graveyard caretaker. When the larger cemetery, nearer the road, had gone in, this shack must have been abandoned.

"Seamus, how did you find this place?" she asked.

"I told you," he answered, standing near Rose and looking down at her with some concern. "I widened my search last summer, and I just chanced upon it. I sometimes zone in on cemeteries. I'm not sure why."

"You pick up on cemeteries?" Eleisha moved toward him, worried now. "But if that's how you found it, the girl ghost could find it, too."

"I don't think so. She'll spend at least several nights searching London, and we're an hour outside the city. Even if she widens her range, there is too much ground to cover. We're safe for now, and I'll keep my senses open."

He sounded so sure of himself that his words made her feel safer.

"I'm glad you're with us," she said simply.

Well . . . they had shelter, in a place where no one would find them, and now it was time to turn to the next problem. Eleisha had always been a firm believer in taking one problem at a time. She briefly wondered what to do and reached a decision quickly.

"Rose, you just rest here with Seamus. Maxim, come in here with me."

He turned from the window, watching her as she backed into the bedroom, and she could not read anything in his expression, but his skin was too white, and she knew he must be starving.

Once inside the bedroom, she slipped down against the front wall, out of Rose's sight line, and he followed, crouching and cocking his head. It had been several hours since any of his actions had caused her injury—not since the attack by the orange cat—but she wouldn't be able to drop her guard just yet, and she had to remain aware that he was unpredictable and dangerous. He was also a great deal stronger than she was, and she'd need to handle this next act carefully.

"Here, sit," she said.

He dropped from his crouch to sit down beside her, and she was positive he was beginning to remember and comprehend more and more words. But there were no words to explain what she was about to do, and she simply put her wrist to her mouth and tore it open to expose the veins. Then she held it up for Maxim.

"Drink."

Her blood would not nourish him as a mortal's would. It was the equivalent of trying to give someone half-digested food. But in the distant past, an-

other vampire had once done this for her, and she'd
done it for Philip, and it did provide life force and
energy.

Maxim hesitated, as if uncertain what she was
telling him to do, and she put her wrist up to his
mouth.

In a flash, he grabbed it and latched on, drinking
in gulps. The pain was blinding for a few seconds,
and she grabbed his shoulder with her free hand,
pulling him around, so he was lying in her lap and
drinking furiously.

"Slower," she said. "Go slower."

But she'd been right, and he was starving. He
gulped several more mouthfuls, latching down too
hard.

Slower.

She sent this as a suggestion, not a command, and
it worked. He stopped drinking for a few seconds,
but he didn't detach himself. Then he drew down
with less pressure and swallowed.

"Good."

She was holding him like that, with her wrist in
his mouth, when Rose appeared in the doorway,
turning to look down at them. She did not ask what
Eleisha was doing. She watched only until Eleisha
got Maxim to stop and pulled her wrist from his
mouth. When he looked at her, something in his
face had changed. Of course, it wasn't so white
now, but there was something more. She could
swear she saw gratitude in his eyes, either gratitude or something close to it. She didn't think she'd

need to drive any more mental commands to keep him at her side.

"The sun will be up before long," Rose said calmly, as if they were a mortal family that had just finished supper. "I think we should all sleep in this room."

Residing in close proximity to Jasper, with nothing else to do, was beginning to grind on Julian's nerves in a way he'd never experienced before. Even in life, he'd required a great deal of privacy. After being turned, this need increased.

Spending three nights locked in a suite with an inferior creature like Jasper was enough to drive him mad. He'd gone back and forth over sending his servant back to San Francisco. Only the uncertainty of tonight's events kept him from doing so.

There was still a possibility that he might require assistance.

But in spite of Mary's unforgivable blunder, as usual, she'd come up with a clever plan to keep moving forward. He'd never tell her, but he had faith she'd find a way to lead Philip right to Eleisha and the feral vampire.

Mary had a way of handling whatever was thrown at her.

"Julian?" she called.

He was in his bedroom at the suite—trying to avoid Jasper—and he was annoyed she had materialized out in the sitting room. Opening the door, he walked out to see her standing by the fireplace with Jasper at her side.

"Well?" he asked, but he could tell from her stance that something was wrong.

She shook her head. "No dice. I got Philip there, but she was already gone . . . with Rose and the vamp. The place was cleaned out. I don't think they're going back." She stood straighter. "I did a sweep of that area before coming here, but I didn't sense anything. I don't know where they are."

He just stood there, staring at her, too over-whelmed for anger.

"I'll keep searching the city, but Eleisha's not stu-pid, and I doubt anyone's going to find her until she wants to be found this time."

"What do you mean, 'wants to be found'?" he asked quietly.

"She won't leave Philip and Wade on meat hooks for long. It's not her way. They all have cell phones. She'll call Wade sooner or later, and I'll stay right on top of him. He'll lead me to her. We just have to wait."

Jasper ran a hand over his face. "No," he whis-pered. "You want me to just sit here? Mary, I can't."

She looked at him with open pity. "I'm so sorry. That's the best I can do . . . I think. I'll go out looking again right away, but . . . ," she said, trailing off.

Julian had no pity for either of his servants, and he was well over his quota for disgust at the mo-ment. Without another word, he turned and walked back into his room, closing the door. But he couldn't help agreeing with Jasper on a certain level, and he didn't know how much longer he could just sit in here either.

Something had to happen soon.

He sat down on his bed. Dawn was not far off.

When Eleisha awoke that night, she found herself lying on the floor of the shack's bedroom with Maxim pressed up beside her. Rose was still dormant on the bed. This was the first moment in twenty-four hours that Eleisha had to really think, to let the ramifications of her own actions sink in.

Was it only last night that she'd awoken on Philip's chest, right before Seamus materialized to tell them he'd found a signature near Westminster Bridge? It seemed like weeks.

And the sight of Maxim lying beside her brought a sharp pain she hadn't expected.

Philip would be waking up alone.

She missed him. She missed how he always woke up a few seconds before she did and she would look down into his eyes as she was already planning events to entertain him for the night.

He must be lonely and angry. He must be so worried.

Her gaze flickered to the backpack in the main room. The cell phone was tucked inside. Should she call him? Better, maybe she should call Wade again and just give him a message that they were still safe?

But even as she ran this option through her mind, she knew it was wrong. She shouldn't call either one of them until Maxim was ready. She couldn't do anything to jeopardize his safety, not now, not when he'd come so far in the span of a single night.

He stirred on the floor beside her, opening his eyes. An instant of blind panic hit him, and he jumped up, looking around the foreign room.

"Maxim," Eleisha said, and he turned on her.

But he didn't charge or lash out. His gaze cleared and then dropped to her wrist. His skin was not so white anymore.

"Leisha?" he said.

She sat up, startled. "Yes, Maxim."

Rose was awake, watching them both. "Have you felt a hint of his gift?" she asked. "Anything at all?"

"No, and he doesn't seem to even know he could push me out of his head if he tried. The only power he seems to have is controlling the behavior of animals."

Rose didn't know that Eleisha had already seen some of Maxim's memories. Eleisha wasn't sure how to tell her that even in life, Maxim hadn't exactly been a poster boy for mental health. He'd been an odd young man, brilliant, but cold to the point of expressing total disregard for others. However, he'd also not expressed any affinity toward animals. When had that started? And what *was* his gift?

Before Eleisha could make any further progress with him, she had to know what had happened to turn a scholarly, fastidious young vampire into a feral creature who'd forgotten how to speak.

Only then would she know how to move forward.

"Rose," she said slowly, "Maxim seems to feel more comfortable outside. I'm going to take him for a walk, and we may be a while. Is that all right?"

Rose watched her for a few seconds. "Yes, of course."

Rose never needed to have anything spelled out for her. Eleisha stood and headed for the door.

Let's go into the trees, she flashed to Maxim.

He didn't need to be asked twice and hurried after her. Soon, they were half a mile from the shack, running through the forest, and Eleisha could not help enjoying the sensation. Since being turned, she'd always lived in cities . . . New York, Seattle, Portland. But in her youth, she had run among the trees at Cliffbracken, and tonight brought back pleasant memories.

Maxim jerked to a halt, his head swiveling. She stopped beside him.

"What is it?"

"Shhhhhh," he said.

His eyes narrowed, and a large rabbit hopped toward them. It kept coming without fear, as if being called. Maxim suddenly stepped forward and picked it up, sinking his teeth into its throat and gulping. For some reason, Eleisha looked away. This brought back different memories.

Maxim fed on rabbits? No wonder his undead signature was so weak. She'd known only one other undead who'd been able to feed on rabbits.

When Maxim finished, he hid the animal's small body under a patch of ferns, but he did not bother wiping his face. His movements were fluid, and he seemed more at ease than Eleisha had ever seen him. He was at home out here.

"Maxim," she said, sinking down beside a wide tree trunk, "come here."

He came to sit beside her, his skin even less pale now, and he pointed back toward the patch of ferns hiding the dead rabbit. "One," he said, "for you?"

She sat up straight. He was combining words . . . and if she understood him correctly, he was offering to bring a rabbit for her. The rapid forward movement of his progress had begun when she'd forced his memories to surface, leading him to remember Brandon and Adalrik.

"No . . . no, thank you," she said. She leaned toward him. "Maxim, I need to see more, like last night." She reached out and touched the back of his hand, and he did not pull away.

What she asked of him was complicated, and she gave up on speech.

I need you to think back to that night Adalrik took you out to feed in the village. Can you go back to that night?

His face was close to hers, and he was clearly uncertain about doing what she asked. The first session had been brutal for him. But he was a good deal more coherent and aware now.

He closed his eyes, and she slipped deeper into his mind, locking onto the memories and propelling them forward.

chapter eleven

Maxim

Maxim stumbled out of the alley behind Adalrik, feeling better physically, but nearly sick with relief that this whole "feeding" ordeal was done, and they could ride back to the library. His fantasies of traveling with Adalrik were fading by the moment, and he was desperate to go home and lock the doors.

He started toward his horse.

"Not yet," Adalrik said, and his tone brooked no argument. "Follow me."

Maxim looked toward the horse and wavered in indecision. Could he simply flee? Swing up onto the animal and race back to the house?

"Now," Adalrik ordered.

Long accustomed to obeying his mentor, Maxim fell into step.

"This is all wrong," Adalrik said more kindly, "and I know I'm rushing you, but we have no choice."

They passed by a number of closed shops, and Maxim soon heard voices up ahead. Adalrik walked into a busy pub five blocks from where they'd left the unconscious man in the alley.

"No, not here," Maxim whispered in panic. "We're not far enough."

"Quiet."

The place was crowded but clean, with a long polished bar. Several men behind it served drinks and chatted with patrons. A few of the locals turned to look their way, and Maxim's stomach tightened. He almost turned around and walked back out.

"Sit down," Adalrik told him.

He sat.

"When the serving girl comes over," Adalrik said, "I want you to speak to her directly, and I want you to think of feeding at the same time. Imagine her as you would if you pressed against her and fed from her wrist. Think on that image as you speak."

After a year alone with no one but Adalrik, Maxim was overwhelmed by the sights and sounds of so many people. He was overwhelmed with worry that the man in the alley might wake up at any moment and come accuse him. He was overwhelmed by a need to be safely locked away in the library.

"Focus," Adalrik whispered.

A pretty girl with thick brown hair and a clean

apron came to the table. "What'll you have?" she asked.

Maxim was frozen for a few seconds, and then he tried to do as Adalrik asked. Strangely, it wasn't difficult, and he almost could not help picturing himself pressed against her, swallowing her blood.

"Red wine," he said, "preferably in a pewter goblet."

When he spoke, his voice sounded . . . different. She gazed down at him, momentarily shaken, and then she smiled. "Pewter goblet indeed. You think you're drinking with the queen?"

Something warm began to build inside him, and it felt as if it were seeping outward. The girl's eyes locked on him in fascination.

Adalrik was watching them both, and he said to the girl, "My dear, have you ever read 'The Nun's Priest's Tale'?"

Maxim blinked at his mentor. What a ridiculous question to ask a barmaid.

She laughed. "No, sir, I certainly have not."

"Tell her the story, Maxim."

Grasping for a moment of security, safely ensconced inside the words of Geoffrey Chaucer, Maxim began to spin the colorful story of Chanticleer, a clever rooster who outwits a fox. As he spun the tale, several other patrons stopped their drinking and moved closer to listen. The girl's fascination with his face, with the movement of his mouth, only increased.

The warm feeling continued flowing from his body, gaining strength.

When he finished the story, everyone around applauded and cheered. He did not know how to respond, but Adalrik stood up. "We must be on our way."

"No, sir," the girl protested. "You've not even had your drinks yet." She looked to Maxim. "Please, tell us another."

"The hour is late," Adalrik said. "We must be heading home."

Against other protests, Maxim followed him numbly to the door, wondering what had just happened. He knew it was something important. He simply did not know what.

They mounted their horses and rode out. Once they were well away from the village, Adalrik finally said, "I suspected. But I had no idea you would be so strong, so soon. You were meant to exist as one of us."

"What are you saying?" Maxim cried, unable to keep the questions and the fear inside any longer.

Adalrik started slightly at the outburst and pulled up his horse. "Your gift." He paused. "We all have gifts. Some are straightforward and easy to name, such as mine. Did you feel it in the alley? Mine is trustworthiness. When I speak while hunting, any mortal within earshot will trust me absolutely, and so I am able to seduce him or her quietly. We could not survive without our gifts."

Maxim turned his horse to face Adalrik's. "Then what is mine? I felt . . . something back in the pub."

"I'm not sure I can name it, although I could feel it as deeply as everyone else. It is a kind of awe. Everyone there saw you as brilliant, gifted . . . a scholar. They wanted to be near you, to be part of the world you were spinning with those words." He paused. "I cannot help feeling envious. I could only hope for such a gift. Do not squander it."

Maxim rode in silence the rest of the way home, thinking on all of this, even growing slightly excited.

He could inspire awe by simply opening his mouth.

The following night offered no time for literary discussion, and to Maxim's further anxiety, Adalrik seemed determined to quit this place as soon as possible. There was a great deal of packing to be done—mainly books—and instructions to leave and arrangements to be made. The two of them would be traveling light, but Adalrik was having a number of boxes shipped to wherever they were going. As of yet, he would not say the destination.

"Must we go?" Maxim asked, wringing his hands. "No one bothers us here. I don't see why we cannot stay."

"It's not safe," Adalrik answered. "It is too well-known among my family."

Who was this family he always spoke of? Part of Maxim wished to know, and another part wished they didn't exist. The library looked ugly with so many books missing from the shelves, like an old woman who'd lost half her teeth.

"Come and sit for a moment," Adalrik said. "There are important things to tell you."

He sat in his chair by the fire, and Maxim joined him reluctantly. So far, with the exception of Maxim's gift, every "important" thing Adalrik had to tell him had been unpleasant.

"There are a number of others like us," his mentor began, "and we have existed in secret for centuries among mortals by following four unbreakable laws. As I tell you each one, you must swear an oath to uphold it. Do you understand?"

Laws? Maxim had never broken a law in his life. Well, until last night. But hearing about laws sounded safe. Perhaps tonight's lesson would not be so unpleasant after all.

"I understand."

"I've already told you the first law," Adalrik went on. "No vampire shall kill to feed. This assures our safety and secrecy. Swear this to me. You will never kill to feed."

"I swear."

This was the first time Adalrik had used the word "vampire." Somehow, it did not startle Maxim.

"The second law," Adalrik said, "is that no vampire shall make another until reaching the age of one hundred years as an undead, and no vampire shall ever make more than one companion within the span of a hundred years. The physical and mental energy required is so great that any breach of this law will produce flawed results. Do you swear your oath?"

"I swear."

"The third law is that no vampire shall make another without the consent of the mortal. Do you swear?"

"I swear."

"The fourth and final law is that the maker must teach the new vampire all methods of proper survival and all four of the laws in order to protect the secrecy of our kind. Do you swear?"

"I swear."

This rather lengthy exercise struck Maxim as pointless. With the exception of the first law, he gave no thought to any of this. He certainly had no desire to make another vampire—even if he knew how.

"There is a reason I am telling you all this tonight," Adalrik said. "One of us has broken the laws and placed the rest of us in danger."

The word "danger" got Maxim's attention.

"One of our most trusted elders lost his reason, and he made three sons in the span of a scant few years. As a result, one of them was born unto us with no telepathic abilities at all. None. His name is Julian. He cannot follow the first law."

This puzzled Maxim until he remembered how Adalrik had replaced the man's memory the night before. "Oh . . . so he cannot . . . ?"

"You understand." Adalrik's eyes drifted. "None of us would ever harm another, but this situation has no precedent, and his maker refused to destroy him. Several of us had decided to take matters into our own hands . . . and then Julian began murdering us."

"Murdering? You said we would live forever."

"Some things can still kill us: fire, the sun, and decapitation. Julian is coming from the shadows with a sword and taking heads. No one knows quite how he always succeeds. But no one he's attacked has survived."

"Taking heads?"

The very thought of this, the image of some great vampire coming from the darkness with a sword, filled Maxim with a dread he'd never experienced. It almost made him ill.

"Do you see now why we have to leave?" Adalrik asked. "Why we must go someplace no one would associate with me?"

"Yes," Maxim said, nodding. "I will help you pack the books."

The following night, the deliveryman from Shrewsbury arrived after dark so Adalrik could discuss some final details for closing up the house. Maxim no longer feared leaving. Rather, he couldn't wait to get away from here—the sooner the better.

Finally, a few hours past dusk, everything seemed settled.

"I think we're ready," Adalrik said. "We'll ride into Shrewsbury, sell the horses, and hire a carriage for the journey to the coast. We'll be more comfortable in a carriage."

"The coast? Will that be far enough?"

"No." Adalrik smiled. "I don't think anywhere in Europe will be far enough. We'll book passage on a ship and spend a few decades in the New World."

When Maxim shook his head, Adalrik's smile broadened.

"New York," he said.

This left Maxim uncertain. He had no knowledge of New York. But then . . . perhaps Adalrik was right. If they wished to avoid Julian's sword, the farther away the better.

As if reading his face, Adalrik grew more serious. "Listen to me. I've told no one, no one among our kind, that you exist. Should anything happen to me, you must disappear. You mustn't let anyone know of your existence."

The very thought terrified Maxim. How could he travel without Adalrik? Survive in a foreign land?

"I need a few travel documents from my desk in the library," Adalrik said. "You get your bag, and I'll meet you in the foyer." He looked around. "I will miss this place. You and I have spent many happy hours here."

The night before, Maxim would have agreed. Now he just wanted to saddle his horse.

"I won't be long," he answered, heading off to his room.

His bed was made, and a small bag of his clothes

was neatly packed with a spare suit, toiletries, and undergarments. All his other clothes were boxed for shipping. His long coat lay across the bed, and he slipped it on before turning to leave. His attachment to this place had vanished the moment Adalrik told him of Julian. Now it was a house of threats.

They had not bothered lighting many candles tonight, and the hallway was dark, but as he stepped from his bedroom, a cool gust of air blew against him, and he turned to see the back door was open.

He frowned, certain he'd locked it earlier, but when he moved to close it, he looked down to see the jam was broken. Someone had forced the door. His throat began to close up, and he did not call out. Instinct told him to remain silent and to locate Adalrik immediately. The safest place was behind Adalrik.

He put down his travel bag and walked silently down the hall. The library had two entrances, and he headed for the main one. The door was half-open, and he could see his mentor standing inside, shuffling through a desk.

This seemed a pleasant, normal sight, and Maxim walked faster. He was only ten steps away when something caught his eye . . . a glint of reflective light from the other entrance on the east side of the library, very near to Adalrik. The same survival instinct surged up in Maxim, causing him to change plans, and he stepped behind the door, peering through the crack beside the wall only a few seconds before the fear hit him.

He'd never experienced anything like it in his life—and he knew a good deal about fear. Waves and waves of gut-wrenching fear poured from the library, hitting Adalrik at the same time.

Adalrik staggered back from the desk, attempting to turn around, and a tall, broad-shouldered man with dark hair stepped from the shadows of the other doorway and swung with both hands gripping the hilt of a sword.

His blade sliced right through Adalrik's throat, severing his head, which flew off and bounced against the red carpet. Maxim pressed against the wall behind the door, willing himself not to scream.

Then the memories hit him.

Image after image of Adalrik's life erupted inside his mind. But the fear was still choking him, and few of the images even registered. He saw foreign places and countless people. A gypsy girl. A hardened soldier with a broken nose. Scene after scene of Adalrik leaning over a book with some stranger, and then . . . images of Brandon. Many images.

Maxim wanted to scream, but something, some shred of survival instinct, kept him silent.

Then he saw memories of himself here in the house, studying in the library, and his panic increased. Was Julian seeing these memories, too? If so . . . he would know! He would know about Maxim.

The pain and the images faded, and he forced himself to open his eyes. Julian was standing over Adalrik's body, looking down. He did not appear to

have suffered the same onslaught. Perhaps he had
not seen any of the memories?

Adalrik's words came back to Maxim.

*Should anything happen to me, you must disappear.
You mustn't let anyone know of your existence.*

Julian had not heard Maxim out in the hallway
and didn't know he was there. Maxim looked behind himself toward the broken back door. Then he
peeked back through the crack. Still gripping the
sword, Julian watched Adalrik's headless body as it
began to change, to lose its form. While Julian's attention was so absorbed, Maxim slipped silently
down the hallway and out the open door, leading to
the untended gardens behind the house.

The fear that Julian had projected was still with
him. It permeated deep inside his mind, mingled
with his own natural fears, and became trapped
there. All Maxim could feel was terror. All he could
see was the sword swinging and Adalrik's head hitting the carpet.

Maxim ran.

Within seconds, he reached the beginning of the
dense forest behind the house. He'd never cared for
forests, but now the trees and the darkness were a
haven—the only place to offer safety. He had to disappear.

He ran.

Shortly before dawn, he stopped running. He didn't
know where he was, but it didn't matter. As long as
he stayed in the forest, away from people, Julian

would never know he existed. All he could feel was fear, and all he could see was the glint of the swinging sword.

But he was safe here, alone among the trees.

Yet dawn was coming, and he needed to survive the day.

He chose a spot with loose soil and dropped to his knees, digging. The strength and durability of his slender hands surprised him. He dug himself a grave.

Once the hole was deep enough, he crawled inside and buried himself completely. Feeling safe for the first time in hours, he fell dormant.

He woke up that night with a stab of fear piercing through his brain. In the darkness of the grave he saw Julian's cold, pale face.

He quickly dug himself out, not caring that he was filthy—barely even noticing. The fear in his mind had only increased during his sleep, and he began looking around for a place to hide. Yes, that was the answer. Find a place to hide, somewhere Julian would never find him.

He found a patch of heavy shrubs beneath an oak tree and crawled inside the prickly branches. He could see in front and to the sides, and the tree was behind him. He felt safe here and remained hidden like that all night.

He buried himself in the hole again before dawn.

That night, when he awoke, he decided it was time to change to a new location. It wasn't safe to remain in the same spot for too many nights.

Heading deeper into the forest, he found a new place to hide, beneath a new patch of bushes.

This pattern continued for six nights, and then he realized he was hungry. He needed to feed. Somehow, he knew the direction back toward the house without even thinking about it, but he could not go back there, never back there. Instead, he headed in the same general direction, until he reached the road that he and Adalrik had taken to the village.

The thought of Adalrik almost paralyzed him with fear. He could not think of Adalrik without seeing Julian.

Slipping through the trees beside the road, he kept moving until he smelled smoke, and he peered out through the edge of the forest to see a small, isolated house. By now the hour was late, but he could hear people moving inside. His hunger grew, and he forced himself to creep up and peer through a window. Being out in the open was the worst thing he could imagine now, but he peeked inside a window to see an old woman, a young woman, a man, and several children. The children were sleeping.

He longed to feed on any of them, but to do so would mean luring someone outside, and he did not know if he could replace a memory as Adalrik had done. And what if someone else in the family saw him? His existence would be exposed. Julian would find out about him. He knew it.

But Maxim was so hungry.

What if he simply killed the victim or even the

whole family? That would silence them. Adalrik's laws no longer seemed to matter.

Yes, this prospect seemed best.

But . . . if he couldn't replace memories, he'd have to kill every time he fed. Adalrik's logic about secrecy tied to the four laws drifted through the terror in his mind. Stories of blood-drained bodies would reach Julian.

His thoughts shifted again. He could hide the bodies or burn the house down afterward?

No, that would only buy him time. Sooner or later, Julian would know. The fear grew stronger amid his hunger.

Should anything happen to me, you must disappear. You mustn't let anyone know of your existence.

He slipped away from the window, running back into the forest in despair. How could he feed? How could he survive if he could never expose himself to mortals? The hunger and sorrow and terror caused him to stumble and fall. When he looked up, he saw a rabbit staring back at him from under the brush. The creature was frozen still, as if it could hide itself by virtue of not moving. Maxim didn't blame it. He'd subscribed to that philosophy for the past six nights.

But he could smell the blood, the life force in the small creature, and he imagined himself biting through its fur.

"Have I ever told you the story of Chanticleer?" he asked, and then he laughed, hearing madness in his own voice. The rabbit darted, but Maxim reached

out for its thoughts, as he had for Adalrik's that
night in the alley.

Wait. Don't go.

The rabbit stopped.

Come.

It turned and hopped toward him. As soon as it
was in reach, Maxim grabbed it with one hand, bit
down, and began feeding. He'd fed on a mortal only
once, but he was aware that the taste and the entire
experience were different. He did see some flashes
of memories, but they were simple . . . mating, eat-
ing clover, sleeping in a deep den. However, the
blood quelled his hunger, and he felt better afterward, not as strong or as sharp as when he'd fed on
the man, but he wasn't starving anymore.

And rabbits could not speak.

None of the animals in the forest could speak.

He'd found a way to survive.

Here, Eleisha became aware of herself again as she
almost lost the connection, and she fought to keep
his memories flowing forward. But his nights began
passing in a blur, one after another, almost always
the same, of Maxim using his telepathic ability to
call upon animals, of him feeding, and running in
the trees, and burying himself before dawn.

Decades slipped by, and he never left the forest.

Eleisha realized the difficulty in channeling his
memories came from his mental processes breaking
down between a combination of his twisted fear,
feeding only on the life force of animals, and his

complete separation from humans. She had no way of accurately knowing how much time was passing, and his clothes appeared to almost rot off his body overnight. He didn't like being completely naked, and so when his clothes were beyond tatters, he would sometimes creep up to an isolated house and steal what he could. He didn't care about shoes after a while.

He forgot how to speak. He forgot his gift. He forgot his name. He even forgot about Julian—except for the shadow of absolute belief that he must remain in the forest.

Still aware of herself, aware she was reading memories, Eleisha began to gauge time better as the number of dwellings he stumbled upon grew more numerous and more modern. The forests began to feel smaller and smaller. The population of England was growing, and the forested areas were vanishing at a rapid pace.

Without warning, Maxim hit upon a more cohesive memory, and Eleisha was lost inside him again.

He was hungry and knew he could call a rabbit, but he smelled something good—something better. Crouched on all fours, he listened as the good thing came toward him.

She walked on two legs like him, making strange sounds like the birds as she came through the trees while moving her mouth. Something in the back of his mind told him to stay hidden, but he was hungry, and she smelled so good.

A bright light flashed from her hands. He blinked and looked away as it hurt his eyes.

He tried to call her with his thoughts, as he would a deer or a rabbit. She didn't hear him. But when she walked right past the place where he hid, he couldn't hold himself back. Launching at her, he was surprised by how easy it was to knock her down, to hold her down even while she fought him and made much louder noises—which did not sound like the birds.

He bit down on her throat, gulping and drinking as fast as he could. The taste was unbelievable, so different, so much better than a deer or a rabbit. He drank and drank, feeling his body grow stronger, more alert, more aware. Unwanted thoughts tickled the back of his brain—thoughts that he should not be doing this—but he pushed them away and drank until he could take no more. When he finished, she stared up at the night sky with dead eyes.

He felt different.

He knew he'd done something wrong, but the taste of her blood was still in his mouth, and he already wanted more.

Over the following nights, he tried to feed on rabbits and squirrels and deer again, but they tasted like sand in his mouth. He knew where many of the two-legged things lived, and he began to seek them out, to try to catch one alone.

This proved more difficult than he'd expected.

Sometimes he succeeded and sometimes he had

to settle for the animals of the forest. They were so easy to call. They always heard him. The two-legged things did not.

After he'd drained a few more of them, the voice in the back of his mind grew stronger, telling him he was doing something wrong and he should flee once he was finished feeding. He moved south, farther and farther, leaving the forests behind. He learned to hide among the dwellings of the two-legged things. He learned he could call the creatures that lived to serve them. The animals always came to him when he called. They would always do as he asked with his desires. They heard him.

The bright lights and rushing squares of metal frightened him at first, but he used every bit of knowledge from the forest to find places to hide, to lie in wait, to try to feed.

One night he found himself in a place bursting with light and rushing metal squares and countless numbers of the two-legged things. He was starving that night, and he smelled someone alone.

He moved between two solid walls to a dark place where he saw her walking. He rushed her, trying to pin her against a wall, but her clothes were slippery, so he lost his grip for an instant and she made a very loud, high-pitched noise. He dived in again, snapping for her throat, biting her hard, but more of the two-legged things came running toward him, including two big ones with large animals held by some kind of thin rope around their throats.

He panicked, the fear of discovery driving him forward.

Using his mind, he cried out to the four-legged beasts to protect him. They did. He heard the snarling and the tearing teeth as he ran away, disappearing into the darkness.

He was still hungry.

chapter twelve

This time, Eleisha pulled away because she had to. She couldn't stand to see any more—and she didn't need to. He'd taken her right up to the point where he'd attacked the woman outside of King's Cross Station and then turned the police dogs on their human partners.

Maxim was choking on the ground beside her, and his black eyes were open, staring out in horror. She'd brought him out of the fog-filled stupor last night by making him remember the distant past, and now she'd made him see himself as he'd been in the recent past . . . made him aware of it.

"Maxim," she whispered as the reality of the situation began to truly sink in.

His gift was useless. He could barely speak, and even if he learned to function well enough to pass among contemporary society, he was never going to be able to spout Shakespeare, Milton, or Chaucer.

He was a different person now.

After well over a century of feeding on animals and connecting only to animals, he also seemed to have bypassed developing any ability to telepathically influence humans. What was she going to do? How could she possibly teach him to feed?

"Leisha," he said.

She tried to understand his self-imposed degeneration.

No, that was unfair. He'd been sent into madness by Julian's gift. Maxim had already suffered from a pathological fear of men, and Julian had just driven him over the edge.

"I'm sorry I did that to you," she said, "but I had to know."

He lay there, looking at her. Wanting to offer him some comfort, some method for him to stop reliving what she'd just put him through, she reached out and touched his arm, flashing images into his mind of the church, of the sanctuary she and Rose had turned into a library, of the kitchen and the bedrooms.

"That is my home," she said. "I want to take you there, to live with us."

His head tilted to one side. "Home," he said as if contemplating the word. Then his eyes grew sad again. "Where . . . where Brandon?"

Again, he was asking for Brandon. Eleisha suspected that after spending nearly two centuries of near-identical nights in the forest, Maxim had no idea how much time had passed.

"Dead," she answered. "Long ago." He sat back stiffly, and she knew he'd understood her. "But I'll look out for you," she said. "I want you to come home with me."

"Home," he said.

When they got back to the shack, Eleisha was not surprised to find that Rose had cleaned and straightened and was attempting to make the place livable. She'd found a broom in the closet and begun sweeping.

Maxim seemed fascinated by the process and moved closer to watch.

In spite of all the progress they'd made, Eleisha could no longer push down the guilt over leaving Wade and Philip behind. Sometimes the end justified the means, but that still didn't make it all right.

She dug through her backpack and pulled out the cell phone. "Rose, I'm going . . . to step outside."

Rose stopped sweeping. "Are you sure?"

"Yes"—she nodded—"but I won't be long."

Heading back outside, she crouched beside a tree, flipped open the phone, and dialed Wade, knowing his caller ID would let him see it was she. He deserved more than one brief warning about a ghost.

He picked up on the second ring, and she braced herself.

"Where are you?" he asked without saying hello. His tone was cold.

She didn't speak for a moment, not having had much of an idea how he would react.

"Eleisha?" he asked.

"I'm here." Then she focused on the only reason she'd called him. "I just wanted to let you know that we're safe, and we're making progress. I didn't want you to worry."

"You didn't want us to worry?" He sounded incredulous now. "I watched him rip your throat out."

Her first impulse was to start apologizing, but he and Philip had forced her into this position, and she had nothing to be sorry for.

"He's getting better. I've got him talking," she said, "but I think he's lost his gift."

The line was silent for a little while, and then he said, "He's talking? What do you mean he's lost his gift?"

She didn't know where to begin, and she couldn't bring herself to start telling him everything over the phone. "You'll understand all this better than I do. He's been through a lot, Wade. I'm going to need you so much once I've gotten him a little further along—far enough that Philip won't just kill him."

"Far enough that . . . Eleisha, you tell me where you are, right now!" His voice exploded into the phone. "I'm not sitting this one out! Not again. Tell me where you are, and I can help you tonight."

The offer was so very tempting. Wade had a doctorate degree in psychology. He understood phobias. He understood mental illness, and he would certainly know how to proceed with Maxim far, far better than Eleisha ever could. Should she just tell him where they were? Get him on a train?

Seamus suddenly materialized in front of her, looking down at the phone and slowly shaking his head.

He was right.

If Wade came, Philip would come, too. As much as Eleisha missed Philip, Maxim was not ready for him yet.

"I can't," she whispered. "Please, Wade, just give me a few more nights. Just stay there in London, and I promise I'll bring you here as soon as I can."

"Stay *there* in London? Are you not even inside the—?"

She heard a door open on the other end of the line, and then Philip's French accent.

"Is that her? Give me the phone!"

She could hear his angry footsteps on the floor, and she clicked her phone shut with a stab of guilt and loneliness. But talking to him right now wouldn't help.

Eleisha spent the following two nights in and around the quiet shack, helping Rose improve Maxim's vocabulary. She'd briefed Rose on his unusual past—even showing her several memories—and they both spent some time communicating with him telepathically.

He could hear their thoughts when they linked

with him, and he could project scattered thoughts himself, but as of yet, he'd not been able to reach into either of their minds on his own.

At first, he'd flinched or started every time Seamus appeared, but that soon improved, and he grew accustomed to Seamus' blinking in and out.

Maxim seemed fond of the shack, perhaps too fond, and Eleisha could feel how much he liked the combination of a safe shelter nestled among the forest. She worried it might be difficult to get him to leave when the time came.

Linked with his thoughts, she was not surprised by how much time he spent going over and over the memories she had forced him to bring to the surface. He focused a good deal on Brandon, which was understandable, but he also could not seem to reconcile that the young man in those memories was himself.

This was a difficult dichotomy, and she thought if he could just accept who he had once been, he might become more of himself again.

However, a part of her wasn't sure that would be an entirely good thing. The Maxim of the past may have been brilliant, but he was also a self-centered coward willing to say or do anything to get past an uncomfortable moment.

The present Maxim was capable of reciprocation. He was capable of gratitude. She liked him.

Just past dusk on the third night, all four of them were outside the shack, and Maxim looked upward. A flock of geese was flying overhead.

"Look," he said, narrowing his eyes in concentration.

Suddenly their V shape broke up, and they formed two circles in the sky. Then they formed a star while still flying.

"Oh, Maxim," Rose said, smiling. "Very clever."

Was he trying to entertain them?

But Seamus wasn't watching the geese. He was watching Maxim.

"What is it?" Eleisha asked.

"As soon as he linked into the geese . . . I almost couldn't sense his signature anymore. Could that be the trick? When he's connected to animals, he's so much a part of them that a hint of their life force becomes part of him?"

Eleisha pondered this. "I don't know. Maybe part of it. I think so many years of feeding only on animals may have weakened his signature, too."

Maxim was different from any other vampire she'd known. Perhaps like mortals, the evolution of an undead was also based on conditions and environment.

"But unless he can redevelop his gift," she added, "he'll never be able to hunt on his own."

"Would that be so terrible?" Rose asked, looking down from the geese to Eleisha.

"What do you mean?"

"If he couldn't hunt on his own? If you or I had to go out with him every time and use our own gifts and replace a memory for him. Would that be such a tragedy?"

Eleisha had not considered this—at least not for the long term. "No," she answered, "it would not."

She and Rose could simply trade off taking him hunting . . . but of course, they'd have to get Philip on board as well.

The possibilities drifted through her mind, and she came to a decision.

"I'm going to take him out tonight. We passed some houses on the way to that newer cemetery . . . what was it called, Caufield?"

Maxim stopped playing with the geese and turned to look at her. Sometimes she thought he understood a great deal being said around him.

"Will you come with me?" she asked him directly. "Come hunting . . . as you did with Adalrik?"

He flinched at Adalrik's name, as the image of his second mentor always brought a memory of Julian's sword, but Eleisha wanted him to remember that night in the alley, the only time he'd ever fed by the first law.

"Come with me," she said.

When she began walking toward the path back to the road, he followed.

After two straight nights of hanging around the Montague hotel—while Wade and Philip did basically nothing—Mary teleported back to Great Fosters to give Julian a report, whether he wanted one or not.

But when she materialized in the sitting room of the suite, it was empty. Julian's bedroom door was closed, and she sensed his presence on the other side.

Where was Jasper?

Focusing, she felt his signature up above her somewhere, and she blinked out, blinking back in on the hotel's rooftop. Jasper sat near the edge of the roof, gazing out over the painstakingly landscaped and manicured grounds.

The English certainly knew how to design a garden.

"You okay?" she asked.

He turned his head quickly, and his face lit up. "Mary? Is something happening? Are we moving in?"

Sorry to disappoint him, she shook her head. "Not yet, but I just had to get away for a few minutes. Wade and Philip are just sitting there, waiting."

He grimaced. "So are we. I couldn't stand it in that suite another minute. It's no big thrill up here, but it's better than staying in there with him."

The venom in his voice caught her attention. He'd never spoken of Julian with anything but respect, and he'd made it crystal clear that he was more than pleased with his current lifestyle and would do anything to keep it.

"You sound as though you hate him," she said.

"I don't like the way he talks to you. I don't like the way he treats you."

That threw her for a loop. Jasper was pissed off over the way Julian talked to her? "He doesn't mean it," she said. "That's just the way he is. He came from a different time."

"Well, this is now, and you're the one doing all the work."

No one had ever put her first like this, and she wasn't sure what to say, but maybe . . . maybe he was getting sick of working for Julian?

"He promised he'd let me go if I served him, that he'd let me stay on this plane but cut me loose from him."

Jasper turned his head toward her. "When?"

"I don't know. I think when he's sure Eleisha's found the last elder."

His face fell. "That will take forever."

"No, there couldn't be too many more. From what he's told me, only a few could've slipped him— maybe not even that many. He just wants to be sure."

"What will you do when it's over?"

"Depends on what you do." She hesitated, not sure she wanted an answer, but finally asked, "Could you be happy without the money . . . the cars and the clothes and condo? Just fending for yourself?"

He was quiet for a little, and then answered, "Yeah, I could. When this is over, I don't think I'd mind being cut loose either."

A shadow of hope flickered inside her.

"I always wanted to go to New York," he went on. "You think you could give that a try?"

"Yeah." She nodded. "I could."

Eleisha had planned to travel inside the tree line down the road for a while before finding a house where someone lived alone, but as they emerged from the path into Caufield Cemetery, she saw a light on in the shed near the small cottage.

Reaching out with her mind, she picked up thoughts from only one person—a woman.

The isolated situation was ideal . . . but this place was only a ten-minute walk from where they were hiding out. However, if she succeeded tonight, they wouldn't be here long.

Maxim sniffed the air, seeming uncomfortable at being so out in the open.

"It's all right," she said, grasping his hand. "Let me do the talking." She walked past several stone headstones and called out, "Hallo?"

The shed door opened, and a large woman with shorn hair came out, frowning. "Who's there?"

Maxim tensed and began to pull away, but Eleisha gripped down on his fingers. "No," she whispered. "Stay with me."

Then she called out, "Here! Over here."

The large woman strode toward them, carrying a flashlight. She wore jeans and a heavy flannel shirt. "I didn't hear a car." She didn't sound happy. "What you doing out . . . ?"

Six feet away, she got her first clear look at Maxim, and Eleisha wondered if this had been a good idea. While he was clean and dressed now, and his slender features were almost pretty, she hadn't quite realized how his demeanor might appear to someone unaccustomed to him. He didn't make eye contact, and he constantly shifted his weight between his bare feet.

"My brother got lost in the woods," Eleisha said. "I've been looking all day, and my cell phone is dead. I just found him. May I use your phone to try and call our father? There are still other people out looking."

Maxim didn't look remotely as if he could be her brother, but as Eleisha spoke, her gift flowed out, making the woman see her as someone small and helpless and in need of assistance. Unfortunately, as Maxim stared tensely at the ground, he growled softly. Eleisha gripped down harder on his hand.

The woman tried to get a glimpse beneath his bangs, to see more of his face. "Is he . . . is he all right?"

Her meaning became clear in seconds, and Eleisha latched on to the idea. The woman was wondering if Maxim was somehow "challenged." That could work.

Eleisha feigned distress. "Yes, he's very special. Please, could I use your phone?"

"Of course," the woman said, shifting into helpful mode. "You both must be freezing. Did he lose his shoes? You came from the woods? Do you know where you are now? You come inside, and I can give your father directions."

Eleisha could sense a kindness under the woman's gruff, cautious exterior. She must be the caretaker of the cemetery here. The house was small, but warm and clean, and Eleisha pulled Maxim inside the front door. Had he truly wanted to flee, he certainly could have jerked away from her, but he seemed to be fighting his fear and reluctance in order to stay with her.

"Phone's over here," the woman said, walking past her couch toward a low table.

"Wait," Eleisha said, reaching into her mind. "You're tired. You need to sleep."

The woman was strong and wavered on her feet until Eleisha sank the suggestion deeper, and then she fell forward onto the couch.

Letting go of Maxim's hand, Eleisha connected with his thoughts.

Stay with me. Stay inside my mind as you did with Adalrik. Remember that night with Adalrik, but stay with me.

With the woman unconscious now, Maxim seemed calmer, and he looked at Eleisha intensely. She flashed images of him feeding from the man's wrist in the alley.

Like that. You have to be careful, and take enough but not too much. Listen for the heartbeat.

She hurried to the couch and turned the woman over, positioning her on her back.

Over here.

Maxim seemed interested now and came to kneel beside her. His dark eyes were shifting back and forth at the images she was sending, and when she lifted the woman's wrist, he grasped it.

Be careful.

Putting his teeth to her wrist, he bit down. Eleisha stayed sharply on guard, ready to freeze him if this got out of hand, but for the most part, she just con-

tinued showing him his own memories of the only
other time he'd done this.

He began sucking and swallowing, and Eleisha
also kept a good sense of the woman's heartbeat.
She was just about to tell him to stop . . . when he
pulled out on his own.

Good! she flashed. *Stay with me.*

The woman had been out in the shed when they
arrived, and Eleisha assumed she owned shears for
gardening. She took the woman back before they'd
arrived. The woman accidently cut her wrist on a
pair of shears and came into the house before realizing the depth of the cut. She'd seen no one, met no
one. Then she passed out.

Eleisha disengaged her mind from Maxim's.

He sat close to her, his eyes still intense.

"You feel better?" she asked.

"Better." He studied the woman's chest as it rose
and fell. "First law."

"Yes." She took his hand again. He was beginning
to comprehend some of his own memories, and Eleisha was reteaching him the old ways. Robert
would be proud of them both.

Only on the way back to the shack did Eleisha
remember that while feeding, Maxim had seen none
of the woman's memories—none at all.

chapter thirteen

The past two nights had been hell for Wade.

For once, Philip had no interest in being entertained. He didn't want to watch movies or play cards . . . or do anything. He either paced or he sat and stared into space. Philip had always been hot-tempered, even explosive, but this was different.

He was angry—deeply, silently angry.

Upon waking the third night, Wade wasn't sure he could go through another ten or eleven hours like this. In addition, he didn't feel able to nurse his own feelings of anger and his own fears that Eleisha viewed him as a mere appendage that had its uses—as long as he didn't get in her way.

Philip came down the stairs wearing nothing but a pair of jeans. His normally flawless hair was a mess, sticking out in several directions.

"Put on a shirt," Wade said, unable to keep the irritation from his voice. "I'm calling room service for something to eat. Do you want tea or a glass of wine?"

Maybe a bottle of wine would do them both good.

"No," Philip answered, dropping down onto the couch and staring into space.

Wade couldn't stand it anymore. "Are you going to start that again?"

"I am thinking."

"About what?" Wade tried to keep sarcasm from his voice. He didn't expect an answer.

But Philip said, "A memory Eleisha showed me."

Wade stepped back. "A memory?"

"From Robert. She thinks I've forgotten, but now I think it is the core of all this. I am not what she wants me to be, or she wouldn't have disregarded my judgment so easily."

Wade stood tense, partly annoyed, partly filled with pity, partly feeling something else . . . something he couldn't quite name. "Philip, she did what she did because of the mission. This isn't all about you."

Just then, Wade's cell phone rang. It was lying on an end table.

Philip jumped up, but Wade dived for it. He was closer, only a few steps away, and he grabbed it, holding his hand out to Philip. "Stay there!"

Wade flipped the phone open.

"Eleisha?"

Philip's whole body was trembling slightly, but he held off.

"We're outside of Oxford," she said immediately, "and I really need you. I've taken him as far as I can, but you need to take over now. If you promise you'll help me, I'll give you directions."

"Of course I'll help you." He couldn't believe she was asking him this. What? As if he were some kind of monster? That vampire had tried to kill her. How had she expected them to react?

"And you won't let Philip hurt him?" she asked.

That was another matter, but he said, "I won't. Where are you?"

"Go to Paddington Station and take a train to Oxford . . . ." She went on, giving him careful instructions to Caufield Cemetery northeast of the Farmoor Reservoir. "Seamus will meet you there and guide you the rest of the way."

"All right."

"Can you bring our luggage? We all need clean clothes. The back of my shirt is torn, and Rose has been in the same dress since we got here."

Eleisha sounded so tired, and for the first time, Wade's anger wavered. Was it possible that he and Philip really had driven her and Rose to such drastic measures?

"Yes, we'll bring everything."

"Okay, thanks. See you soon."

They both hung up.

Philip was staring daggers at him.

"I know where they are," Wade said. "We need to catch a train."

Philip grabbed up his machete and his coat. He didn't say anything.

Mary didn't realize how close she'd cut her time until about four seconds after materializing on top of the Montague . . . just as Wade and Philip walked out the front door carrying their luggage.

Due to her short visit with Jasper, she could have missed them leaving.

Yikes.

But that recrimination didn't stay with her long. She hadn't missed them. They were on the move, and they seemed to have checked out of the hotel.

Finally.

She watched them climb into a taxi, and then she floated upward, high in the sky, keeping an eye on their cab as she followed. They went all the way to Paddington Station.

Interesting.

She couldn't wait to see where they went next.

For Wade, the train ride seemed short, but he was growing more and more concerned about Philip— who hadn't said a word since Eleisha's call. Wade tried to engage him a few times, but he got no response.

After completing a taxi ride from Oxford Station all the way to Caufield Cemetery where Eleisha had instructed them to get out, Wade paid the driver and watched him drive off; then he turned to Philip.

"I promised Eleisha we'd help her," he said, "and she's trusting me. She says she's gotten this vampire calm and able to speak, so it's possible we were both wrong. When we get there, you need to at least listen to what she has to say and not start yelling . . . or anything else. Do you understand?"

Philip studied the headstones all around them.

"Philip! Do you understand?"

"I understand."

Well, at least he'd said something. Wade didn't begrudge him his anger, but they were not guiltless here, and it seemed now that Eleisha may have been right all along. He'd just have to make an assessment and see if she was overstating the vampire's progress.

The air shimmered, and Seamus materialized with a guarded expression. He didn't move for a long moment and then looked at Wade.

"You're here to help?" he asked.

"Yes."

Philip didn't say anything, and Wade wondered if his silence was simple agreement to the answer. But even if not, Eleisha had always been able to handle him. She'd be ready to placate him now, and they couldn't go back. They could only move forward.

"This way," Seamus said, heading down a path through the trees that Wade had not noticed before.

*   *   *

Eleisha was standing in front of the shack, waiting as Seamus, Wade, and Philip came out of the trees and began walking through the smaller, older grave-yard. She braced herself. Rose and Maxim were still inside, but Eleisha needed to get a feel for what she was up against.

Both men were carrying luggage. That was a good sign. They'd done as she had asked, and they seemed prepared to stay here if need be. But as she got a clearer look at Philip, some of her hopes fell. He put down the suitcase. His hair was a mess. His coat was buttoned only halfway up his chest, and he wasn't wearing a shirt beneath it. Had he ridden to Oxford like that?

That wasn't a good sign.

Still, just the sight of him sent a jolt up her spine she did not expect. She was surprised, almost ashamed, of how much she'd missed his handsome face, his need for fun . . . the feel of his chest beneath her head.

He wasn't looking back at her. He wasn't looking at anyone.

"Wade?" she asked anxiously. "Everything okay?"

"Yes," he answered.

The gratitude she felt for him at that moment could not be measured. No matter what breaches or difficulties passed them, he would put the mission first—or at least as he saw it. She knew he would always protect her above any other vampire they found, and this had motivated him earlier to side with Philip. But now he was ready to help her: solid as a rock, ready to forgive and forget.

Healing mutual wounds with Philip might take longer, but at least he wasn't in a rage.

She nodded to Wade, reached back, and opened the door.

"It's all right. You can come out."

Tentatively, Maxim came toward her and stepped out the door. On seeing Philip, he stopped.

"This is Maxim," Eleisha said.

Then Eleisha heard a whooshing sound.

Philip opened his coat with his left hand and jerked out the machete with his right.

He was the only one capable of doing what was necessary, and he had no intention of shirking that responsibility.

Eleisha was not a fool in most ways, but she had a blind side when it came to other vampires. She had trusted Simone back in Denver. . . . She had tried everything to help Simone, and the result had nearly been her own death.

That was not going to happen again.

He strode forward without hesitation, even as Wade called out.

"Philip! What are you doing?"

The black-haired vampire's eyes widened, and then it bolted left, running for the trees.

"Philip!" Eleisha shouted.

But he didn't listen. Better he hurt her now than let that feral vampire hurt her later. He broke into a run, keeping the creature in sight as it passed the tree line. This time, it would not escape him. It was fast, blurring among the dense greens and browns of the forest, but Philip increased his own speed, gripping the machete. This would take only one swing.

Freeze!

Every muscle in his body went rigid at the same time, and he fell forward into the dirt. Eleisha was inside his head, and his mind roared back at her. How could she? How could she side against him even now?

Raw anger such as he'd never felt before exploded inside him, and he used all his internal strength to push her out. She fought him, trying to keep him frozen. But he pushed back harder, feeling her control give way, and he jumped to his feet.

The vampire was gone.

Whirling around, he saw Eleisha standing about twenty feet behind him just beyond the tree line. Wade, Rose, and Seamus were behind her, nearer to the shack.

Rage kept coming in waves, and, nearly blind with anger, he roared at Eleisha with his voice this time. Striding back toward her, he felt his lips curl up into a snarl.

Wade almost couldn't believe what was happening, but Philip was closing in on Eleisha, snarling and carrying a machete.

He started to run toward them, but Rose grabbed his arm, dragging him back.

He shook her off, scrambling forward as she cried, "Wade, no! Look at his face!"

Something in her voice stopped him, and she grabbed his arm again.

"He'll kill you in that state!" she said. "She's the only one safe from him! He might knock her out so she won't try to stop him again, but that's the worst he'll do."

Her hands gripped tighter as he hesitated for just a second.

Eleisha could hear Rose shouting behind her, but Philip was coming straight at her, and for the first time since the night she'd met him . . . she was afraid of him. He had a full block up, and she couldn't get a command through.

He was closing the distance between them rapidly, but she wouldn't run—not from Philip.

Then a high-pitched cry, like that of an animal, rang through the night, and a black and white blur came from the trees at high speed. Before Eleisha really understood what was happening, a loud thud sounded, and Philip pitched forward again, hitting the ground.

She realized the black and white blur was Maxim; he dashed around Philip to get in front of her . . . and he was holding a tree branch. Philip's head was dripping blood, but he jumped to his feet again, his eyes lost in a mad rage.

"Leisha, back!" Maxim shouted, gripping the branch with both hands. He snarled at Philip. "No!"

Philip stopped when Maxim spoke, taking in his stance and the branch in his hands.

"Can't you see?" Eleisha cried. "He's protecting me! He thinks he's protecting me from you!"

Don't move, she flashed to Maxim. *Don't attack him*.

Philip stood there, staring at Maxim, and Eleisha knew this might be the only moment she'd have to get through to him.

"Philip, please. He can already feed without killing. I know I was wrong before, in Denver, but trust me this time. He can function." She choked. "He's been alone nearly two hundred years, and I can't finish this by myself. Please."

Philip moved his gaze from Maxim to Eleisha. His head was still bleeding, but slowly, he lowered the machete.

Mary floated in the darkness of the trees, close enough that at one point, she might have run her hand through Maxim as he dashed past.

Seamus was too preoccupied to sense for her, so she watched the whole scene play out, thinking that any moment Philip was going to end this, and she'd be able to teleport back to Julian with good news.

Then, Philip seemed on the brink of turning on Eleisha—something Mary had not thought possible—and Maxim ran back into the fight . . . to protect Eleisha.

And he was speaking.

The sound of his words, and the sight of him defending Eleisha, brought Philip to a screeching halt. Mary felt her hopes begin to sink.

"He's been alone nearly two hundred years," Eleisha cried, "and I can't finish this by myself. Please." She was choking, and if she'd been mortal, she would have been sobbing. She was begging Philip—and he always responded when she begged him.

As Mary watched the rage fade from Philip's face, her hopes died.

He lowered his blade.

Cursing quietly, Mary blinked out. This was far from over.

chapter fourteen

Ten minutes later, Wade decided to follow Eleisha's lead—in however she wanted to move through the following hours of this night. Although the crisis seemed to have passed, the situation was far from resolved.

They were all still outside.

But Philip stood back, away from everyone, and Maxim wouldn't go near him. Eleisha had somehow gotten Maxim to put the tree branch down, and she was leading him back toward the shack. Wade couldn't help being fascinated by the difference in this tragic creature from the last time he'd seen him.

Eleisha had not been exaggerating.

She was holding Maxim's hand as she led him closer. "Maxim, this is Wade," she said. "You'll like him. He's nice, like Brandon."

Maxim looked up. "Like Brandon?"

"Yes, very much like Brandon."

Wade had no idea what this meant, but he didn't interrupt.

"Can you go inside with Wade and Rose, and maybe show Brandon to Wade?" Eleisha asked.

"With memory?"

"Yes, with a memory."

Rose reached out to help guide Maxim back inside, and suddenly, Eleisha flashed into Wade's mind.

He can speak telepathically if you link with him, but he can't instigate. Don't go anywhere alone with him yet. Stay with Rose. I don't know how he'll act around a mortal, but he always responds to her gift.

Wade nodded and then asked aloud, "Aren't you coming in?"

"Not yet."

She was already walking backward . . . toward Philip.

Wade should have known. No matter what happened, no matter who it was they needed to help, no matter how grateful Eleisha might be to Wade, in the end, she would go running to Philip.

It would always be Philip.

Eleisha walked through the aged headstones.

Philip's coat was still open, and his ivory chest shone in the moonlight. His head had stopped bleeding. He saw her coming toward him and glanced away, as if he couldn't bring himself to look at her. She was still unsettled over being so affected tonight by the mere sight of him.

His physical appearance was just part of his gift, part of the illusion he needed to hunt. She'd never let herself think much on it before.

Or had she?

Maybe because she had spent so much time in Maxim's memories, among the vanity of vampires, and love of personal beauty, this thought was foremost in her conscious mind as she looked at Philip now. In her opinion, Maxim's beauty had been a shadow next to Philip's.

Philip was tall and fierce and strong. The clean lines of his face and his red-brown hair were perfect to her—even with his gift turned off.

When she reached him, neither one of them spoke at first, but she pointed to a large headstone near the trees. "Over there."

She walked over and sat on the ground, leaning against the back of the headstone and thinking it poor manners to sit on the other side, on top of someone's grave.

He followed and crouched down. "You don't trust me," he said finally, and from the pain in his voice, she knew what this had cost him to say.

But his words struck her as unfair, considering how determined he'd been to kill Maxim.

"You didn't trust my judgment," she answered, regretting her response instantly as his face closed up. Attacking Philip was never the answer, and she knew it. Talking was not going to fix this.

Let me in, she flashed. *Let me show you how I've felt, what I've thought.*

She could feel his hesitation, and then his mind opened up. She rushed inside him, showing him her perspective from the night he'd first tried to take Maxim's head, how Philip looked to her eyes, sounded in her ears. She showed him the dilemma of lying on that bed at the suite with her throat torn open, trying to decide what to do . . . and how difficult the final decision had been. She showed him scenes of her and Rose washing Maxim, and trying to trigger his ability to speak, all the while hoping Philip would understand later.

She showed Philip how much she feared his tendency to act first and ask questions later.

She showed him how much she'd missed him.

Suddenly, he pushed his own thoughts inside her mind. The onslaught was intense, and she had trouble absorbing the images and emotions at first, nearly falling over and catching herself on one hand. He started with the night Maxim had attacked her, showing her the same scenes from his own point of view. The scenes from his viewpoint were ugly, but she didn't push him out. He saw Maxim as a feral, mad creature that had to be put down.

It was the only way.

Then Eleisha manipulated Philip several times and abandoned him, putting herself and Rose in danger, leaving him and Wade in limbo with nothing to do but worry. He bitterly resented that she'd chosen Maxim over him, and he was embarrassed by this resentment, but he couldn't help it, and he didn't know what the future would hold if Eleisha continued down this path. . . .

"Stop," she said, putting both hands on the ground.

He stopped.

She wondered how other couples might be able to bridge vast divisions if they could share viewpoints like this. She felt terrible, having seen herself through his eyes, but he'd seen himself through hers.

"I didn't put Maxim before you," she said softly. "But I put the mission before everything else. That won't change."

He was quiet for a while and then said, "You saw that memory in Robert. The one of . . . me when I was like Maxim."

Each word sounded torn from his mouth. Why did he care so much about that? She didn't. As far as she and Philip were concerned, only one of Robert's memories mattered.

"I don't care about that memory," she whispered. "I care about the one I showed you. The one you won't even talk about."

He rocked back on the balls of his feet. "The memory you . . . is that why you've been . . . don't you know I . . . ?"

Without warning, he moved forward and gripped the back of her head, pressing his mouth down against hers. The sensation was shocking, and she stiffened, but then her mind became tangled with his again, and she could see that he had thought about Robert's memory, over and over while he sat on a couch for the past few nights.

He'd felt her stiffen, and he stopped.

"What's wrong?"

Now he sounded uncertain, confused.

"Nothing."

She reached up, kissing him this time. Neither one of them knew how to do this, but she wanted it more than anything else in that moment. She ran her hands down his chest, and he moaned. The sound was electrifying, and she kissed him harder, startled when he pressed his tongue into her mouth.

But she tried to respond, licking the tip of his tongue with her own. He pushed her back against the ground, and she could feel his weight on top of her, but she wasn't afraid.

Turn on your gift.

Almost instantly, the glow of his gift washed over and through her, making her want him even more. For the first time ever, she regretted her own gift. She didn't want him to see her as helpless.

But he pushed her shirt up, running his hands up her back, touching her skin in a hungry rush, and she turned her gift on to join with his, only she channeled it and altered it slightly, focusing it upon how helpless she was without *him*.

On how much she needed him.

He moaned louder at that, pushing harder against her, moving his hands over her breasts, then down her lower back, over her hips. He pushed deeper with his tongue. She lost herself inside his gift as Jessenia had with Robert, letting hers combine with his, until a great release burst inside her mind, flowing rapidly down through her body until she jerked and gasped. Philip had stopped kissing her, and his teeth were tightly clenched. He had a hold of the back of her neck with one hand, with his temple pressed up against her cheekbone as his body jerked several times.

When the sensation finally faded, they stayed locked together for a while.

Then he lifted his head and looked down at her. His eyes were full of wonder.

Wade was growing more fascinated with Maxim by the moment—to the point where he was beginning to suffer guilt over having ever agreed with Philip that Maxim might be a hopeless case.

Not that Wade was ignoring Eleisha's warnings. He was well aware that he was dealing with an unstable vampire. Somehow, Maxim looked smaller than Wade remembered. Maybe this was because he was wearing Philip's too-large sweater and rolled-up pants?

"How did you get him talking?" Wade asked Rose quietly. He'd been inside Maxim's mind back in London, and he'd seen no concept of language then.

"Eleisha forced his memories to surface. He started speaking soon after. She said he'd forgotten his own name."

Wade looked around the shack. It was somewhat decrepit and long abandoned, but adequate for their needs, except for the temperature, which was cold. He wondered if the fireplace's chimney was clear, and if he might start a fire. He looked through an open door at the back of the main room, spotting a mattress on the floor.

"Maxim," he said, keeping his voice soft, "is that where you sleep?"

"Yes."

Maxim walked into the bedroom and lay down in the center of the mattress, but the short way, across it, so that his head, torso, and thighs were on the mattress, and his feet stretched out over the floor. He pointed to the left side. "Leisha." Then he pointed right. "Rose."

Oh, they'd all been sharing the mattress. That made sense, but it still surprised Wade. Eleisha and Rose seemed to have accepted Maxim rather quickly— not that he blamed them.

Maxim motioned his hand around the room. "Safe. No sun."

There were no windows in this room. Wade could almost not believe this was the same vampire from the streets of London. Rose was in the doorway, smiling at Maxim, and suddenly, Wade wanted to be alone with his new "patient" in spite of Eleisha's concerns.

"Rose, would you excuse us for a little while?" he asked.

She had not heard what Eleisha said outside. "Of course."

Wade sat down cross-legged on the mattress. Maxim sat up to face him, and Wade slipped inside his mind.

Can you show me Brandon?

Maxim started slightly, and Wade wondered why, until he realized that his mental voice must sound so different from Eleisha's inside Maxim's thoughts.

I'm sorry. I should have warned you.

The answer came clearly, and although Maxim's speech patterns were still rudimentary, his mental voice was not hoarse like his spoken one.

Is all right. I show Brandon.

He closed his eyes, and Wade locked into a memory of a fishing village in Hastings. The shack around him vanished as he was swept inside the image.

Rose didn't wish to intrude, but she wanted to keep an eye on Wade. Once Wade launched into "a project," he could be quite capable of losing perspective. She peered through the open door to see them both sitting cross-legged and sharing a memory. Good. The sooner Wade fully understood the situation, the better he could help restore some of Maxim's former self.

Also, this had been a night of high emotions, and a little quiet time was more than welcome. She sank into a chair.

The air wavered, and Seamus appeared.

"Are they talking alone?" he asked, looking through the open door from a poor angle, so he couldn't see the mattress.

"Sharing memories," she answered.

He nodded.

"Is Eleisha all right?" she asked. Philip had almost lost control of himself earlier, and Rose never wished to see that again.

"I'd say so," Seamus answered. "She's kissing him and rolling on the ground."

"Kissing him?" Rose's mouth fell open, and she closed it quickly. "Are you sure? He's not hurting her?"

"No, he's not hurting her. I think she started it." At the sight of Rose's stunned face, Seamus shrugged. "Ah, Rose, I don't know what she sees in him, but she's not the first woman in history to use her body to solve a problem with a man, now, is she?"

His attitude irritated her. "I hardly think that's what she's doing," Rose answered.

Again, he just shrugged.

Julian was on the verge of calling Mary back to the suite for some semblance of a report—anything—when she blinked back into the sitting room. Jasper had been watching television, and he stood up, hitting the off button on the remote.

But Julian could immediately tell something was wrong. He could always read Mary's face, even when she didn't burst into babbling the second she materialized.

Standing near the couch, close to Jasper, she crossed her arms and made a strange sound, almost as if she were breathing.

"Well?" Julian asked.

"They're all together again, hiding in some old cemetery outside of Oxford."

"Oxford? No, wait. Don't bother with that. Has Philip killed the vampire?"

She shook her head. "It's no good. The vamp isn't so crazy anymore. Eleisha's got him talking now, and Philip wouldn't take the swing."

While her word choices were confusing, the basic facts came through. Eleisha's group was reunited, and Philip was back under her spell—and completely useless. Julian nearly closed his eyes. "What have you learned about the vampire himself? Is he new?"

Again, Mary shook her head. "No. Eleisha said he's been alone for nearly two hundred years, and I think she meant a lot more *alone* than any of them. That's probably why he went so fruit bat crackers. He's been hiding from you someplace where he's been really alone."

Every muscle in Julian's body tightened.

"Have you heard a name?" he asked quietly.

"Maxim. Does that mean anything to you?"

It didn't.

Putting his fist to his mouth, he rolled all the things Mary was relating through his mind. First, he'd never heard of an elder named Maxim, and yet . . . one existed. Second, Eleisha had this elder speaking again, so every moment he spent with her group was a risk for Julian.

Jasper was looking back and forth between them expectantly.

"Mary, where did you find them again?" he asked.

"In an old cemetery outside Oxford. I can guide you."

Jasper turned back to Julian. "Do we go?"

There was little choice now.

"Get your sword," Julian ordered.

Wade pulled away from Maxim's memories through sheer effort, choking and gasping for air. Maxim was lying on his side, gagging, when Rose ran into the bedroom.

She dropped down beside Maxim, stroking his back. "Shhhhhhhh. You're in the bedroom again."

Wade was still absorbing what he'd seen, all the way from Maxim's childhood through Adalrik's death. He hadn't meant to go so far, but once they'd started, he'd just kept going.

"Oh my God," he whispered.

Eleisha should have prepared him. Maxim had been a nineteenth-century literary protégé, and he'd watched Julian take off his maker's head in their own library. Eleisha should have warned him. But then again . . . she'd just told Maxim to show Wade images of Brandon. She hadn't known they'd go so far.

Maxim was still shaking.

"I'm so sorry," Wade said. He seemed to be apologizing to Maxim a lot. "I didn't mean to do that."

Other thoughts passed unbidden through his mind. Eleisha had compared him to Brandon. Was that how she saw him? As a sexually ambiguous, kindhearted scholar? But he also fully realized what she'd meant when she told him Maxim had lost his gift. That aspect was more complicated than he'd expected.

He looked around. "How long were we out?"

"I don't know," Rose answered. "A few hours."

"And Eleisha and Philip haven't come in yet?" He stood up. "Did you check on them?

She looked away. "Seamus has."

As if on cue, the front door opened, and Eleisha walked in. She was a mess, with dirt in her hair. But Wade didn't have time to ponder this. Philip came in after her, and even from the bedroom Maxim could see him and started hissing, jumping up into a crouch.

"It's okay; it's okay," Wade began saying, moving closer to keep Maxim from rushing to the door.

"Stay here," Eleisha told Philip, and she hurried into the bedroom, dropping down beside Maxim. "It's all right," she said.

The back of her shirt and her jeans were smeared with dirt. Maxim's dark eyes moved over her face in relief. "Leisha."

"I'm here. I'm sorry I was so long. Did you show Brandon to Wade?"

He didn't answer, so Wade said, "Yes, and a lot more."

She looked at him. "How much?"

"Too much."

She frowned at him, and then scooted across the mattress to lean against the wall, holding out her arms. "Maxim, come here. Let me show you pictures of the church."

"Library?"

"Yes."

Like a child, Maxim crawled over, sitting beside her, pressed up against her, and they both closed their eyes. Philip stood in the doorway. Wade expected him to react with his usual selfish jealousy.

But he didn't.

His coat was open, and his hair was crusted with dirt, too. He just watched Eleisha with an almost-accepting expression, as if he actually understood what she was doing. Something between them had changed. Wade couldn't bring himself to ask, but he was suddenly worried that Philip might be more human than he'd ever realized.

"It is her mission," Philip said.

Wade turned back to Eleisha and Maxim. True enough; this was the mission. He could always take comfort in that.

By the time Julian's taxi reached Caufield Cemetery, dawn was less than an hour away, and he'd come to a decision. A shed and small house were directly to the left, but Mary had explained that Eleisha's group was farther away, hiding in the shack of an abandoned graveyard from years past. So as soon as the driver stopped the cab, Julian reached over the seat, grabbed the man's head with both hands, and snapped his neck with a loud crack.

Jasper glanced over as the man's head lolled forward.

"Get rid of the car, and meet me back here," Julian ordered, climbing out. He looked up at the sky. "But don't be long."

Without waiting for an answer, he walked through the headstones toward the house, his long black coat swinging around his legs. He heard the taxi pull away. The shed was dark, but he saw a light in the house. Someone was an early riser. He tried the door, found it locked, and kicked it open.

A large woman sat drinking coffee on her couch, watching the early news.

She stared at him in the doorway and began to jump up.

He turned on his gift and hit her with a wave of fear. She fell back, and the sleeve of her right wrist came up, exposing a white bandage. The sight of it bothered him.

She appeared too filled with terror to even scream, but her mouth twisted as she writhed on the couch. He crossed the distance between them and grabbed the back of her head. She wasn't at all to his taste, and he didn't need to feed yet, but he was never one to waste an opportunity. Driving his teeth in, he ripped out part of her throat and then began drinking, gulping until her heart stopped.

But it stopped beating too soon.

He was surprised by how quickly he'd drained

her, and he dropped her body on the floor, watching residual blood leak into the cracks of the hardwood.

Mary materialized, and made a face. "Jeez, Julian, make a mess much?"

He pointed to the woman's wrist. "While watching Eleisha, have you ever seen her feed from someone's wrist and then leave the victim alive?"

"Sure, she does it all the time. So does Philip . . . but he still kills people sometimes, when he's hunting alone."

He couldn't believe what he was hearing. "And it never occurred to you to tell me?"

Her expression shifted to anger. "How am I supposed to know what to tell you unless you ask? You got pissed off when you found out Philip was sleeping in Eleisha's bed, but then you tell me not to speak to you unless you ask me a question. What do you want, Julian? You can't have it both ways!"

He was trembling slightly, wishing he could strike her, and trying to digest this new development. Was he already too late in trying to stop a resurgence of the laws? Should he just take Eleisha's head and then turn to destroying her companions as quickly as he could? If she was feeding and replacing memories and leaving victims alive, she was already practicing the first law, whether she knew it or not.

He closed his eyes. No, not yet. This changed the situation, but she was still unearthing elders—and they responded to her call. As soon as he was certain she'd exhausted her resources and could not find anyone else, then he would catch her outside the church and end this.

Jasper walked in and glanced down at the body.

"What are we doing? You want to attack now?"

"No. Find something to cover those windows." Julian paused. "We'll let them sleep out the day, and we'll move in after dusk, when they have just woken for the night. That is the best time to catch someone off guard."

Jasper nodded, picking up a heavy blanket from the back of the couch, seemingly glad for something to do. "Tonight," he said.

chapter fifteen

Wade woke up a few moments before dusk, lying on one end of the mattress. Rose slept at the other end, with Maxim between them.

Eleisha and Philip were asleep on the floor, curled up on top of Philip's coat.

Before falling dormant that morning, Maxim had objected to this arrangement strenuously, but Wade didn't have much sympathy for him. If Maxim was going to live with them, he'd have to learn to deal with Eleisha's attachment to Philip—just like the rest of them had.

Maxim's eyes opened. Then Rose's.

Wade sat up and looked over to see that both Eleisha and Philip had opened their eyes.

Dusk must have fallen, and their bodies were like

unnatural clocks. He'd never awoken with four vampires before, and the experience was slightly unnerving, almost creepy.

Before anyone could speak, Maxim hissed at Philip, in a clear combination of fear and open hatred.

But Wade understood this better after reading Maxim's memories. Maxim seemed to divide men into two categories: those to be feared and those to be trusted. The latter group was incredibly small.

As Eleisha got up, Philip hooked the machete back onto his belt and picked up his coat. "I'll go outside so you can calm him down," he said.

Wade nearly gasped. Philip was thinking of someone else's feelings? Had the world gone mad?

But he had to admit that the second Philip left, Maxim became much easier to deal with.

"Rose, he looks ridiculous in Philip's clothes," Wade said. "They're too big."

"I wear that sweater all the time," Eleisha objected.

"Yes, and you look ridiculous," he answered. "It hangs nearly to your knees."

Rose tried to hide a smile. "What do you suggest?"

"Can you show him my suitcase," Wade answered, "and help him pick out something else? My clothes will fit him better, and it'll be good for him to start making choices."

"Of course." She motioned to Maxim and let just

a hint of her gift flow. "Come and look at these clothes with me. Tell me what you like."

Curious, Maxim followed her out into the main room, and he crouched beside her as she showed him a pair of black socks.

Eleisha moved over to the mattress to sit beside Wade. "Speaking of clothes, did you sleep in that jacket? I don't think I've seen you take it off since we landed in London."

There was a good reason he kept his jacket on—and buttoned—but he had no intention of sharing it with Eleisha. "It's freezing in here," he answered.

"Hopefully, we won't be here long." She looked at him more seriously and lowered her voice. "What do you think?"

He knew what she was asking, and he glanced out at Maxim. "The time frame makes it harder," he whispered back. "A mortal alone in the forest for even twenty years would be nearly impossible to re-habilitate, but Maxim . . ."

"I know," she said. "Decades upon decades. Do you think you can bring him back at all?"

"Yes, but I don't know how far, and I can't make any promises about his gift."

She seemed troubled, and he wished he had better news for her, but she said, "I do want him to get better, but I hope you don't revert him too much."

"What? Why?"

"You saw him before he was turned . . . and just after. I like him the way he is now. The old Maxim wouldn't have grabbed a tree branch and jumped in front of Philip."

Well, that was certainly true.

Wade nodded. "Maybe we'll end up with a combination of the old and the new."

She smiled at him. "I'm so glad you're here."

He had no response to that, so he watched Maxim trying to pull on a pair of jeans and a long-sleeved T-shirt. Eleisha moved to help.

"Let him do it," Rose said.

The jeans were still too long, but otherwise, they fit. Once he was dressed, Maxim reached out for Eleisha. "Outside."

She turned back to Wade. "He wants to go running in the forest. We won't be long."

They both slipped out the back door, leaving Wade and Rose alone. Seamus had not appeared yet tonight.

"She's too easy on him," Rose said. "He needs to do things for himself, and she shouldn't always give in to whatever he wants."

"Don't worry. I'll be the bad guy if need be." Wade had seen down the corridors of Eleisha's life all the way to her childhood, and he knew how exactly she'd spent much of the last two centuries. "It's just her way. She took care of someone a lot like him . . . for a long time."

But this was part of their need for the mission, and Maxim was a perfect fit. Eleisha needed someone to take care of, and Wade needed a new patient.

He had no delusions about this at all.

*   *   *

Mary materialized in the graveyard of Caufield Cemetery just as Julian and Jasper stepped out the front door.

She couldn't help studying them for a moment; they were so similar and yet so different. They were both pale with dark hair, wearing long black coats and swords on their belts. But Julian towered over Jasper, and his shoulders were broad, while the smaller Jasper moved more easily, as if his bones were liquid.

Although she was sure they'd never meant to or planned it, the two of them made an impressive-looking pair.

"You'll have to split up the group," Julian ordered the moment he saw her. "I need Maxim as isolated as possible."

"Already done," she answered, glad to give him some good news for once. "Philip's out walking alone in the old graveyard, looking at headstones. Wade and Rose are still in the shack. Eleisha and Maxim are in the woods."

At first, this news did seem to please him, but then he frowned. "Eleisha's with Maxim?"

"Yup."

Mary didn't know why, but Julian was most afraid of Eleisha.

"How do you want to play this?" Jasper asked. He looked so confident, so very cool, standing there, ready for orders. She wished she could tell him how he looked.

Julian was still thinking, but he finally said, "Wade and Rose are nothing. Ignore them. I'm going after Maxim. Mary, you guide me and keep a close watch. If I miss on the first swing, you'll have to drive him away from Eleisha and keep her from getting a direct sight line to me. Do you understand?"

"Why can't she get a . . . ?" His face clouded, and she said, "I understand."

God, he could be a pain sometimes. If he were not so secretive, she could probably provide him with a lot more useful information. Half the time, she didn't know what was important to tell him and what wasn't.

"Jasper," he went on, "you go to the old graveyard and keep Philip busy."

That got her attention, and she floated closer to Julian. "To Philip? No way. You're not sending Jasper after Philip . . . alone in some graveyard. Jesus, Julian, no way."

Before Julian could bark a retort, Jasper cut in. "Stop it, Mary! I can handle Philip."

"No, you can't."

Of all the stupid ideas. Philip gripped that machete as if it were part of his hand. He'd have Jasper in three pieces before Mary could even blink in.

To her shock, Jasper glared at her, and he was about to say something else when Julian raised one hand. "Quiet!" His mouth tightened, and he grew more thoughtful. "Mary is not entirely wrong. Jasper, don't engage him. Just keep him busy. Keep him from going into the woods. That's all."

"Why can't I fight him?"

"Because his father started teaching him to use a sword when he was six years old, and after he was turned, his body remembered every lesson." He lowered his face toward Jasper's. "Just keep him busy. Make him chase you, but don't let him catch you."

Jasper looked away, pissed off.

But then he nodded and headed for the old cemetery, and Julian headed into the trees. Mary blinked out, following Julian. She didn't care how this played out as long as Jasper stayed safe.

Eleisha and Maxim ran together for a little while and then slowed to a walk, moving through the dense trees, and she tried talking to him about the future.

"We'll be going home soon," she said.

Maxim pointed back to the shack. "Home."

She had to admit that he looked better in Wade's clothes. Both the jeans and the long-sleeved T-shirt fit him well. She'd buy him his own clothes in Portland, and she made a mental note to pick up some long-sleeved T-shirts in dark colors.

"No, that's not our home," she told him. "Home is the church I showed you. Remember? With the library?"

"That is home?"

"Yes." She had told him this before, several times. But he seemed concerned now, anxious. "Where?"

"A long way," she admitted, stepping over a

fallen branch. Getting him to Portland was going to be a nightmare, and she didn't want to think of that just yet. A large raven came down through the treetops and landed on a low branch slightly ahead of them, on a small aspen tree just across from a large spruce.

Maxim was a half step in front of Eleisha, and he looked at the bird intently. It, in turn, seemed focused on the spruce, and suddenly Maxim gasped loudly, holding his arm back to stop her, and he shouted, "Leisha!"

She saw the glint coming down as a dark shape beside the spruce flowed into movement. On instinct, she shoved Maxim as the sword swept past. The tip sliced his face, and he hit the ground, but Eleisha didn't watch him fall. She spun around, looking up into a pale face with cold eyes. His arms were already drawn back again.

Stop!

She drove the command into Julian's mind with every ounce of anger and strength rising inside her. His sword stopped midswing.

Freeze!

His body went rigid, and her satisfaction at the sight of it was almost alarming. She wanted to hurt him. He'd just swung a sword at Maxim.

I told you what would happen if you tried to hurt me or mine again, she projected.

Even frozen, Julian's face shone with fear.

But the air shimmered beside Eleisha and a scream sounded in her ear, breaking her focus and sending her falling to one side. The magenta-haired girl ghost materialized, still screaming.

Maxim was writhing on the ground, lost in terror, and he scrambled up to his feet.

"No, don't run!" Eleisha called to him.

But he ran.

Eleisha looked around wildly.

Julian was nowhere in sight.

The girl ghost blinked out, and then blinked back in on Eleisha's other side, aiming a kick at her. Even while knowing the ghost couldn't hurt her, Eleisha flinched, then jumped to her feet.

Seamus materialized beside the girl ghost, shouting, "Get away from her!"

The girl blinked out, and so did Seamus. Julian was still nowhere to be seen, and Eleisha needed a direct sight line to reach into his mind. As he had no telepathic ability, he was like a blank wall to other telepaths. They could not locate him mentally.

So she ran after Maxim, hoping to protect him, and without bothering to focus or even trying to pinpoint Philip's mind, she sent out a mental cry.

Philip! Hurry! Julian's in the woods.

Jasper had reached the old cemetery quickly, and he was crouched behind a headstone, watching Philip stroll toward him.

Philip did not seem to be doing anything in particular, just walking and looking at the old epitaphs on the graves. It galled Jasper beyond words that he was supposed to run from Philip again. The only other two times he'd met Philip, he'd run like a little girl—with no choice then.

But now he was ready for a straight-up fight, and Philip didn't look so tough anymore—tall maybe, but not so tough.

However, Julian had been crystal clear, and Jasper always followed his orders, so he glanced around, wondering about the best time to move into Philip's sight line and start running away from the forest, leading Philip in the other direction.

He was just about to move, when Eleisha's voice burst inside his mind. He couldn't believe the clarity of her words, and he could almost "hear" the direction she shouted from.

Philip! Hurry! Julian's in the woods.

Philip's expression shifted to alarm, and he whirled around, looking into the trees, and Jasper knew he'd heard the voice, too.

The game had just changed.

Jasper pulled his sword, and dashed forward, hoping to catch Philip with his back turned.

Philip was walking through the headstones, thinking on Eleisha, thinking on what had happened between them last night, when her voice erupted inside his head.

Philip! Hurry! Julian's in the woods.

He froze, thinking she was in the shack with Wade, but her telepathic voice sounded far away. What was she doing in the woods?

It didn't matter.

Julian.

He jerked out his machete and took a step forward, ready to break into a run, when a sound behind him caused him to dodge and turn on instinct, and a silver blade missed him by inches. He swept his own blade upward with force, sending sparks flying as the metal connected, and then he found himself looking at a familiar-looking vampire—but he couldn't quite place him.

The vampire snarled and swung again. He was fast, and his motions were smooth, but Philip blocked him easily and began driving him backward. Philip didn't have time to be fighting some puppy. Eleisha was alone in the trees with Julian, and Philip was ending this quickly.

He just kept swinging, forcing the vampire to step back and back, confusion and worry growing in his eyes when he couldn't get an opening to attack Philip.

Then Philip feinted left with his blade and swung hard with his right fist, catching the vampire across the jaw and knocking him off his feet. Philip had the machete ready to stab downward, through the vampire's chest to stun him—just long enough to take his head.

But when he drove downward with the point of his blade, his attacker rolled with incredible speed and came up on all fours; then he shot into the forest, running so fast that Philip had trouble seeing him.

Philip didn't bother following. He bolted into the forest himself, heading toward the sound of Eleisha's mental cry.

*   *   *

Wade was repacking his suitcase when Eleisha's cry burst inside his mind.

Philip! Hurry! Julian's in the woods.

Rose stumbled in shock, and he knew she'd heard it, too. He ran for the door.

"Wade, no!" Rose called. "You don't know where she is, and you can't stop Julian. Philip and Eleisha both know exactly what to do. You'll just get yourself killed."

He turned on her angrily. Did everyone view him as useless?

"I'm not going to just leave her out there with—"

"Wade!" Seamus shouted, materializing near the door. "Run for Caufield Cemetery. That's where Maxim's heading, and Eleisha's right behind him. Julian and that girl ghost are out there!"

Before Rose could say a word, Wade ran out the door, heading down the path for Caufield Cemetery.

Blind with panic, Jasper ran, wondering how to salvage this. Mary had been right about Philip. A few months of training with an instructor had not left Jasper remotely prepared to take on someone like Philip.

He understood that now, but it was too late.

Philip was on the loose somewhere in these trees, a threat to Julian.

Jasper had failed again in the one thing Julian asked him to do.

The air wavered up ahead, and Mary appeared.

He skidded to a stop in relief. She always knew what to do.

"God, I screwed up, Mary. I really screwed up!"

"Run that way," she said, pointing south, "to that cemetery where we arrived. Everyone's heading that way, and Julian's going to need help."

His eyes followed her transparent finger. He could still pull this off if he jumped in to help Julian at the right moment.

He bolted south, crashing through brush and not even trying to be quiet.

Eleisha nearly flew through the trees, ignoring branches hitting her in the face as she tried to catch up with Maxim. She could only imagine what he was feeling. All the years of hiding in terror had now culminated with his greatest fear of Julian swinging that sword from the darkness.

She caught a glimpse of Maxim in a break in the trees up ahead, and she tried calling to him telepathically.

Maxim!

She didn't want to send a command and freeze him in case Julian was near . . . and she needed to save her own mental strength to fight.

Maxim, please, wait for me.

To her relief, he slowed and looked back. His eyes were mad with panic, but she caught him quickly, pulling him down to a crouch, realizing they were at the edge of the tree line and looking out over the graveyard of Caufield Cemetery. Until now she hadn't even realized they'd been running south.

He clung to her, and she clung back, her thoughts racing for what to do next.

Something loud was rustling through the bushes about forty feet away. It couldn't be Julian. He didn't make noise.

Then Philip's voice shouted in her mind. *Where are you?*

But he sounded farther away than forty feet.

Here! We're here at Caufield Cemetery!

"It's all right," she whispered to Maxim. "He's coming."

But the air wavered beside her, and the girl ghost appeared, shouting, "I found them!"

With hiding no longer an option, Eleisha grabbed Maxim and tried pulling him into the open. At least that way, if Julian attacked, she'd see him coming.

"No!" Maxim shouted.

He held back, terrified of the open space, and she couldn't pull him. Something dark moved from the bushes beside her, and she looked up just in time to see a fist coming down.

She didn't even feel pain.

The world just went black.

Julian heard a satisfying crack as his fist connected with Eleisha's face, and she dropped, lying in the dirt with her eyes closed.

Letting out a strange cry, Maxim bolted out into

the graveyard—it was the only place to run—and fled through the headstones at high speed.

Julian started after him, wondering what was causing that rustling sound in the forest about forty feet away, when Jasper burst from the trees with his sword in his hand. What was he doing here? Where was Philip?

But Jasper spotted Maxim immediately and blurred into motion, running after him, and Julian could not help being impressed by his servant's fluid speed. Jasper sailed over the headstones as if he could fly, and he cut off Maxim's escape almost effortlessly.

Maxim wheeled and began running back toward Julian . . . until he saw Julian and then cut left. Julian broke into a jog, moving faster with each step.

He rarely had call to run, but he could if necessary. By this point, he knew he'd never seen Maxim before, but it didn't matter. If Maxim had been hiding for nearly two hundred years, he was an elder who had once practiced the laws and might teach them again. He was a danger. He was an enemy.

At the sight of Julian running to intercept him, Maxim wheeled again, and this time, Jasper caught him, using a roundhouse kick to knock him off his feet. Jasper didn't waste any time and raised his sword to strike. Julian moved closer but didn't interfere. If Jasper wanted to take Maxim's head, Julian had no objections.

Again, he couldn't help being surprised by the sight of his once shabby, useless servant now standing there in his long black coat with his sword raised, ready to destroy an enemy. This would all be over in a matter of seconds.

An explosion sounded. Blood sprayed from Jasper's shoulder, and he stumbled backward. Another explosion followed immediately, making a hole in his chest.

He choked in shock and called out, "Mary!"

Julian swiveled his head to see Wade standing at the mouth of the path and holding a gun in both hands. Another shot rang out. This time Julian's chest sprayed dark blood and another shot followed, catching him in the stomach.

Maxim bolted, darting away through the headstones. Julian stumbled after him but quickly lost sight of him.

Philip burst from the tree line about twenty feet from Wade, and he spotted Julian before he'd even slowed down.

He carried a machete in his right hand.

Mary materialized next to Jasper, who was still on his feet but reeling, with blood pouring from his torso.

"Oh my God," she said. "Jasper! Oh my God!"

Julian . . . stop.

A weak command reached his mind, and in horror, he swiveled his head again to see Eleisha up on all fours, regaining consciousness and trying to get up.

Philip was running through the cemetery at high

speed toward Julian, trying to close the gap between them.

Julian forced himself to think.

In the blink of an eye, an easy victory had shifted to a defeat so stunning he might not simply lose the battle, but lose his life. The same survival instinct that had caused him to commit the near-genocide of his own kind rose up through the blood and the pain in his chest, and he could see only one way to stop Philip and Eleisha.

Gripping his sword in both hands, he took a few steps back and swung hard, slicing through Jasper's throat. He watched his head fall to the ground, the body falling to its knees and dropping right after.

As Jasper's psychic energy burst, Philip stumbled and dropped his blade. Then he cried out and grabbed his head. So did Eleisha. So did Wade. Julian was never affected by the psychic release of an undead.

But Jasper had been a young vampire, and Julian knew he would not have much time.

He turned and fled, hearing only the sound of Mary's wailing behind him.

Seamus did not feel the psychic blast. He'd heard the younger vampire call out for Mary, seconds before, and he now had a name for the girl ghost.

But everything happened so fast.

From the time Wade fired the first shot to the instant Julian had beheaded his own companion, only a few blinks could have passed.

Seamus' companions were all holding their heads

in what appeared to be agony. He could not see
Maxim, who had run through the headstones. But
the girl ghost was in far more pain than Eleisha or
Philip or Wade.

She was on her knees beside the dead vampire,
sobbing as if she were mortal and crying out over
and over again, "No, Jasper, no!"

Seamus was moved by this sight. He understood
loss, and he teleported beside them.

"Mary," he said softly.

She looked up, her features twisted and transparent tears on her face. "Seamus, where is he? Where
is his spirit? I don't see it!"

She let out a long, low-pitched sound of pain, and
he wondered how to answer. Had she expected this
Jasper to come to her as a ghost?

"I don't know," he said. "Mary, I don't know."

She made the low-pitched sound again.

After the last of the blast faded, Eleisha climbed to
her feet, feeling dizzy and sick. She stumbled out
into the graveyard.

"Maxim?"

Searching with her mind, she felt him on the
other side of a tall headstone, and she stumbled onward, finding him huddled there, frozen in terror.
She dropped down, grabbing him and pulling him
close.

"It's over," she said, rocking him back and forth.

But it didn't feel over. She was shaking and
couldn't seem to stop. All she could think of was the

sight of Julian murdering his own companion and running away.

All she could hear was the sound of the girl ghost's sobbing.

She looked up, dimly aware of the sight of Philip and Wade running toward her. The sobbing faded.

When she turned her head to look back, the girl ghost was gone.

Thirty minutes later, Eleisha was sitting on the mattress inside the bedroom of the shack, with Maxim beside her and Rose in front of her.

"That's a bad bruise," Rose was saying. "Has Philip looked at this? Did he think the cheekbone was broken?"

Eleisha did not remember leaving the cemetery or coming back here. She didn't know why she'd have a bruise.

Wade and Philip were speaking in low voices in the main room, but she couldn't see them.

Bits and pieces of the night began coming back to her, and she remembered Julian's fist coming toward her face.

Julian.

She gripped Maxim's hand. He was safe. Julian hadn't hurt him. He gripped her fingers back.

Philip came through the bedroom door with Wade on his heels. They both looked at her with concern. Why were they concerned?

"Are you all right?" Wade asked.

She just looked at him.

"Philip thinks I should call a taxi," he went on, "and we should get cleaned up, and try to go home tonight. It's still early, and we can make Heathrow before midnight. We'll be traveling west, so we'll land in the dark."

For some reason, Eleisha's voice didn't seem to work, or maybe it was her mind. She couldn't answer him, but his words brought a flood of relief. Home. Yes, she wanted to go home more than anything and leave this place behind. She wanted to lock them all away in their fortress of a church, with its heavy doors and bulletproof glass.

"Maxim can't fly to America yet," Rose said.

Wade turned on her, almost angry. "We can handle it. I'll help you on the flight, and Eleisha can help Maxim."

"I think we should go, Rose," Philip said quietly. "Tonight."

"I'm not talking about fears and phobias," Rose answered, growing angry herself. "He doesn't have a passport. He doesn't have any identification. We won't even get him through security."

Despair flooded in, washing away Eleisha's relief. They couldn't go home . . . and how could they ever get proper documents?

But neither Philip nor Wade appeared alarmed. Wade seemed slightly chagrined, and he said, "I think we might have that covered." He glanced at Eleisha. "But you might not like it."

He walked out into the main room and came back in carrying a long black coat and a pair of boots.

"The vampire Julian killed was about Maxim's size, and he was turning to dust, so we took his coat and boots . . . to help Maxim fit in better on the way home." He reached into the coat's pocket and took out a wallet and a passport. Opening the passport, he crouched down to show it to Rose. "They look about the same age, same height, weight, slender face, pale with dark hair. Maxim's hair is darker, but this Jasper Nesland had very short hair, so the color isn't so visible in the photo. I think this passport will work if we book a plane ticket in Jasper's name." He glanced at Eleisha again. "I know it's ghoulish, but I just can't think of—"

"No, it's good," Eleisha said, finding her voice as bits and pieces of the night still came back to her. She could hear the explosions in her ears. "Where did the gun come from? You didn't bring it with you."

"Yes, I did." He didn't look remotely chagrined at this. "I hid it in the lining of my suitcase, checked it in, and got lucky. Nobody found it. Why do you think I've been wearing this jacket since we got here?" He opened one side, exposing a small holster strapped to his rib cage.

"Oh . . ." She felt brittle, like a dried leaf. "Philip?"

He crouched down beside her, and for once Maxim didn't hiss at him. Eleisha leaned over, putting her forehead on Philip's knee. "Take us home. I want to go home."

chapter sixteen

Two weeks later, about a half hour past dusk, Wade made his way up the staircase to the top floor of the church to check on Maxim.

It always took a while for Eleisha to recover after a mission, and this last one had proven no exception. Success or failure, every time she faced Julian, it seemed to take a little more out of her, and Wade couldn't stop going over the events of that night in the cemetery, wondering what they might have done differently so that Philip might've taken Julian's head.

If they didn't have to fear Julian, their missions would take on a whole new light.

But . . . Maxim had also proven a welcome distraction from dwelling on such possibilities, and Wade looked forward to their time together. So far,

Maxim had not exhibited any ability to instigate telepathic contact on his own, and his language skills were progressing slowly—but they were progressing.

Eleisha had taken him out hunting, and as long as she handled the telepathy and memory replacement, he was able to feed by the first law.

However, Wade felt somewhat guilty over having to create "rules," such as Maxim's being permitted to walk alone in the garden but not being allowed beyond the gate by himself. His behavior was still completely unpredictable, and he reacted badly when panicked or confused; the last thing Wade needed was the police knocking on their door.

It seemed heavy-handed to treat a two-hundred-year-old scholar like a child, but secrecy and safety had to come first.

Reaching the upstairs hallway, Wade walked to the first room on the left and knocked.

"Maxim?"

He cracked the door. Upon returning from London, Eleisha had decorated this room with soft blankets and numerous pillows and heavy forest green curtains. She'd hung framed photographs of woodland scenes on the walls and around the room had placed a number of "normal" items, such as a digital clock and a calendar on the wall by the light switch.

Wade stepped inside. "Hey, Maxim, tonight, I thought we might . . ."

He stopped.

Maxim, wearing a pair of dark blue pajamas Eleisha had bought for him, was sitting on the bed and petting a small cat. The cat looked a bit ragged, as if it had been outside for a while, but it was maybe eight or nine months old. Its body was a soft shade of gray with white patches.

Maxim looked up.

"Tiny Tuesday," he said.

Wade shook his head. "What?"

"Her name." Maxim held both his hands up with a small space between them. "Tiny." Then he pointed at the calendar. "Tuesday."

"Oh, she's tiny, and you found her on Tuesday."

Interesting.

"She have no home. Hungry," Maxim said. "I keep her."

Wade pondered that for a moment, wondering what Philip might say, but there was no reason why Maxim couldn't keep a little cat.

"All right," Wade said, "I'll go to the store and buy her some food and a litter box. Did she come to you out in the garden?"

Maxim nodded and put his hand on her side. "Babies."

"Babies? She's pregnant?"

That did color matters slightly. "You can keep Tiny Tuesday, but I'll have to find homes for the kittens, okay?"

Maxim didn't answer, and Wade decided to press it.

"Maxim, if you agree, you need to say 'okay' back to me."

"Okay."

Watching Maxim sit there, gently petting the small cat, Wade couldn't help a flash of seeing him sitting beside Adalrik, debating Shakespeare. Did he remember anything at all on a conscious level, or was his former self forever locked away, only to be viewed in memories? He'd once loved *Macbeth*, and Wade had read it back in college. He'd always liked the opening with the three witches.

On impulse, he moved closer to Maxim and quoted the first witch. "'When shall we three meet again? In thunder, lightning, or in rain?'"

Maxim was still stroking the cat, gazing down at her. But when he spoke, his voice sounded different, clear and smooth, "'When the hurly-burly's done, when the battle's lost and won.'"

"'That will be ere the set of sun,'" Wade responded, surprised and hoping for the next line.

But Maxim, seemingly unaware he'd even spoken, looked up again. "Not wait to go for store. She hungry now."

Disappointed, Wade moved for the door. "Is she? I've got some milk in the fridge and maybe a can of tuna in the cupboard. I'll find her something."

Heading back down the staircase, Wade thought about what a houseful they were gathering . . . and now they had a pregnant cat named Tiny Tuesday.

He could still hear Maxim's smooth quotation in his head.

Maxim was still in there somewhere.

Wade just had to find him.

Vale of Glamorgan, Wales

Julian was blind without Mary.

He'd managed to make it home to Cliffbracken and take refuge inside the manor, but the holes in his chest had been so extensive, they'd healed completely only a few days ago.

Now, with fear in his heart, he had more time and energy to dwell upon what had happened that night in the cemetery.

And in addition to everything else, it now seemed he had lost Mary.

He sat in his study, staring at a burning candle and cursing fate.

His failure had been absolute that night . . . beginning with a raven landing on an aspen branch. He had pulled back from the brink of disaster after that, only to find himself wounded and bleeding and facing three opponents with different weapons or strengths.

What choice did he have?

Taking Jasper's head and releasing his memories was the only possible option. While he had no intention of explaining himself to an underling, surely Mary could see he'd had no choice?

But every time he'd called her since that night,

she'd shouted profanity at him, called him unspeakable names, and then vanished. One night, he'd called her back three times, and every time was worse. He'd finally given up.

Somehow, he had underestimated her attachment to Jasper.

Then he thought that if he left her alone, let her stew on her own for a while, she might come back to herself and see reason.

That had not happened, and he was growing desperate. He had no idea where Philip or Eleisha might be. He assumed they'd taken Maxim home to the church in Portland, but he didn't know, and he'd become very, very accustomed to *knowing*.

He could feel desperation leaking in on the edge of his mind, and tonight, an idea had come to him.

Standing up, he called, "Mary Jordane!"

Since he had brought her over from the gray plane—the in-between plane for troubled souls who were not yet ready to move on to the afterlife—he had power over her and could call her to his side when he wished.

She materialized, and upon realizing what had happened and where she was, she pretended to spit at him. "Leave me alone, you son of a bitch!"

"Wait."

"No! You killed Jasper. I'm never doing anything for you again."

Her colors began to fade as she dematerialized, and he called out, "He's on the gray plane."

For a moment, nothing happened, and then her

colors grew bright again, but her face still shone with hatred. "What did you say?"

"His spirit will be on the gray plane, waiting for yours. He's hardly ready to go on to the afterlife."

"What do you care where he is? You murdered him like he was nothing!"

"Would you like to join him there?"

This had been a threat he'd used against her in the early days, that since he'd called her, he could send her back if she didn't obey him.

But now might he not use it as a reward? Having to resort to offering her something was almost more than he could stand . . . almost.

She glared at him. "What do you mean?"

"If you assist me through one more of Eleisha's so-called 'missions,' I'll send you to the gray plane. You can reunite with Jasper and move on to the afterlife together."

He had no idea where Jasper's spirit might be— or indeed if the souls of vampires went anyplace at all—but he could see Mary's mind working.

She looked at his face again, and her expression closed up. "I'm not doing anything for you. You may as well send me back now."

"No. One more mission. Then I'll send you."

"Oh yeah, well how about if I just teleport to Philip and tell him exactly where you are? How would that be? If you run, I'll find you. Maybe I should do a few favors for him?"

The fear in his chest was almost painful now. But he kept his face still.

"He cannot send you back. I can."

She turned away, crossing her arms, and the hatred vanished, replaced by loneliness and pain.

He had her.

"Only one more?" she asked.

"Only one."

She looked back at him. "If you're lying, and you don't send me back after one more job, I will go get Philip . . . and Eleisha. Do you understand?"

"Of course I understand. Now go the church and make sure they're all there."

Her eyes narrowed, and he thought she might try to spit at him again—foolish effort. But she blinked out.

Only then did he let himself sink down in the chair. He was no longer blind, at least not for a while.

Seamus sensed a presence out in the garden, and he materialized beside one of the rosebushes. All the blooms were gone, and it had gone dormant for winter. A light rain fell from the sky, passing through him and soaking into the ground.

He could see her in profile, standing beneath the stained glass windows of the church, sad and angry and alone.

"Mary," he said gently.

She turned to look at him. The rain fell through her magenta hair and black mesh overshirt.

"Don't spy for him anymore," Seamus said. "Don't do anything he asks."

She didn't answer, and her face gave nothing away. Her colors simply faded and she vanished. Seamus didn't try to follow. He floated just above the ground, staring at the empty spot for a long time.

Philip took Rose out hunting. They'd both gotten wet in the rain, so once back home, Rose went to her room to change clothes, and he started searching the church for Eleisha. His new coat kept his clothes dry, and he never minded if his hair was damp. He didn't know what Eleisha had planned for the night, but he hoped it was entertaining—or at least that they might head off to her room early. He found that since returning from England, he liked retiring with her early. She'd started locking the door once they were both inside.

"Eleisha?" he called out the back door to the rose garden. Sometimes, she still pulled weeds in the rain.

But she wasn't out in the garden.

She wasn't reading to Maxim in the sanctuary—it was empty.

She wasn't in the bath.

He decided to check with Wade and opened the office door. To his surprise, Eleisha was sitting at Wade's desk, using the computer. She was the only one in the room.

"Where's Wade?" he asked.

"He wanted a few hours to work with Maxim alone."

"What are you doing?" he asked, an uncomfortable feeling creeping through him.

"Wade taught me how to use this machine. I'm doing a search myself."

"That's Wade's job."

He'd come to terms with the fact that she'd never abandon this search for lost vampires, and that if he tried to force her to choose between the "mission" and himself, he might not like the answer.

But at least during the in-between times, he'd hoped everything would go back to the way it had been before the search for Maxim, when Eleisha spent most of her time with him. He understood she sometimes had to help with Maxim now . . . but this . . . this business of her using Wade's computer was unsettling. How long would she stay in here looking at that screen?

"I know it's Wade's job," she answered, "but I may see things he doesn't, hints he might not recognize."

"Have you found anything?"

"Maybe . . . but I'll go over it with him later." She stood up and turned off the monitor. "I didn't know you were back yet." She smiled at him. "Your hair's wet. All that gel you use will turn it spiky."

"I don't care."

He liked seeing her smile. She hadn't smiled much since returning, but she was coming back to herself more quickly than the last time—from that bloody mission in Denver.

"We never did watch *Vertigo*," she said. "You up for some Hitchcock?"

Ten minutes later, she was curled up beside him on the couch, watching Jimmy Stewart's name in big letters on the screen, and his tension began to ease.

"You like to be with me," he said, as if making a statement.

She glanced at him and hit the PAUSE button.
"Why would you even need to say that?"

He shrugged. Maybe because she'd abandoned
him in London and chosen her mission over him.
Maybe because she'd fought him to protect Maxim.
Maybe because now that they were home again, she
was taking over Wade's job so they might launch
into a new search even faster.

But . . . she was also sitting here with him now,
and he couldn't wait until an hour before dawn
when she'd lock them both away, run her hands up
and down his chest, lick the end of his tongue with
her own, and let her gift rush inside him.

"I always like being with you," she said. "I just
need to start trying to help Wade more in between
missions. But you and I have a lot of time together
now, at least until . . . until we find the next lost one."

She pulled her knees up, pressed in closer to his
arm, and pushed PLAY on the remote.

He nodded. He was content.

At least until they found the next lost one.

Just past dawn, Wade left his bedroom and walked
out into the hallway. Eleisha's room was one door
down, but he didn't try the handle.

The morning after returning from London, he'd
been stunned—even hurt—to find it locked. The
next morning, he'd been angry. The third morning . . . he realized it was for the best, and he hadn't
tried to open the door again. Without ever saying a
word to him, she seemed to have closed both a lit-

eral and a symbolic door, and he'd accepted her decision without saying a word to her.

However, she was actively assisting him with Maxim, and she was working to locate new targets for investigation; he realized he could live with this. He could deal with anything as long as she was still dedicated to the mission.

Now he headed upstairs to briefly check on Maxim, who sometimes didn't make it as far as the bed and fell dormant on the floor. But on reaching the top level of the church, he heard a soft scratching sound and walked over, cracking open Maxim's door.

Tiny Tuesday pushed her body through the crack and looked up at him. She had blue eyes. *Meow.*

Peering inside, Wade saw Maxim dormant on the bed, and then he looked back down at the small gray and white cat. In spite of Maxim's affection for her, Wade realized he'd be the one to clean her litter box and make sure she had fresh food and water.

Strangely, he didn't mind at all. He should probably make her an appointment with a vet today, just to get her checked out.

"Come on," he said, heading down the hallway.

She followed him down the stairs.

So . . . for now he had Maxim to work with and a cat to care for, and Eleisha seemed determined to help him search. That was enough for now.

He could cope and wait and make it through the days, waiting.

Until they found the next lost one.